THE CHANCER

'Hilarious and heart-warming, *The Chancer* sparkles and hooks you in from the first page. A dazzling debut from Fiona Graham. I devoured it'

– EMMA HEATHERINGTON

'Chance would be a fine thing. But *The Chancer* is the finest— and funniest—thing of all'

– OLAF TYARANSEN

'Fantastic book! Sharp, funny and extremely enjoyable'

– SEAN MAGUIRE

'Outstanding! Full of heart and packed with humour'

– ANITA STRATTON, *Radio Broadcaster*

'You'll smile, you'll gasp, and you'll laugh out loud. *The Chancer* is a rollercoaster ride with a heart of pure Irish gold. Graham's debut is pacy, punchy and a pure joy'

– CHRIS HARVEY, *STV*

i

First published in 2023 by Sonny & Skye Productions

Copyright © 2023 Fiona Graham
All rights reserved

The moral right of the author has been asserted

Cataloguing in Publication Data
is available from the British Library

ISBN: 978-1-7392884-0-2 (Paperback)
ISBN: 978-1-7392884-1-9 (E-book)
ISBN: 978-1-7392884-2-6 (Hardback)

Cover design and typesetting
by Vanessa Mendozzi

He was born to be a star.
Pity no one else thought so.

THE CHANCER

A Novel

FIONA GRAHAM

FIONA GRAHAM lives in County Galway, in the west of Ireland, with her husband and daughter and their two dogs. Fiona grew up in Scotland but has lived in Ireland for most of her adult life. Fiona wrote and produced the award-winning Irish feature film *Songs for Amy*.

The Chancer is Fiona's debut novel.

WWW.FIONAGRAHAMWRITER.COM

For Sean and for Sheena
With love and laughter

CHAPTER 1

NOW, 1989, LOS ANGELES

Donnie scanned the stage for somewhere inconspicuous to puke, but it was too late. He was being ushered closer towards his big moment and felt utterly paralysed with fear. He swallowed the acidic puddle of vomit in his mouth and blessed himself. Holding his clammy hands tightly together to stop them from shaking, he prayed for success to the God he desperately now hoped existed.

Randolph Lettering strode onto the stage as the announcer belted out a welcome around the venue.

'It's Randy! I can call him Randy because I know him. It's Randolph Lettering!'

Randolph stood in the centre of the stage, lit up in a halo of light. He gave the audience a hearty wave.

'Welcome to our music special at The Troubadour! And it definitely will be special! We've got some amazing music on the show tonight, and our guests include The Bangles!'

The crowd cheered, but Randolph was a little disappointed with the LA crowd, grungy and dressed in black. He was used to the slick, colourful New Yorkers. So Randolph upped his game, hoping to rally some enthusiasm.

'And all the way from Australia, we should be so lucky, Kylie Minogue!'

A more spirited cheer—they were warming up.

'And as well as our musical guests, we have a couple of guests from the movie business ... here to save the world, Bill

Murray! And our *Big* guest, Tom Hanks!'

A few exuberant whistles filtered through thunderous applause. Randolph knew Bill Murray and Tom Hanks would achieve that but wasn't sure how his next guest would go down.

'But first up, we have someone you have never heard of because this is his first film.'

The audience fell silent.

'He's landed on his feet in a new George Lawless movie, *Cracked* ... Maybe he'll join the walk of fame one day, but it all starts here. Ladies and Gentlemen, please welcome ... Donnie McNamara!'

Donnie shielded his eyes from the white glare of the lights and peered at the audience—row upon row of black silhouettes, like crows on a telephone wire at dusk. He thought his bowels were going to explode or implode. Either way, he shuffled onto the stage, clenching his buttocks. Randolph smiled broadly, disguising his instinct that this would be an onerous interview ... but a favour was a favour.

Donnie managed to sit down without falling and, perched in front of Randolph Lettering, his adrenalin finally kicked in. *This was it!* He gave the audience a coy little wave of his hand, grinning so hard he thought his lips would rip. Donnie felt that every second he had spent dreaming, every time he had ignored rejection, deflected humiliation and upheld his self-belief, had led to this moment. This was the beginning of his journey to The Oscars.

'Good to meet you, Randolph!' Donnie seemed to have no control over his shrill voice.

'It's okay, I won't bite,' Randolph smiled. He shook Donnie's damp hand and subtly wiped the residual sweat on his suit trousers under the desk. 'So, Donnie, you're a farmer from a remote village in Ireland, and now you're making a George Lawless movie! Tell us— how did this all come about?'

Donnie cleared his dry throat and tried to remember at least some of the script Sable Vonderhyde, the scary publicist, had given him, but his mind went blank, and instead, he stared at Randolph ... Randolph Lettering. He was sitting right in front of him, being interviewed ... about a movie he was making. Donnie's dream had been on borrowed time, and if he didn't hit the jackpot now, he would have to retreat, bury his dream forever and accept the fact that he was going to spend the rest of his life knee-deep in cow shit. But here he was, with success in sight, being interviewed by the legendary talk show host. The question bounced around Donnie's head—*how did this all come about?*

Was it on the annual family pilgrimage to Dingle for summer holidays when they had watched in awe as an entire village was built for the set of *Ryan's Daughter*? Or was it his first-ever trip to the cinema? The magnificent wonder of the big screen had been a feast for his senses, transporting him to a cliff top, his heart in his mouth as he evaded the enemy and plunged into the water with Butch and Sundance.

His memory of that day was so vivid he could still feel the rain trickling down the back of his cagoule as he queued with his elder cousins and big sister in the pouring rain. There was a busker with thick sideburns and long hippy hair that flapped in the wind. He belted out tunes on his guitar to those queuing, hoping they might relinquish their precious money to show their appreciation. Donnie had clenched his fist over the coins in his hand, partly to conceal them and partly to ensure a fit of inadvertent generosity didn't overcome him—any surrender of coins would mean no tin of coke for the film. His cousins, PJ, Antony and Liam, wanted to light up, so they had led his big sister, Kathy, and him to the back row. Donnie was pushed into the row first, and to his disgust, he was seated next to a couple slurping at each other's mouths. Purple smoke swirled around the beam from the projector, but as soon as the movie started, he forgot about the pair snogging next to him and marvelled at Paul Newman and Robert Redford blowing up trains, galloping under gunfire and kicking up one hell of a storm. That could have been that day it *all came about,* or it could have been his first stage appearance in the nativity play. It hadn't been a question Donnie had ever considered.

Randolph Lettering wanted to click his fingers in front of his guest's face, but he resisted the temptation.

'Donnie? How did it all come about?'

Just as Donnie's brain kicked into gear to answer the question, he heard a hideously familiar voice from the audience shout out.

'Everyone knows you can't fucking act!'

As Randolph's eyes darted towards the heckle, Donnie felt like someone had stabbed him in the chest. He managed a nervous laugh and tried again to speak, hoping the voice was an anxiety-induced hallucination.

'Well, Randolph, for as long as I can remember, I wanted to be an actor, and I don't think anyone really took me seriously—'

The heckler boomed over Donnie from the crowd, 'Took you seriously? Why would they? You suck, you useless, little, lying bollox!'

Donnie felt he was falling from a great height even though he was still sitting in the chair. Wide-eyed, he stared into the black depths of the audience as Randolph looked round to Paul, the keyboard player. Paul shrugged back at him. Randolph was used to the unexpected happening on live television, and at first, he thought the heckler might be some prank, but now with this language, it was clear he was not, and why the hell had the producer not cut to the ads?

Being a pro, Randolph continued undeterred, 'Seems you have a bit of a fan already.'

The audience laughed and then gasped as a hulking figure made straight for the stage.

The producer, aware that he should be cutting to ads, felt the urge to let it play out for a little longer. He could see the security heading straight for the figure, and although he may well be fired for this, it could make ratings soar. The risk was worth taking.

Donnie saw him coming, signalling the imminent collapse of his new world. He had a feeling of being sucked through the floor into the jaws of humiliation. He felt dizzy as he tumbled into a career death roll. There was no time to filter his thoughts.

'WOULD YOU EVER FUCK OFF, FRANCIS!' Donnie shouted at the top of his voice, slid from his chair, and hid behind Randolph, covering his face with both hands.

The producer was about to yell, '*Cut!*' when two security guards hauled the man away. Donnie crawled out slowly from behind Randolph. The producer held his hand up—he wanted just a few more moments of this television gold, and Donnie was about to deliver it.

Donnie stumbled, stupefied, towards camera one. Then, looking directly at the camera, he whispered, 'Hi, Mum, Dad, Kathy, Sheena. I've got a lot to tell you.'

CHAPTER TWO

BACK THEN, 1971, BELLVARA, IRELAND

Sheets of rain lambasted the streets of Bellvara and pelted down on the few unfortunate people still outside. This wasn't soft Irish drizzle—it was biting rain that hurt, whipped up from the Atlantic, and menacingly hurled at the shore. Some people huddled in doorways; some stood under the thatch, waiting for the storm to abate before running to the next shelter en-route home. Others dashed into The Pier Head bar and made a mental note to hunker down there for the remainder of the day.

A red Zetor tractor pulled up behind a donkey and cart carrying the milk churns. The tractor was Mickey-Joe McNamara's pride and joy. He was a powerful man with a face that looked like it had always lived outdoors. Excessive beatings as a child meant that Mickey-Joe grew into a man who didn't take any shit from anyone. He operated on the edge and had a complete disregard for caution. With an unusually broad smile, he helped his daughter, Kathy, steer from his lap. His wife, Elizabeth, was squeezed in beside them. From the nettled look on Elizabeth's face, the journey had been somewhat hazardous.

Mickey-Joe climbed out and shielded his wife and daughter from the Atlantic storm as they ran to the steps of the school.

Through the rain, Elizabeth saw a familiar figure hobbling purposefully towards them.

'Mickey-Joe, it's your mother!' Elizabeth called out to her,

'Nuala, what are you doing out in this weather? You'll catch your death.'

Mickey-Joe's mother, Nuala, wore a thick woollen coat which was bulging from the weight of the rain. Jam-jar glasses enlarged her smiling eyes, and her cheeks had been slapped red by the wind. Mickey-Joe caught her arm, and she leaned on him to climb up the steps.

Elizabeth looked worried.

'The doctor said you were to stay at home. You need to keep warm, Nuala.'

Nuala beamed, revealing shiny, white, false teeth.

'Nothing would warm me more than seeing the little chiseler's play.'

'Right, let's get this over with,' Mickey-Joe sighed as he opened the door of the school hall. Mickey-Joe had no idea how it had happened that he was here, at Donnie's nativity play, when he distinctly remembered telling his wife he hadn't a notion of going.

They opened the doors into a big, stuffy hall that smelt damp from all the drenched people lined in rows on uncomfortable wooden chairs. At the front of the hall, there was a makeshift curtain made from an old bedsheet and a dimly twinkling Christmas tree that had already shed most of its needles. Elizabeth, Mickey-Joe, Nuala and Kathy found some empty seats near the back of the hall. Mickey-Joe sat down with a breathy grunt and took off his sodden cap. He knew he would be here for longer than would be bearable. Beside him, Elizabeth placed her hand on his arm. Mickey-Joe wasn't sure if the pressure she was exerting was a display of gratitude that he was there or a warning not to leave. Kathy rested her head against Nuala's sopping coat as Nuala strained to see the stage through her fogged-up glasses and waited for her grandson's big moment.

At the front of the hall, Lorcan and Delia Brawley sat on the best seats in the house. Their only son, Francis, was in the play.

The Brawleys had inherited old Jack Brawley's estate and had moved back from London with big plans that never materialised. Lorcan was generous to a fault, helping locals whenever someone was on their uppers. His wife, Delia, provided a tight-fisted balance, underpaying staff and overspending on herself. Lorcan had long since realised he had married the wrong woman. Delia's initial beauty and charm were short-lived, and by the time they had their first child, Francis, they were sleeping in separate bedrooms. By then, they both knew that Francis would be the last offspring. Despite their private lack of affection, they kept up public appearances, and many wondered how a gentleman like Lorcan coped with his acerbic wife.

Lorcan reached into his pocket and felt the flask that provided him with his coping mechanism. Subtly, he took a small swig when Delia wasn't looking. Not just because she was likely to disapprove to keep her Holy Joe image intact in public but because he had no wish to share it with her.

'I still can't believe they didn't give Francis the part of Joseph,' Delia whined. 'After everything we've done for this school. Do you know *who* got it?'

Lorcan shook his head. He wasn't sure what the question had been and hoped that a shake of the head was an appropriate response. Sometimes he wasn't sure if Delia had spoken at all or if he just had a constant recording of her whining in his brain.

'It was Donnie McNamara. I can't get over it. I think that kid is retarded.'

She stared at Lorcan for his agreement, but none came.

Behind the makeshift curtain, Donnie felt an adrenalin rush. In that moment, he knew this was what he was born to do. His purpose in life was to act. His talent had finally been recognised because the part of Joseph usually went to the most popular kid or the most good-looking kid, and Donnie was neither. He was far from ugly, but he had a clumsy face, as if God had been in a bit of a hurry when he put it together. The good Lord had blessed him with bright blue eyes and thick dark hair, but not much thought was put into fine-tuning the arrangement of the rest of his features. In Donnie's opinion, God had bestowed him with talent, and when the teacher recognised this and called out his name for Joseph, Donnie was so ecstatic he thought he would burst. This achievement was made all the sweeter because Francis Brawley, whom Donnie despised, had wanted the part of Joseph, but he had been given the part of the Innkeeper as a small consolation. Francis wasn't clever, but he was good-looking, athletic and rich, which seemed to make him very popular, and he got whatever he wanted. He lived at Brawley's estate with his parents. His parents wanted him to experience 'local life' at Bellvara's national school before enrolling in Ballycraven Boarding School. So Donnie eagerly awaited the day Francis would be shipped off, a heavy trunk in hand, out of Donnie's life. Donnie didn't know how the torment from Francis had started, but he could still taste the dirt in his mouth and hear Francis's taunting laugh as he tried to scramble to his feet and run away. He later found his school bag up the tree, missing a couple of sacred sweets, and every school book inside the bag had missing pages.

The curtain tumbled down, and the show was on! Donnie was ready to walk onstage with the very pretty Roísín O'Donnell, dressed perfectly as Mary. She offered Donnie her charming elfin smile as he linked arms with her. She elevated Donnie, and he squared his shoulders and looked straight ahead at Francis. To Donnie's surprise, Francis gave him a thumbs up.

Donnie and Roísín walked in front of the audience towards a prop door made from wooden pallets. Donnie knocked, and Francis, as the Innkeeper, opened the door.

'Is there any room at the Inn?' asked Donnie.

Francis smirked and, in a voice that boomed across the hall, answered, 'There is for Mary, but you can fuck off, Joseph!'

CHAPTER THREE

EIGHTEEN YEARS LATER, 1989, BELLVARA, IRELAND

Donnie sauntered around the harbour, scuffing stones under his feet. He often went for a walk, paced the pier, looked across the bay into the waves beyond, and willed himself to see beyond the limiting horizon.

For anyone visiting Bellvara, it was a mystical place of rugged beauty with stark, limestone-paved hills decorated with wild orchids and spring gentians. A feeling of ancient history felt embedded in the landscape—from the fossils in the rock to the castle commanding the bay. The village was a vibrant rainbow of painted houses and pubs, emitting a vibe that nothing happened here at any great pace. For the town's locals, it was simply home, but for Donnie McNamara, Bellvara felt like a hand-me-down coat he would rather not be wearing.

Some people might have said Donnie McNamara had 'notions', but Donnie felt God had made a mistake. He was born into the wrong family, on the wrong side of the Atlantic, and what made it worse was that he was perched on the edge of that ocean, taunted by the chasm between him and his dreams. He wanted to be somewhere exciting, flashy and modern, where life moved forward rather than stood still. A place where wanting to be a star wouldn't land him in the lunatic asylum. To be somewhere that he wasn't seen as the good-for-nothing farmer's son, a small-town nobody, the family disappointment.

For Donnie, that somewhere was America.

Donnie felt the wind nipping his skin and wished he had brought a jumper. He turned and headed home, passing The Pier Head without any temptation to join the 'early in the week' hardened drinkers.

Teresa, the publican, rolled out a keg to the pavement like she had hundreds of times before. Teresa was heavy-footed, but her face had once been beautiful. The years of working in a smoky bar and drinking her share of the profits caused her beauty to fade—blotched like a watercolour painting left to rot in a damp attic.

'Do you want a hand, Teresa?' Donnie offered.

Teresa shook her head with a tired sigh. She was happier when everyone saw how hard she worked.

'No, you're all right. C'mere, how's your mother, this weather? She's not been around much.'

'She's grand, thanks for asking, Teresa.'

Teresa shook her head to indicate his answer had not satisfied her curiosity. 'Oh, and I hear your uncle Pete is coming back today!'

This was news to Donnie.

'Well, if you've heard it, Teresa, that's probably right.'

'Probably,' Teresa replied matter-of-factly. 'Must be nice,' Teresa continued.

'What's that?' Donnie wasn't sure what tack she was taking.

'Having a rich uncle. Tell me, is he a millionaire or a multi-millionaire?'

Donnie stared at her for a moment before answering with a smile, 'Well, I heard that he was one of the largest donors in Ronald Reagan's presidential campaign, so make of that what you will.'

'Oooh,' Teresa giggled, unsure if this gossip was real and could be repeated, 'and a bachelor too!'

Donnie carried on up the road, mildly amused about Teresa's status as the *village oracle*. Communication happened by three means: telephone, television and *teleteresa*. He walked a little faster, delighted to hear that his uncle's visit was imminent.

UNCLE PETE WAS Donnie's father's brother and had emigrated to the States to work as a labourer in New York. He was the epitome of the American Dream—having swapped his shovel for a bar towel. His electrifying personality was dynamite in the pub trade, and before long, he was a partner in one of the busiest pubs. Irish bartenders were already at legendary status in New York as the pub culture had been ingrained since birth. They knew the pub was a sanctuary: a place to be entertained and have the craic, to catch up on social news and perhaps meet the right people to help with life's opportunities. It was a place to unwind from hard living, reminisce, dream, sing, and ultimately to drink. Pete's listening ear, combined with humour and stories that should have been destined for the stage, drew a huge crowd who would roar with laughter when a new customer entered and ordered a bowl of the infamous rabbit stew.

Pete would plonk the bowl down in front of the punter and declare,

'You've read the book, you've seen the film, now eat the cast.'

Uncle Pete visited Bellvara yearly. He would arrive in a big, fancy car that drew looks up and down the street. He would play his guitar and sing rebel songs with locals crowding around him like the homecoming of a celebrity. He made up songs on the hoof about the people around him, causing much hilarity. He got away with talking about taboo subjects and saying the most inappropriate things because that was 'just Pete'. He bought round after round for everyone in the bar. Children were savvy to stay close by when the notes fell from his wallet as he would regularly tell them to keep whatever he had dropped. Despite his colourful personality, he had never married and didn't ever bring a girlfriend home. Many had speculated that he was freer to be himself in America, away from an intolerant church's judging eyes and preachings.

Donnie's father, Mickey-Joe, had inherited the family farm, but it was Pete who was held on a pedestal by the village. One of their own 'done good' in America and regularly returned to be amongst his own people. Rumour had it he was a millionaire. But, regardless of the cash he clearly had, the village loved him, and so did Donnie.

Meg, the family collie, greeted Donnie at the red gate that led home. The McNamara's house was an old stone farmhouse flanked by a large shed and several old outbuildings. Hanging up on one of the outbuildings was an artistically decorated sign that read *Kathy's Bakery*.

Donnie kicked off his boots at the door and pushed them into line with the other boots. No matter how much mud or cowshit was outside, no one dared bring it over the door. His mother, Elizabeth, kept an incredibly tight ship and was obsessed with cleanliness—there wasn't a cup out of place or carpet hair pointing in the wrong direction.

Donnie called out to his mother.

'Mum, Uncle Pete is coming!'

Elizabeth stuck her head around the door from the living room. Her hair was tied up with a kerchief, and she looked harassed.

'So I heard! He hasn't called. I heard it from just about everyone in the village. I'm sure he does this to annoy me. The place is a kip.'

Donnie shouted after her as she disappeared back into the living room, 'Maybe he just doesn't want you running around like a mad thing, cleaning a perfectly clean house.'

Elizabeth rounded the door again with her rubber-gloved hand on her hip.

'Your idea of clean and mine are as close as an ass and a thoroughbred. Your father's outside. He could do with your help.'

Donnie went out to the field to help his father mend the wall by the old well—two hours too late, Mickey-Joe told him. Mickey-Joe was twice as strong as Donnie, lifting two stones to

Donnie's one. Nothing was said about this, but Donnie felt it puncture his masculinity, so he tried to equal his father's efforts, which resulted in dropping a large stone on his dad's toe.

'Stupid fecker! Just as well I've got steel toe-caps. Christ!'

Donnie saw his uncle's car hurtle down the driveway in the distance, like a chariot charging to save his nephew from further ridicule. He lobbed the last stone on the ground and ran towards the house. Mickey-Joe shook his head, replacing the stone in the wall before sauntering down the field after his son.

Pete pulled up in front of the farmhouse in a black Grenada. Pete always felt a pull to the place that made him feel more homesick when he was there—a sadness of days gone by and a life that had moved on. The farmhouse belonged to Mickey-Joe, making him feel like a visitor in his own home. Pete's old bicycle was still in the shed, rusted with flat tyres. He could see himself as a child climbing the walls and scraping his shins, hanging from trees, and raking the hay with all the other local teenagers. It felt like someone else's life.

Pete's blocky figure filled the doorway, with his welcoming arms open and a small blue suitcase at his feet. He hugged and kissed Elizabeth and then slapped Donnie's back as he greeted him in a bear hug.

'Still not too old for a good hug!' Pete said, laughing.

Mickey-Joe couldn't help himself when he spouted, 'He's twenty-four, Pete and not growing up at all.'

Pete looked at Mickey-Joe a second longer than was comfortable.

'Good to see you, MJ!'

Donnie noticed immediately that Pete did not look well. He had a grey pallor that Donnie recognised—either very hard living for too long or a lingering shadow cast by the Grim Reaper himself. Whatever was causing it, Donnie was concerned. Pete's laugh still boomed, and his eyes still danced, but the energy that once swirled around him was dimmed, like the fading out at the end of a raucous song.

'Still got the fishing rod I got you?' Pete asked Donnie.
'Sure.'

'Tomorrow then. We'll go fishing, just you and me, but tonight your dad and I have some things to discuss.'

Mickey-Joe nodded, indicating to Donnie that things were going on that he had deliberately been told nothing about.

Mickey-Joe and Pete headed into the living room and shut the door as Elizabeth pulled out the best crystal glasses and a bottle of whiskey from the press.

THE NEXT DAY Donnie and Pete took the winding road south into County Clare. The road hugged the mountain on one side and provided panoramic views of the wild Atlantic on the other. A muted sun danced between the clouds, casting heavenly beams through the cracks in the grey sky, making the stone walls on either side of the road look like silver ribbons in the distance.

Pete pointed to the sunbeams.

'Angel rays!' he declared. 'I always love to see angel rays. You don't see much of them in New York—the sky isn't big enough.'

Donnie found Uncle Pete's enthusiasm for the west of Ireland infectious. Pete saw wonder in everything, like a child collecting shells on the beach, each one prettier than the last.

'I think you're blessed,' sighed Donnie. 'I'd love to live in America.'

Pete let out a low cynical laugh.

'Beauty is in the eye of the beer holder. New York is a racket of sirens, cars, horns and people. It's a lot of fun, it's edgy and exciting, and now it's home ... a home where, on average, every single day, five people are murdered, nine are raped, and almost two hundred people are assaulted.'

Donnie stared at him, trying to compute the information that sounded like another planet.

Pete continued, 'There's whole neighbourhoods where you

can't go—a giant chasm between the haves and the have-nots, living beside each other. There's a crack cocaine pandemic and constant muggings. Take a wander to Times Square, and depravity will punch you in the gut: peep shows, brothels, perverts getting their kicks watching live sex shows. If New York had a moral compass, it rode out on a horse with the saddle flapping long ago.'

Donnie felt crushed with disappointment. Pete was his hero, living the life of his dreams. He didn't want to hear about this dark, depressing side of his fantasy of bright lights and excitement.

'Did Dad ask you to put me off America?' Donnie mumbled.

Pete laughed, 'No, I'm just saying. That's all.'

He pulled the car into a tiny lay-by just outside Bally-vaughan, and they clambered over the flagstone rocks with their rods to the perfect spot Pete had found decades before. Although the sea was calm, waves beat gently against the rocks, throwing droplets of salty spray onto their faces.

Pete attached the bait to the hook as Donnie watched and copied him exactly. Donnie had been fishing several times before, but he knew Pete was a veteran at this, and he would learn all he could from him today, whether it was about fishing, America, or life in general. The fresh air had not changed the ominous colour of Pete's face, and Donnie wondered if this visit might be his last.

'New York isn't all bad,' Pete conceded as he cast his line out. 'I've made a lot of good memories there, and the city has been good to me … but it's not what it used to be. Maybe I'm just getting old.'

They sat down on the rocks together, looking very much like father and son.

Donnie grasped onto Pete's positivity.

'You left here with nothing and were a huge success out there. Everyone talks about it—Dad too.'

'Ah yes,' Pete replied as he lit the cigarette dangling on his lip, 'Pete the millionaire, Pete the *multi*-millionaire. So

I've heard. It's all shite, you know, but let them talk and tell them fucking nothing!' Pete winked at Donnie. 'If I were a rich man, you and your sisters would be inheriting a fortune, would you not?'

'I haven't thought about it,' Donnie said, and he genuinely hadn't. Up until recently, Donnie thought Uncle Pete would live forever. 'I've been too busy thinking up my own plans.'

'I see. Well, your sister has found her passion here with the bakery, and I know she'll do well with her plans to grow it. What about you?'

'My dream has never changed, Uncle Pete. I want to go to America. I want to be an actor. I want to be so good at it that I win an Oscar, and then I plan to come home and put that Oscar on my Dad's mantlepiece.'

Pete's face betrayed his frustration.

'It's a pipe dream, Donnie. Do you know how many young people fantasise about the same thing? Sure, wouldn't I like to be Clint Eastwood? Is there nothing here that interests you here?' Pete threw his arms out in front of him. 'I mean, look at this place, Donnie, home is fucking paradise, and you've a family responsibility to the farm.'

'Right, but so did you, and you live in New York.'

Pete exhaled a deep sigh. Translating his years of experience into a short conversation was a struggle.

'It was different in our day. For so many of us, there were no opportunities here. So we had to leave.'

'Things haven't changed that much, and the farm is exactly as you left it,' Donnie retorted.

Pete accepted in his mind that there was only so much his generation could teach the one before it. Humans, he deduced, are hardwired to want to make their own mistakes—and so, history repeats itself, and the young think they have all the answers, just as the old did when they were young.

They sat in silence for a moment until Pete turned to Donnie with a bright smile and said,

'Don't be listening to the likes of me, Donnie. I'm battle-worn. Go to America! Follow your dreams and do what makes you happy because one thing is for sure … life is too fucking short. Just don't forget where you're from.'

Donnie felt a pull on his fishing line.

'Got something!'

He reeled it in, but the hook dangled, devoid of a fish. 'I was sure I had something.'

Pete chortled, 'First lesson on fishing with me— it's not really about catching fish.'

CHAPTER FOUR

MEANWHILE, IN LA

Abe Nelson sat his ass down on a stool in Mike's dive bar. Mike nodded a welcome and reached for the bottle of Jack Daniels as Abe pulled out scrunched-up dollars from his pocket and placed them on the counter. Once a man of spontaneity, this ritual had become a daily occurrence. Abe was aware, when he caught sight of himself in the mirror behind the bar, that his reflection betrayed his lifestyle but consoled himself with the fact that people barely recognised him these days. His greying hair was long and unwashed; he had a shadow of stubble across his face, and sunglasses covered his trademark blue eyes. At fifty-nine, he was boozed, bedraggled, and barely present. From a distance, he bore more resemblance to a hobo than a Hollywood actor, but close-up, his face stubbornly held its handsome structure. Abe didn't speak to anyone in Mike's bar. Instead, he drank to numb the pain and block the memories, merging the days into weeks of emptiness.

Four years had passed since the incident, but four years is a long time in Hollywood—sufficient time to fall far enough into the pit of disgrace to prevent any possibility of climbing out. Not long before that, he'd been surfing a wave of success—he had friends, a wife, a son and a place to call home.

Abe downed the Jack Daniel's Mike had poured him and found his mind once again back in the limo on that fateful night. Jack Daniels had featured that night, too ... and coke, but not the kind that was poured into his drink. Unlike many of his peers, Abe had side-stepped drugs most of his life on the basis that he had thought he'd probably be a candidate for taking them too far, but when he met Sophie Silver, who was young and full of adventure, he called his own bluff and proved his own point. Now he was attending the film premiere, battling bad headlines and befriending booze and drugs, while Sophie stood on a podium of glory, the new princess of Hollywood who bedazzled and bewitched.

Fate hadn't been any less kind to Abe than it had been to the next man. He had triumphed from the unplayable hand he'd been dealt as a kid. He'd been on top of his game, sought-after by studios, snowed under by fan mail, regularly interviewed on top-rated shows, and suddenly incredibly desirable to women—but that was after years of hard slog, rejections, flipping burgers, cleaning windows, digging holes, evictions, and having to pull some belief in his future from a hat full of nothing.

But his career turned around, and life had been sweet for a long time—until he fucked up. It had started with a regrettable mistake, an act of infidelity, that led to a guilty conscience. The remorse gnawed at his soul, making itself known to those around him through the sweat on his brow, his bitten lip and his words tumbling too fast from his mouth.

Abe wasn't stupid; he knew Sophie was a fling. She would dispose of him once he had served his purpose and would move on to someone younger and higher in the ratings. However, he hadn't expected Sophie to sell him out and share his story and secrets as fodder for the masses. She did so in such a way that she looked compassionate, even humorous at times, but underneath that angelic loveliness was a toxic, selfish soul who would trample anything and anyone to fulfil her ambition.

Abe's publicist, Terri, had been there when he poured out from the limo. She effortlessly shielded his stagger from the public glare. Professional, poised and a heart of gold—that was Terri, but even Terri had a breaking point.

'Where is Crystal?' she had asked with concern. 'I thought she agreed to come with you.'

'I think she just told you that. I knew she wasn't coming,' Abe had slurred. 'She's fucking gone, Terri, and she's taken Steven with her.'

Terri let out a small gasp before catching Abe's arm and guiding him forwards.

'She's taken everything too. I haven't got a fucking chair to sit on or a plate for my dinner. Jesus Christ, she even took the toilet roll holder.'

'Okay, Abe. Let's chat about this later. Put your smile on, and let's move.' Terri had smiled at him as if showing him how it was done.

'I don't know where they fucking are, Terri. She isn't letting me talk to my own son.'

'He's seventeen, Abe. He's not stupid.'

'Before they left, he told me hated me.'

Terri noticed a tear drip down under Abe's sunglasses.

'It'll be okay, Abe. You'll see. She'll calm down, and you can work things out one way or another,' she whispered, hoping to God Abe's public persona would kick in soon.

Abe had not just made a promise to Crystal; he had trusted himself not to succumb to the advances of other women and certainly not to go out looking for them. The latter he managed. The former had not taken 'the Sophie factor' into account. Sophie was an upcoming actress that snagged the lead in his latest, Oscar-nominated film. She was a stunning dancer with a mystical aura. At twenty-eight, she was almost twenty years his junior and *seemingly* besotted by him. She showed her adoration by holding his gaze a few moments too long, bowing her head to the side and smiling broadly every time he spoke. She was intelligent, graceful, and the embodiment of youth. A youth that had faded in Abe. The first time they slept together, he had found it hard to feel any guilt—he scanned his conscience, but nothing would filter through the elation and vivacity he felt when he was with her. The second time, Abe knew he was dangerously close to the edge, but when he hit double digits and was still left wanting, the lies spiralled; deceit was his shield, and his opponent was himself. Crystal had suspected the worst from Abe's tortured expressions, but she waited, nursing her mistrust until she had gathered her ammunition to annihilate him. Loss of his wealth was, of course, going to inflict some pain, but her pivotal weapon of destruction was using their son, Steven, as a pawn in her check-mate. Crystal plotted to break that relationship beyond repair.

Perhaps if Crystal had been Abe's first wife, there might have been room for forgiveness and a possibility to rebuild trust, but Crystal was lucky number three, and unlike the first two, Crystal thrived on revenge and showed no mercy.

Abe had come to a grinding halt, a look of torment on his face. Terri followed his gaze to a crowd forming around a young, striking woman clad in a slinky golden gown.

'Sophie's further up, doing interviews,' she had said, trying not to point. 'Are you sure you want to do this? We can say you're not well. Although, I think it's better to face it.'

'Never better,' Abe said as he staggered backwards.

Terri failed to catch him this time as cameras closed in. Abe pulled himself up as the cameras flashed with unrelenting scrutiny. His head spun as darkness crept from the corners of his eyes, blurring his vision and disorientating him. Down he went as if he was at sea, battling currents and tumbling waves. He struggled to his feet, unzipped his trousers and pissed all over the red carpet.

And that was the night Abe's career was over.

Losing his son created a nuclear landslide that obliterated his life as Abe knew it, culminating in a momentary loss of control of his mind and his bladder for all the world to see. Abe had seen the footage: struggling from the limousine, cameras flashing, staggering and crashing into people. He watched in shock as he saw himself fall and crawl around the red carpet before grappling to his feet, leaning back, laughing manically and urinating on the red carpet, surrounded by Hollywood's nobility. Whatever gaps were in his memory, the recorded footage could remind him and the rest of the world forever. He felt he had been watching an imposter ruin his life. To wake in the morning with the fear that someone else had been out there pretending to be Abe Nelson and damaging his life beyond all recognition was a terrifying thought. Even more horrifying was the reality that there was no imposter, and Abe had done it all to himself.

Abe was no stranger to the bottle. His confident exterior had always hidden baggage that had never been properly unpacked. Abandonment was at the core of his deepest fears, having suffered at the hands of his parents, who regarded him as both a mistake and a secret. Newly born, Abe had been shipped off to live with a widowed aunt, Peggy, in Canada. Peggy had one daughter, Melanie, thirteen years older than Abe. When Abe was five, his beloved Peggy died, and Melanie traded her future dreams and freedom at eighteen to raise him because his birth parents would not acknowledge his existence. These were the secrets Sophie had shared with the world. She had betrayed him and had been applauded for it, as the public devoured every scrap of his personal life, but worse than that, Sophie had given the mosh-pit access to Melanie's life, and there wasn't a woman alive that Abe loved and protected more than Melanie. It had been Melanie who drove to his house, pushed past the paparazzi, and found him face down in a pool of vomit on the living room floor. She unplugged the televisions, threw away the papers and nursed him back to semi-sobriety. She was his gatekeeper, his confidante, his cousin, his sister and his mother.

Abe's beach house in Malibu had already been sold before the film premiere, and he was living out the final weeks among boxes and bottles, seeing ghosts of a happy family chatting in the kitchen, drinking wine on the deck, surfing the waves in front of the house. It wasn't the house he would miss, but the memories made there. Memories that his son had discarded as irrelevant—love that his son rebuffed, phone calls left unanswered, and hateful words spouted were what led to the debacle at the premiere. Crystal knew she'd hit the vengeance jackpot.

SITTING IN MIKE'S bar, Abe lifted his sunglasses briefly to wipe the tears that were forming again.

'Same again?' Mike asked, knowing the answer.

Abe nodded and pulled more dollars from his pocket.

CHAPTER FIVE

A WEEK LATER, 1989, BELLVARA, IRELAND

onnie walked into the living room where his nine-year-old little sister, Sheena, was cartwheeling around the room, narrowly missing the furniture.

Elizabeth appeared in the lounge, dressed to the nines in a glamorous pink chiffon skirt and white blouse. She seldom dressed up now, so when she did, it gave her a rush of excitement, making her feel frivolous as if she was trying to recreate the magic of her giddy youth. She would fight these high spirits with her mature and sensible alter ego, not realising that she was the warden suppressing her own happiness.

'Donnie, we're going out tonight. I've been looking forward to seeing Big Tom all month, so I don't want any shenanigans.'

Mickey-Joe leaned against the door frame, looking sharp in his pressed trousers and pale yellow shirt. As Elizabeth passed in the doorway, he pulled a cigarette packet from his pocket.

Elizabeth flicked her hair, waiting for the compliment that didn't come.

Pete arrived by Mickey-Joe's side, dressed more casually in faded jeans and a checked shirt.

'I think we've all scrubbed up well. You look great, Elizabeth,' Pete said cheerfully.

Elizabeth smiled, glad that someone had noticed.

Mickey-Joe tapped a cigarette from his packet and lit it. He exhaled blue smoke as he turned to Donnie.

'Keep an eye on Áine while we're away. She's in the shed.'

'What?' Donnie was a little alarmed.

'I don't think she'll calf tonight, but I've put her in the shed all the same. She might. Keep an eye. Any problems, you can call Gerard.'

'What if she does calf?'

'Call Gerard, like I said. I wouldn't be expecting you to calf her, and your big sister is out with Francis tonight, so you are on watch.'

Pete looked at Mickey-Joe imploringly.

'Come on now, MJ. The lad is well able to calf the cow.'

Mickey-Joe gawped at Pete as if he had two heads.

'Áine is my prize cow. I'd have more confidence in Sheena.'

Sheena grinned, but Donnie looked away, hurt burning his cheeks.

'Don't be a bollox, Mickey-Joe,' Pete muttered, but Mickey-Joe either wasn't listening or chose not to.

'Come on, Elizabeth, we don't want to be late for the gig,' grouched Mickey-Joe.

Donnie caught his mother's eye as she left. She smiled at him, defusing his embarrassment.

'You do look lovely, mum. Have a great night,' he said, smiling back.

THROUGHOUT DONNIE'S LIFE, his father had tried, in vain, to instil in Donnie a passion for the farm. Heated arguments, cock-ups and Donnie's inability to foresee what needed to be done on the farm resulted in his father relenting and releasing Donnie to college to study computer science. Donnie didn't share his parent's petrification of computers and had happily embraced new gadgets and technology. He demonstrated adeptness in programming, but the driving force behind his push to attend college was to join the drama club. The year Donnie spent in college centred around plays, theatre, pubs, the drama club and very little on computer science. That summer, his

results had been posted to the farm and were handed to his
father by Frank the Postman. His father passed the envelope
to Donnie and stood expectantly in front of him. Donnie had
felt his face burn on seeing the lamentable F for FAIL.

He had looked up at his father with trepidation and
choked out,

'Not so good.'

Mickey-Joe had turned on his heel and walked out the front
door muttering,

'Well, that's that then.'

And that had been that. The end of the heady days in Galway
at the college drama club, watching plays, sipping pints outside
The Quays bar with a heart full of hope, wondering where life
would take him next. Life took him backwards like the snap of
an elastic band, and he had no idea how to move beyond the
gravitational pull of his father and the farm. Because despite
Donnie's farming incompetence in his father's eyes, his father
could not bear the idea of Donnie being anything other than
a farmer. Donnie was his only son. The farm had been passed
through generations, and now, as it lingered above Donnie's
head, Mickey-Joe was crushed by his son's lack of interest
and ineptness.

DONNIE SAT WITH Sheena on the sofa, watching *Planes,
Trains and Automobiles*, but had paused the film twice to
check on the cow. He wasn't going to give his father any more
ammunition against him. Eventually, the movie finished, and
Sheena leapt about the room to the credits, showing no sign
of going to bed.

'You should probably go to bed,' Donnie half-heartedly
suggested.

'No way!'

Armed with Opal Fruits, Revels and Tayto crisps, Sheena
bounded around the living room.

'I'm going to check the cow again,' Donnie told her.

'You've done that twice.'

'And I'm doing it again. Go and brush your teeth and I'll come up and say goodnight.'

Donnie pulled on his wellies, picked up the torch and headed out to the shed. As soon as he opened the kitchen door, he could hear the cow. Áine's bellows got louder and more frantic.

'Fuck, fuck, fuck,' he shouted to no one but himself.

Donnie looked in on the cow, dazzling her eyes with the torch and saw her on her side grunting loudly—her brown coat shiny with sweat.

He ran back to the house and straight into the kitchen with his wellies caked in mud, lifted the handset from the phone on the wall and dialled Gerard, feeling sick with fear of losing the cow.

Gerard answered the phone, his voice foggy with sleep, 'Yes?'

'Gerard, it's Donnie. Dad's out, and the cow's calving. Please, come quickly.'

'Right then,' Gerard said.

Donnie heard the dial tone at the end of the phone and was left wondering if Gerard was fully awake and on his way or had rolled over and gone back to sleep.

He headed back out to the cow, shone the torch on her again and pleaded,

'Hang in there, old girl. Gerard's on his way.'

The cow made a noise Donnie wasn't sure cows were supposed to make, followed by a guttural groan.

'All right, Áine, hang the fuck on.'

A final bellow and Donnie jumped over the metal barrier, crawling on the straw to reach Áine.

Gerard finally arrived, in his overalls, sucking a pipe. Gerard was around the same age as Mickey-Joe, but the years had been less kind. His glasses hung on his face at an angle, with the hinge on the left leg held together by nicotine-stained

sellotape. Gerard was the most depressing man Donnie had
the misfortune to know. According to Gerard, if it wasn't
raining, it was going to rain, and if it wasn't dying, it was
going to die. Some people were 'glass half full' or 'glass half
empty'; Gerard's glass was the one that fell from the shelf and
got smashed to smithereens.

He shone his lamp into the shed, and his face turned to
sheer disbelief when he saw Donnie cradling the calf as Áine
licked her clean.

'Look at that,' Gerard exclaimed, 'she's done it all by herself.'

Annoyed, Donnie blinked in the glare of the lamp in his eyes.

'No, she didn't. The calf was stuck. I had to ratchet it out.'

'Well, you brought a little bit of luck. Maybe your dad will
call him Donnie.'

'It's a girl,' Donnie replied curtly.

'Donnie will do,' Gerard mumbled, taking another suck of
his pipe. 'What about a dropeen of whiskey then, to wet little
Donnie's head?'

Donnie was pouring the whiskey for Gerard when he heard
the loud voices of his parents and Pete arriving home.

His mother was shouting as she walked through the hall.

'For God's sake, Sheena's fast asleep on the stairs! And
there's mud everywhere!'

They burst through the door of the living room as Donnie
grinned back at them.

'Hi, Dad, we've got a new addition to the family. Áine had
a baby girl.'

Mickey-Joe, delighted, turned to Gerard.

'Oh, thanks be to God you were here, Gerard. Thanks a
million.'

Donnie stared at Gerard as Gerard was taking too long to swig
his whiskey, seemingly contemplating how much glory to take.

'To be fair,' Gerard finally said, 'it was Donnie who calved
her. He had to use the ratchet. She calved before I got there.'

Mickey-Joe beamed at his son, which was so rare, Donnie

felt very peculiar.

'Well done, son,' he said, clapping him on the back, 'we could have lost that calf. We could have bloody-well lost Áine.'

His father's praise felt warm but perilous, like the heat under a dragon's wing.

Pete chipped in from the doorway,

'Little bit of faith, MJ, that's all.'

A sudden commotion from the kitchen was heard as Donnie's older sister, Kathy, flew in with a flurry of excitement. She waved her hand about, triumphantly showing off a vintage diamond ring on her finger.

'I'm getting married!' she screamed as Mickey-Joe's eyes lit up.

Francis, once the Innkeeper in the nativity play and still despised by Donnie, stood behind Kathy and stretched his hand out towards Mickey-Joe.

'I'm sorry, Mickey-Joe, I was coming to talk to you before Kathy announced it. I didn't mean any disrespect.'

'Disrespect,' Mickey-Joe replied, throwing his arms around Kathy and Francis. 'I couldn't be more thrilled.'

Donnie wanted the floor to suck him up. *This was a fucking disaster.*

Pete suddenly clutched his chest and fell against the door frame, the colour draining from his face.

'Pete!' Elizabeth screamed as she grabbed onto him. He slumped to the floor, pulling Elizabeth down with him.

CHAPTER SIX

TWO MONTHS LATER, IRELAND, 1989

It had been two months since Pete had died. Mickey-Joe had spent thirty minutes trying to revive him while Elizabeth paced the road for the ambulance. In the end, the paramedics could do nothing except offer their condolences and take Pete's body to the hospital. That night, Donnie had heard his father howling like an injured animal. Donnie had never imagined his father could feel such emotion and pain, but after that night, Mikey-Joe didn't cry again. He just worked longer, drank more and laughed less.

Elizabeth was worried about Mickey-Joe. Every night in bed, he turned the light out and turned his back on her. She tried not to take it personally. She knew what it was like when the black dog of depression had its jaws around your throat, and she understood that grief was different for everyone, but Mickey-Joe had built walls around himself that no one could penetrate. Lately, she saw a lot less of Mickey-Joe, but the whole family was always together every Sunday at Mass.

Donnie and his friend, Tic, sauntered out of Mass, past the groups of people catching up on the week's news, the hurling won and lost, and complaining about the weather. Mickey-Joe was ahead, hot-footing it straight to the pub with Gerard. Elizabeth made sure Mickey-Joe's mother, Nuala, was looked after. She wheeled her about from person to person, who shared happy stories about Pete that made Nuala smile as she held on tightly to every hand that took hers.

Donnie couldn't believe two months had passed since Pete had died. The loss didn't seem any less, but the involuntary tears had finally abated. Time had fixed the pressure valve in his emotions so that now he didn't have to bite his lip at a memory or dig his fingernails into his hand when he thought he saw him in the distance on the street.

'All right, Donnie?' Tic asked, giving Donnie a light shove.

Tic, not unlike Donnie, was a bit of a misfit, but with the added stumbling block of having some form of Tourettes syndrome. It was currently undiagnosed except by Tic himself. His mother had tried counselling, the doctor and even the priest, but Tic was one of eleven children, so there was only so much time his mother had to search for a solution. In the end, she hoped he would grow out of it. The priest had a vested interest in curing Tic as his frequent, inadvertent heckles at Mass were causing distress and hilarity among his parishioners, but not in equal measure.

'I got my invitation to the wedding!' Tic laughed.

Donnie sighed, 'I had hoped Kathy might see through him by now.'

'A party is still a party! Pity about the divorce referendum, though, isn't it? A positive vote might have come in handy.' Tic then twitched somewhat violently before adding, 'Fucking pious bastards!'

After each cursing outburst, he would mutter 'sorry' and raise his auburn eyebrows as if he wasn't sorry at all.

'I'm glad you're going, Tic. It will be a lot more fun if you're there.'

Tic slapped Donnie on the back.

'I wouldn't want my sister to be marrying that gobshite either, but what can you do?' Tic unwittingly slapped his own face and let out a high-pitched squeal.

Donnie paid no attention. He was too busy watching his sister, Kathy, clamber into Francis's red Jaguar XJS. Tic followed his gaze.

'Have you ever seen the likes of that?' Tic mused.

Donnie looked on in disgust.

'Probably swindled some vulnerable old uncle in England out of his last great joy.'

Francis sped off down the street, the only noise piercing the birdsong outside the church.

'Prick!' Donnie and Tic said in unison.

'You coming for a pint?' Donnie asked. 'Big day for me— Tommy the Thesp is announcing the roles for the play.'

'Ha! Good luck with that. No, I've got to go round to my Nan's. She's not been well. She's had some sort of gastric problem. Stinking! Rotten! Can't even make it to Mass.'

'Okay, I'll see you after. Tell your Nan I hope she's better soon.'

'Good luck with the play! Next stop Hollywood!' Tic then uncontrollably added, 'Un-fucking likely!'

Donnie sighed. He had long since realised that although Tic's outbursts were allegedly irrepressible, they usually had legs.

Donnie walked over to his mother and grandmother, said his goodbyes, and then wandered down the street towards the pub, thinking about his sister and what he saw as the cataclysmic mistake she was making. Kathy and Donnie had always been close. She was the apple of her father's eye but didn't look down on Donnie from her pedestal—she always tried to help him up. She had his back, which was why it was so hard to understand how she could fall in love with someone Donnie loathed.

Donnie could see right through Francis Brawley. Donnie wasn't envious—perhaps jealous as hell of the car, but he knew Francis was a charlatan. He'd listened to Teresa, from the Pier Head, expose how the Brawleys gained their fortune, swindling family and unsuspecting friends. Through rumours from the next village, he had heard about Francis ripping off youngsters by telling them he had a great tip on a horse and then pocketing their money. Everyone knew the Brawleys were stinking rich, so why did Francis need to pilfer from those less

fortunate? Donnie had witnessed his bullying ways and Mach-
iavellian manoeuvres. As for the car … who in Ireland owned
a Jaguar XJS? Absolutely fucking no one. Donnie didn't know
a single person with a convertible, let alone a Jaguar, reasons
for which were fucking obvious in Ireland if you looked at the
sky. Where would he even get it serviced? Where did it come
from? He had tried to share his concerns about Francis with
Kathy, but she would respond simply by saying,

'You don't *know* him.'

But Donnie was sure it was Kathy who didn't know
Francis—she was so trusting and gullible. Francis was wangling
his way into their family, and Donnie felt it was Kathy who
would be a casualty in the train wreck that was coming.

Donnie tried to turn his thoughts to the drama club they
had formed in Tommy the Thesp's shed. Tommy lived next
to the care home, where Donnie's grandmother Nuala was a
resident, and they had come up with a genius idea to rehearse in
front of the residents. It was a win-win; they had an audience,
and Donnie's grandmother and the other residents had a break
from their otherwise monotonous day.

Tommy was older than Donnie and a bit of a joke in the
community. He had followed his sister to Glasgow some years
ago and allegedly managed to secure a place at the prestigious
Royal Scottish Academy of Music and Drama … for about
two months … before getting kicked out and resorting to a
job at a bakery. He managed to land the odd extra role in
some of Glasgow's Christmas pantomimes and played a corpse
in a detective series once, so he had more acting experience
than anyone Donnie knew, and he made a mean sausage roll.
Tommy had come home broke and set up the drama club, and
Donnie had been the first to join. Having spent time acting
in Scotland, Tommy the Thesp was the most exotic person
Donnie knew.

Donnie was excited about today. He knew the play wasn't
Broadway, but every acting role was a step forward, and his

burning ambition in life had always been to be an actor. This was not a dream he could share or discuss, as it led to ridicule or annoyance from his family. His enjoyment of computers over farming had already led to disappointment. Still, pursuing a career in acting could have resulted in being locked up in the asylum in Ballinasloe. Acting was a passion that Donnie had to underplay, and being in a community play was probably about as much as his father would endure. The performance was an adapted version of *Grease,* and Donnie was quietly confident he would get the part, given that only two people had auditioned for the role he wanted.

He neared The Pier Head bar, brightly painted yellow, a welcome beacon for all those weary with their day, and saw old Alfie just ahead of him, pulling up in his tractor for his usual Sunday pints. Sunday was the only day Alfie didn't wear wellies, but the bailing twine that held his trousers up was a daily accessory. He walked into the bar, whistling a tune of his own making while tapping his pocket, reassured by the noise of the jangling coins that would be exchanged for pints of porter. Alfie tipped his cap to Donnie with a wink as he opened the door to the pub.

Teresa owned the Pier Head with her husband, Bernie. Bernie was waiting for Teresa to die. Luckily for Bernie, he was a patient man, as Teresa had the constitution of a horse and showed no signs of departing the world any time soon. Few people liked Bernie. While Teresa may have been a thorn in their side and an incurable gossip, she wasn't a bad soul. Bernie, on the other hand, was a grumpy fucker. His moods would swing from silent and disengaged to black and unholy. Many sympathised with Teresa's fondness of the drink, believing that she had been driven there by Bernie and his cutting snipes towards his wife.

Mickey-Joe and Gerard were already sitting at the counter, drinking Guinness. Donnie casually pulled up a stool beside them. Alfie gave them all a little wave from across the bar.

Mickey-Joe nodded to Teresa behind the bar.

'A pint for Alfie over there, Teresa, and whatever Donnie is having.'

'Hi, Teresa,' Donnie said, 'Guinness and black, please.'

Mickey-Joe and Gerard exchanged a look.

'Sacrilege!' cried Mickey-Joe.

Teresa added blackcurrant cordial to Donnie's Guinness with a little smirk in his direction.

Mickey-Joe often wondered if Elizabeth had had an affair because Donnie couldn't be less like him.

Donnie always felt uncomfortable sitting at the bar with his father. He could have chatted to anyone at the counter, but his father left him constantly feeling judged, yet every time he opened his mouth, he tried to say something that might please him.

'I thought I'd work on a new accounts package for you,' suggested Donnie. 'You know, for the farm. Save mum doing the books all the time.'

'I don't need computers. I can't work the damn things,' Mickey-Joe replied.

'I can teach you,' Donnie offered, but his father scoffed and looked away.

'Didn't you fail computer science? After all the money we spent on university fees?'

'I know how to do accounts packages, though,' Donnie persisted calmly, trying to ignore his father's modus operandi of treating him like a half-witted loser.

'Books. You know where you are with the books,' asserted Mickey-Joe. This old dog wasn't learning any new tricks.

Donnie was relieved to see Tommy the Thesp breeze in the door.

'You got the part! You got the part!' Tommy hollered from the door.

'Oh God, it's that sap, Tommy the Thesp,' muttered Mickey-Joe to Gerard.

Donnie beamed as Tommy strode over and put his arms

around the shoulders of Mickey-Joe and Gerard. Every muscle in Mickey-Joe's body tightened.

'He's only gone and got the lead role!' trumpeted Tommy, and then, as if he had no social understanding of his audience at all, he rubbed the top of Mickey-Joe's head.

'In what?' asked Mickey-Joe, pushing Tommy away.

'*Grease*,' Tommy answered, staggering backwards from the force of Mickey-Joe's shove.

'Got a John Travolta on our hands, have we?' offered Gerard.

'No,' whispered Tommy. Tommy was excited about his big reveal and leaned in really close, invading their space at the bar. 'He's playing Sandy. Olivia Newton-John's part.'

Mickey-Joe wasn't sure if Tommy was joking because Mickey-Joe did not understand Tommy's sense of humour.

'We're cross-gendering the parts. See? To make it funnier,' Tommy enthused.

Mickey-Joe and Gerard didn't see, but Donnie and Tommy shared a laugh all the same. It was going to be funny, all right.

'I'll put you down for a couple of tickets,' said Tommy, eager to press on.

'What night is it on?' asked Mickey-Joe, already figuring out an excuse not to make it.

'June tenth.'

Donnie's face fell. 'No, not June tenth!'

'Why? That's the only night I can get the hall,' Tommy explained.

'That's Kathy and Francis's wedding,' said Mickey-Joe, with a smug smile.

Donnie panicked. This was terrible. Another stake was driven hard into the progression of his dream.

'I don't have to go to the wedding. They won't even notice if I'm not there.'

Teresa tittered from behind the counter.

'You are going to your sister's wedding!' Mickey-Joe was aghast. The boy was soft.

'Francis doesn't even like me!' Donnie protested.

'Of course, he does. He speaks highly of you.'

Donnie looked his Dad squarely in the eye.

'No, he does not.'

Mickey-Joe shrugged.

'Maybe not, but you're still going. Tommy, you'll need to find another cross-dresser.'

And that was it. Lead part gone.

Old Alfie had been watching the scene unfold at the other end of the bar, although no one would have known. Alfie had an uncanny ability to pick up conversations that were seemingly far out of human earshot and could observe everyone in the room—down to the colour of their socks—while looking the other way.

Donnie was on his way to the toilet. He didn't need to go, but it was the only natural way to break the conversation with his father.

Alfie tapped Donnie's hand on the way past.

'Come and keep an old man company.'

Donnie nodded, delighted to have an excuse to move to the other side of the bar, and took a seat beside the old-timer. He nodded to Teresa behind the bar.

'What are you having, Alfie?' Donnie asked.

'He's on the Jameson,' Teresa answered.

'Do you want anything in that?' Donnie asked Alfie.

'Another one,' Alfie replied, laughing but hopeful.

Alfie always reeked of silage, but people stomached the smell partly because of its familiarity but mostly because his kindness eased the stench. There wasn't a soul in the village that had a bad word to say about him. There was something about his blue eyes that emanated a mixture of kindness and devilment that made everyone warm to him.

'Y'know, some people don't know what they want to do in life, and so they are happy to follow a path that others might lay out for them ... but I don't think that's you,' Alfie said, tapping the bar in front of Donnie.

Donnie shook his head as Alfie leaned in.

'You can let them be your excuse as to why you are not doing what you want, or you can get up off your arse and go and do it. Simple as that,' he said, smiling, negating any harshness in his tone.

'I can't do it. The wedding is on the same day as the play,' Donnie moaned.

Alfie rubbed the stubble on his face.

'So that's it, is it? You're going to leg it back to misery at the first hurdle?'

'I'm not following you. The wedding is on the same day. Are you saying I shouldn't go to my sister's wedding?'

Donnie kept his voice low as Teresa put the Jameson down in front of Alfie, giving them both a withering look as if she knew their pointless conversation.

'My father was a farmer,' Alfie said, 'and I have inherited his farm. I was the only boy, you see, and I'm a grateful man. That farm has kept the wolf from the door, and there's many a man who would want to be in my shoes ... but do you know what I think about every day when I'm checking the cattle or putting out feed?'

Donnie shook his head, and Alfie gripped his arm tightly for effect.

'I think about London and singing at the Palladium. I was good. You've heard me sing. I was even better back then. I was living my wildest dream.'

Alfie stared into Donnie's eyes, holding him hostage to his point.

Donnie shifted uncomfortably in his seat, not wanting to disappoint the old man.

'The thing is, Alfie, it's the same day. I want to do the play. I really do, but how?'

A waft of silage was burning Donnie's nostrils as Alfie edged even closer and whispered to avoid Teresa's tuned-in ear.

'Can't you see what I'm telling you? You'll probably be on your farm the rest of your days. Think a little bigger than the community hall. Don't live your life in a monotone like so many before you. Leave this village and be proud to call it home when you return. But, if you never go, it will become your prison. I am happy here now, and I've a mind packed with colourful memories.'

Alfie rested his hand on Donnie's and winked at him, making Donnie feel that if he ignored this man's wisdom, he would live to regret it.

Meanwhile, now that Tommy the Thesp had left the bar, Gerard listened as Mickey-Joe rattled through his disappointments with Donnie.

'It's all right for you, Gerard. Your son is a grafter. Mine is more interested in dressing up for a fucking play. His sister is ten times more capable than he is, and no doubt little Sheena will be as well, if she's not already. He needs a good kick up the hole.'

'We get the hand we're dealt, MJ,' replied Gerard joylessly. 'What can you do?'

The phone rang behind the bar. Teresa looked at the clock and then over to Mickey-Joe. 'Will I tell her you're on your way home, or that you're not here, or that I haven't seen you at all today?' she asked.

Mickey-Joe looked down at his half-empty pint.

'Tell her I'm on the way home and then fill them up again, would you, Teresa?'

The door of the pub opened, and Kathy appeared looking distraught. She called out to her father,

'Donnie is dead!'

Donnie jumped up from his barstool and shouted,

'I'm right here, Kathy!'

'No, not you—Donnie the calf!'

CHAPTER SEVEN

SEVERAL HOURS AFTER THAT

Donnie had returned to the farm with Kathy, Gerard and his Dad, but it wasn't long before he felt unwelcome, as if his name had cursed the calf. His collie, Meg, greeted him on his way back to the farmhouse. There were two collies on the farm, Meg and Nip. Nip was his father's dog, who rudely ignored the rest of the family. She had a fondness for bicycle tyres and Frank the Postman's ankles. Meg, however, was very much the children's dog. She was pushing eight and still leapt around like a puppy, obsessing over balls, sticks and Sheena's shoes.

'Good girl,' Donnie said, rubbing her head. 'Been wandering anywhere today?'

Donnie answered himself in a throaty voice, pretending to be the dog,

'Oh, yes. I went out and took a huge shit on Francis's land.'

'Good girl!' Donnie patted her head again.

Donnie entered the front room. His mother was watching the horse racing, which was not unusual. Elizabeth would watch anything where there was even the slightest hint of gambling. This was a vice that had only started in the last few years.

ELIZABETH WAS ORIGINALLY from Dingle in County Kerry. Dingle was isolated and ravaged by poverty when Elizabeth was growing up, but her father was a clothes merchant. He sold clothes door to door on hire purchase before setting up shop with his wife, a gifted seamstress. They were the lucky ones, not so affectionately known as 'the townies'. Elizabeth and her siblings were picked first for duties at Mass. The nuns and brothers praised them more and hit them less than those less fortunate in the poorer areas. There appeared to be a hierarchy for compassion in the church, and Elizabeth's family was grateful that they were near the top. Her father compensated for the lack of love shown to the poorer families by giving and discounting what he could. Elizabeth also benefitted from her father's kindness; being the baby in the family, she was always spoiled. She grew up seeking adventure outside Dingle, but despite outward confidence, she didn't have the gumption to execute her lofty ambitions. Her older siblings scattered from Dingle: three went to America, two to London and one left for Galway. When Elizabeth was staying with her older sister Joan in Galway while she attended a secretarial course, she met Mickey-Joe at Seapoint dancehall in Salthill. *The Showtime Aces* were playing, and excitement was high. Joan and her husband, Tony, had chaperoned Elizabeth and knew by the way she looked that she wouldn't be waiting long to be asked to dance. She wore a dark green Audrey Hepburn-style dress, her thick hair pulled back in a loose bun. Mickey-Joe had spotted her immediately, and being an alpha male, he made sure no other suitor in the room advanced as decisively as he did. Elizabeth was jived off her feet and felt a giddy sense of intense hope that this man was her future, her salvation, her absolute joy. In the days that followed, she imagined the adventures and fun they would have together, desperately in love. Mickey-Joe courted Elizabeth for three months, cycling miles to see her in Galway, and then on a stormy day on the Salthill promenade, they ran through the driving rain for shelter. Under the awning of the butcher's shop, her feet soggy, her hair clinging to her face, Mickey-Joe proposed. It was less of a proposal and more of an affirmative question.

'What month will we get married?'

He wasn't on bended knee, but Elizabeth didn't even notice. The words were out, and he was hers.

Soon after their marriage, Mickey-Joe's father died, and he inherited the farm as the eldest son. Dreams of working in a glamorous office in the city eluded Elizabeth as she mucked in on the farm. At first, it was just another adventure, and when Kathy was born, she surprised herself with the unconditional love she felt for her child, but when Donnie was born, she felt a dark exhaustion. The daily trudge took its toll, a feeling of isolation overcame her, and the laughter she and Mickey-Joe had shared was seldom heard. A life so full of possibility had become predictable, small and scary. After some time, however, Elizabeth accepted her lot, found her happiness in life's simpler things, and was contented on the farm with Mickey-Joe. But many years later, Sheena arrived—a surprise to everyone. After a difficult birth and re-visiting sleepless nights, Elizabeth felt a shadow overcome her, a murky cloud she couldn't lift, a feeling of pointlessness, despair, and on good days, numbness. She improved the following year but began spending more money, increasing tensions between her and Mickey-Joe. She had learned to hide her favourite coping mechanism—the thrill of gambling. It made her feel alive.

'COME ON, GOLDEN Friend!' she hollered at the TV.

She edged forward in her seat.

'Foyle's Fisherman is in the back marker of fifteen runners,' the TV Commentator quipped.

Elizabeth shouted back at the television, 'Back Marker? Get a move on Foyle's Fisherman!'

Donnie leaned in over her shoulder.

'Hi, Mum.'

Elizabeth jumped. Her cover was blown. She was meant to be doing the accounts. She wondered if Donnie might be preoccupied enough not to notice.

'Oh, hi, Donnie. I was just settling down to do the accounts.'

Even for his mother, this was poor.

'Looks like it. Chosen a nag again?'

Elizabeth shrugged.

'Foyle's Fisherman. I chose him for the name. You should never choose on the name. I know better than that. He's dead last, but I took the tip on Golden Friend as well, and he's going to win. I can feel it in my bones.'

The TV Commentator upped the ante.

'And Golden Friend is in the lead—'

Elizabeth punched the air with delight.

'Thanks be to God!'

Donnie was getting bored and really needed to talk to his mother. He thought he might get an affirmative response while she was distracted, so he decided to go for it.

'Mum,' he said lightly, 'unfortunately, I'm not going to make the wedding.'

Elizabeth found the interruption irritating.

'Are you dying?'

'No, obviously not,' Donnie retorted.

'Then you'll be at the wedding,' she stated, looking back at the TV. 'C'mon, Golden Friend!'

Donnie shook his head at his mother.

'Don't you think this betting is getting a bit out of control?'

Everyone in the family was aware of his mother's gambling to some extent. However, it wasn't so much discussed as dropped in at the end of an argument with Mickey-Joe.

The TV Commentator sounded like he was going to wet his pants.

'And Golden Friend is in the lead!'

Elizabeth was standing now, ready to claim victory.

'I'm winning, Donnie!'

Donnie couldn't care less—whatever was won would likely be lost twice over the next week.

'Anyway, the wedding … you see, I got the lead role in the community play. It's a huge opportunity, and it's on for one night only. June tenth.'

His mother didn't even turn to look at him when she answered,

'Donnie, there are only six people in your *acting* group.' She said *acting* like it wasn't acting at all. 'Tommy the Thesp, you and four people on borrowed time from the care home. It's not that great an achievement to get the lead role.'

'They are not in our drama club. They are our audience!'

Elizabeth shrugged as if that meant the same thing.

Donnie was distraught. From small seeds grew big apples. How could no one in his family see that? He was on his way.

'Anyway,' said his mother distractedly, 'you might meet a nice girl at the wedding and finally move out. You really shouldn't be living with your parents at your age.'

What the fuck did that have to do with his acting career? Donnie thought.

Donnie loved his mother, but at times like these, he wasn't sure if he liked her much. She seemed only to be out for herself and her cheap thrills, shutting out those who loved her, unaware that they needed her attention, her love, and her enthusiasm. They needed her. And while this selfish imitation of the person they knew was an improvement on the dark, detached entity that had wandered the living room in her dressing gown a few years back, it still wasn't the mother he remembered. He believed she was still trying to escape from the imposter who had trapped her soul.

Elizabeth's head swung around as the TV Commentator's voice changed to surprise.

'And first over is Cavvy's clown, then Charter Party and it's Charter Party ahead, and Charter Party leads the way, and Charter Party wins the Gold Cup at Cheltenham!'

Elizabeth hung her head.

'Christ.'

CHAPTER EIGHT

THE MORNING OF THE WEDDING

The letter from America arrived on the morning of Kathy's wedding, and Donnie couldn't help but wonder if the timing signified a divine message being delivered from the other side.

Donnie was putting on the kettle, absentmindedly looking out the kitchen window, and wondering how he would get through the day without a meltdown when he saw Frank the Postman pull up outside. When Frank knocked at the door, Mickey-Joe was on his third cup of tea, eating toast with an inch-thick layer of butter. When Frank entered the kitchen, Kathy was in her room, where she would likely be getting ready for the next few hours. Sheena was still in bed, having, once again, seen midnight because no adult thought to put her to bed, and Elizabeth was hoovering a spotless carpet in the lounge, lest a dog hair might have floated onto the pile. Frank placed the letter in Mickey-Joe's hand with a tip of his cap.

'All the best for today. Me and the wife are looking forward to it,' Frank grinned as he left.

Mickey-Joe opened the letter. There was a card inside and a folded note inside the card. He squinted at the card but couldn't read it without his glasses, which, no doubt, had been tidied into a drawer by Elizabeth. He passed it to Donnie.

'Here, use your eyes to read that, will you?'

Donnie took the card and read it aloud just as Elizabeth entered the room.

'*I'm sorry it has taken so long to get this to you. I found this letter on Pete's desk when I cleared his office in the bar in New York. I'm very sorry for your loss. Pete will be greatly missed. Yours, Pete's friend, Vince.*'

'Vince?' said Mickey-Joe. 'I've never even heard of Vince.'

'Vince was his friend,' piped up Elizabeth.

'So he says,' replied Mickey-Joe, mildly annoyed that Elizabeth knew more than he did. 'Well, what does the letter say?' asked Elizabeth.

Donnie's emotional buttons were easily pressed, and he had to wipe a tear from his eye before unfolding the letter. It was written in a scrawl rather than Pete's usual flowing handwriting.

Donnie read aloud,

'*Vince, when you eventually find this, please pass it on to my brother in Ireland. The address is in my notebook. Mickey-Joe, if you're reading this, I'm six foot under, or if I'm lucky, sitting at the bar in the sky. Either way, get a spade and dig behind the shed, two feet left of the old plough if you're standing with your back to the shed. Love and all that stuff, Pete.*'

Mickey-Joe stared at Donnie. Elizabeth stared at Mickey-Joe, and Donnie stared at the letter.

'Is it definitely from Pete, or is this some kind of joke?' asked Mickey-Joe.

Donnie finally looked up from the letter.

'Well, we won't know until we dig.'

Carrying a shovel, Donnie led the way, with his father trailing uncharacteristically behind him. When they reached the rusty, old plough, Donnie stopped in his tracks.

'Here?'

'Two feet, Donnie, that's more like two inches.' Mickey-Joe took the shovel from Donnie and began to dig, slowly at first and then with more gusto. Finally, his shovel hit something hard.

'Might be a rock,' Mickey-Joe said as they both knelt and brushed off the dirt.

It wasn't a rock but an old wooden box with metal hinges.

'Open it,' Donnie said excitedly as his father lifted it from the ground.

Mickey-Joe looked at Donnie, said nothing, and walked back to the house with the box in his arms.

Everyone else was sitting around the kitchen table in silence when Mickey-Joe and Donnie entered with the box. Kathy's face was covered in a white face mask, which made Mickey-Joe jump as he laid the mystery box down on the table. Then, slowly, Mickey-Joe opened the lid as five heads peered in. Elizabeth gasped and sat down before she fainted. Sheena stuck her hand in, pulling out a pile of fifty-dollar notes.

'Is it real money,' she asked.

No one answered her.

'Are we rich?' Sheena pressed, with a hopeful look in her eye.

On top of the stacks of neatly bundled money was another note. Mickey-Joe handed it to Donnie once again.

Donnie read aloud,

'*Apologies for dying, but there's fifteen grand here for you and Elizabeth, MJ and five each for all the children. Don't let them spend it all in the one shop.*'

'Why didn't he just leave a will?' Kathy asked.

Mickey-Joe half-smiled. 'Never was too fond of the tax man.'

Everyone sat in their own world for a good five minutes before Mickey-Joe collected his thoughts.

'Right, you lot, not a word about this to anyone—ANYONE.'

The family nodded.

'You also need to do something sensible with this money. It's a lot of money. Sheena, we will look after yours until you're old enough.'

'Oh, come on,' Sheena protested, 'can't I at least have some of it?'

'We'll see,' replied Elizabeth, which seemed to placate Sheena for the time being.

Mickey-Joe continued, 'Kathy, you can use it to invest in your bakery, but not a word to Francis. This is all cash earnings, and we need to keep it quiet. Donnie ...'

Donnie looked up, hopefully.

'Donnie,' Mickey-Joe repeated, 'under no circumstances will yours be spent on something arty farty.'

'What do you mean?' Donnie asked, although he already knew what he meant.

'No plays, no acting classes. Nothing like that. This is Pete's hard-earned cash, and I will not have you squander it.'

'I won't squander it.'

'Because you will be disowned, hear me?'

'That's a bit harsh,' Donnie replied, blinking away an unwelcome tear.

'That is a bit harsh, Dad,' Kathy said, jumping to his defence.

Elizabeth had been staring out the window for quite a long time before she turned to Mickey-Joe.

'I suppose we'll be investing in the farm, not going on a nice holiday somewhere.'

'Twenty nice holidays,' Kathy giggled.

Mickey-Joe grimaced.

'Perhaps something towards a honeymoon for you, Kathy, but that's it ... and remember we took a small loan out to pay for your wedding, so that has to be repaid, and, of course, there's the bills from the care home.'

Elizabeth looked a little sad. Why could her husband not just live a little sometimes?

'So, is there millions here?' Sheena asked, which seemed to break the ice.

'No, Loveen,' Mickey-Joe laughed and rubbed her head, 'he wasn't a millionaire or a multi-millionaire, but he liked people thinking he was—just for a bit of devilment.'

'Funny it was today it arrived,' Donnie said.

'Yes,' agreed Kathy, 'what a wedding present.'

Donnie smiled back, but that wasn't what he was thinking at all. He wondered whether Pete had sent him a lifeline from beyond, a way out. All Donnie had to figure out was a plan.

Kathy jumped up.

'Oh, my God! Look at the time! I need to get ready!'

SITTING AT HER dressing table, Kathy removed the last of her white face mask with cotton wool. The sunshine flickered through her bedroom curtains, casting a soft light on her rosy face. Her green eyes were bright and full of hope for a new beginning, an endless romance, a family of her own, and now some investment money for her bakery. Could life be more perfect? Kathy had known Francis since she was eight. As she was older than him, she hadn't paid him any attention except for the exhilaration and shock she felt when he dared to swear at Donnie's nativity play. Francis had gone to boarding school, and she only saw him occasionally in the summer holidays. Kathy had set up a small bakery using one of the outbuildings on the farm and had been making quite a stir with her bread and cakes. One Friday, Francis had appeared at the farm with two horses at closing time. He purchased two slices of her best cake and asked her to accompany him on the horses. Kathy had ridden horses since she was a child, bareback across the fields, so the chance to go out for a ride seemed both charming and fun. She followed him on the horse through the woods until they reached the Turlough—a lake created by underground springs. The sun was setting on a fiery sky, and Francis had reached into his saddle bag and pulled out a bottle of white wine, her cakes, and a rug for them to lie on. He told her he had admired her for years and asked if she would consider being his girlfriend.

Applying moisturiser to her face, Kathy smiled at the memory. She couldn't believe Francis Brawley, the boy who swore at the nativity play, was an incurable romantic, and now she was going to be his wife.

FRANCIS LIVED AT the Brawley manor house, still commonly called 'Old Jack's' by the locals. The once grand house was now reeking of neglect with rotting windows, peeling paint on the door and a weed-ridden driveway. Steeped in history and stories, the old house looked depressed, as if the house knew her glory decades were over, and she groaned with every storm that shook her roof and poured water down her crumbling walls. Today, however, against a sharp blue sky, she gave a little sparkle from her stone and a glint from her windows as if to proclaim there was life in the old girl yet. Today was a wedding day for many couples around Ireland, and the possibility of a 'happy ever after'. It was also Francis's wedding day, but Francis was less interested in 'happy ever after' and more interested in 'rich ever after'.

Francis stood in front of the mahogany mirror in his parents' bedroom. The room felt stuffy as if time had been trapped inside it, a decaying energy of days long gone. Francis smoothed down his suit, checked the buttons on his waistcoat and adjusted his mustard cravat. He liked his reflection—his physique and his face pleased him. Inside his confident, arrogant shell, Francis was scared and insecure. Losing his wealth consumed him like a blanket of shame he wanted to burn. Money had been his cloak of power and freedom, and he felt vulnerable and naked without it. Francis looked down at the threadbare carpet under his feet and smiled. Today was going to change everything. He wanted to marry Kathy, but not because he loved her. Francis wasn't sure he had ever loved anyone, not in the way other people talked about it. He was a survivor, and although Kathy wasn't laden down with riches, she had a farm, a bakery and a big inheritance coming from a loaded uncle. Francis also knew how to win over her father, and so Kathy was his doorway to rebuilding the world he once knew.

Francis's parents, Delia and Lorcan, had died some years back. Delia had drunk her liver into a wreck of an organ, unable to cleanse itself against the waterfall of gin and whiskey.

On days of more sobriety, she drank sherry and perhaps an English Pimms or a Campari if the sun was shining. Many who didn't know Delia thought Lorcan had died of a broken heart some months later, but Francis knew he was just at the end—worn down slowly, like the threadbare carpet under his feet. Constant negativity, whining, and lack of cash were his downfall in the end, and when Delia died and her insidious chatter with her, he had one big knees-up and then wilted like an unwatered plant.

They had left behind the square root of nothing except mounting bills, a manor house that couldn't be heated, a leaking roof, mould, and wardrobes full of mothballs. They did leave Francis with a taste for the finer things in life and a sense of entitlement but had given him no skill set to make the money he needed for his lifestyle.

Before her death, Delia had tried to sell the manor house on several occasions against Lorcan's wishes. She came very close to selling to an American who was insistent on being called Irish despite never having set foot in the country before. He marvelled his way around the manor house, but on his second visit, he pulled the sale when Francis ran around the house screaming about the ghost in the kitchen. Francis's father slipped some money into his son's pocket shortly after.

To the village, the manor house's flagging facade was simply due to the illness and death of the parents, and the locals believed that large sums of money would be passed on to Francis to pick up the pieces and restore the building to its former splendour. But his parents didn't leave Francis a dime, and although Francis was gifted the house, he was also left with all the debt and inheritance tax that went with it. Francis had no intention of selling his home. Someone else had to prop up Francis's spending. Luckily for Francis, he was good-looking and could turn on the charm with an uncanny ability to probe deeply into the heart of another despite having no compassion himself.

Harry Beaker was waiting for Francis in the living room, dressed in the same suit and mustard cravat. With one arm propped up on the mantlepiece, he smoked a cigar and grew mildly irritated by the constant *pip-pip* of water dripping into the buckets in the corner of the room. Harry had been Francis's friend for several years now. They had met at boarding school, and Harry used to invite Francis to shoot on Laverty's estate in Wicklow. Harry had moved back to London, where he was originally from, and had made a mint, which gave him a whiff of luxury hotels, first-class flights, lunches at Rule's restaurant and an endless supply of male escorts. But Harry had lost it all in the stock market crash a couple of years earlier, and Harry wanted it all back.

Harry reached for a bottle of Middleton from the top shelf of the drinks cabinet and picked up two dusty glasses. After wiping the glasses on a faded velvet sofa, he filled them with the last of the Middleton. Harry handed Francis his drink. They clinked their glasses together and downed the whiskey.

'How much inheritance do you think she'll get then?' asked Harry.

'Well, I don't know yet. She's not letting on,' Francis said with mild annoyance. 'I assume it's still with the lawyers. But, of course, these things can take time. When you ask how much … it'll no doubt be divided between Mickey-Joe, her little sister and that fool, Donnie,' Francis surmised. 'I guess it depends on how many millions is multiple.'

'That will come in handy,' Harry smirked.

'Anyway, I should hear any day now. A nice wedding present, I'd say, wouldn't you?' Francis let out a sinister laugh.

A doddery, old man suddenly appeared at the window and pointed at a car in the driveway.

'Who's that?' asked Harry.

'That's Ron, the gardener,' replied Francis, giving the man a half-hearted wave.

Harry looked at Francis quizzically.

'The gardener?'

'Yes,' laughed Francis, 'he's got Alzheimer's, so he's forgotten that it's been at least three years since he's been paid.'

Harry let out a howl of laughter and slapped Francis on the back.

'Let's get on with the show then.'

DONNIE HAD OFFERED to collect his grandmother, Nuala, from the care home on the day of the wedding, partly because he was happy to do so. Still, there was the added benefit of being away from a house filled with wedding excitement that he couldn't feel himself. Donnie was a regular visitor to the care home and knew all the staff and residents by name. Nuala's best friends in the care home were Maureen and Flo. She had known Flo most of her life, just as well as Flo had severe dementia and could only recall the goings-on of fifty years ago and absolutely nothing from the last five minutes. Flo had one foot in this world, one foot in the other, and her mind locked between the two. Nuala and Maureen sat beside Flo every day.

As Donnie entered the living room area, where a few residents stared wistfully out the window to a world they could no longer live in, he saw his grandmother, in her usual seat with a magnifying glass in her hand, reading the paper to an oblivious Flo. Today, Nuala looked glamorous—her hair was styled, and she wore a beautiful blue dress with a pearl broach.

On seeing Donnie, a huge smile crossed Nuala's face, and as always, she attempted to get up from her seat.

'Sit down, Nana,' Donnie said as he bent down and kissed her cheek. The smell of rose perfume and mothballs filled his nostrils. 'You look lovely.'

'Thank you, Donnie. I made a special effort!' she replied, smoothing imaginary wrinkles from her clothes, 'and don't you scrub up well.'

'Are you ready to go?' Donnie asked.

'Just a moment, there's someone I want you to meet. Isn't there, Maureen?'

'There is,' agreed Maureen excitedly.

Nuala beckoned over a nurse from across the room. She was small, barely glimpsing five foot, with a mischievous smile and pastel blue eyes. She had a coyness about her that suggested she was unaware of how pretty she looked.

'Hi, Donnie, do you remember me?'

Donnie shook his head, unable to speak and not understanding why he couldn't remember this beautiful girl.

'I'm Roísín O'Donnell. I was your Mary in the nativity play.'

Donnie could feel his face burning up, and his lips go dry.

'Of course, of course. You moved away to England. Are you back?'

'Yes, my father died, and so my mother wanted to come home. I did, too,' Roísín said as she brought Nuala's wheelchair over.

'That's good. It's great to have you back, I mean. But I'm sorry for the loss of your father.'

'Thank you, Donnie,' she replied.

'It's a pity you're not coming with us to the wedding,' said Nuala, smiling.

'Oh, I would have loved to,' Roísín said dreamily, adding, 'I've had a lip on me all week and could do with throwing some shapes on the dance floor.'

Nuala laughed as Donnie seized his moment.

'Well, you can still come, I mean, if you want to,' Donnie said, and by the slightly bemused look on Roísín's face, he wished he hadn't.

She laughed as if Donnie had cracked a joke.

'I wish I could, but I'm working.'

'Of course. Of course,' Donnie muttered and took the wheelchair from Roísín, turning all his focus onto getting his grandmother into the chair and wheeling her out the door.

Nuala waved goodbye to Maureen, Flo and Roísín as Donnie replayed the conversation: I *was your Mary, your*

Mary, *your* Mary.

'She's a lovely girl, isn't she? You should ask her out,' Nuala said, turning in her chair to try and see Donnie's face.

'I just did, Nana, and she said no.'

'Ah, what are you raving about? Anyway, we'll not worry about your wedding today. It's Kathy's day, after all.'

Donnie stayed silent. He didn't want to say anything that would betray his feelings about his sister's impending marriage.

As they reached the car, Nuala squeezed Donnie's hand.

'It's all right, Donnie. I'm not fond of Francis either.'

CHAPTER NINE

THE WEDDING

Kathy had dreamt about her wedding for a long time, probably since childhood. With every dream, the dress got bigger until it eventually needed its own room. Now that the fantasy was a reality, Kathy hadn't bargained on how hard it would be to carry the hot air balloon on her hips around the hotel ballroom. Glasses were smashed, and small children were knocked over. She had hoped to swish about and be 'oohed and ahhed'; instead, she had to take powerful steps and shove her dress where she wanted to go.

Francis held her arm a little too loosely, so Kathy tightened her grip. Cameras flashed. She was now Kathy Brawley. Kathy suddenly found her arm free from Francis as he strode across the room to greet his friends. She didn't have much in common with his friends, especially Harry, but then Francis wasn't particularly concerned about her friends either, and wasn't it important to both have time with other people? She wasn't going to live in his pocket. She was going to be the perfect wife with the perfect husband.

Francis was delighted to take a breather from wandering around the room, getting kissed by lavender-scented old women, particularly Kathy's Aunt Ester, who smelt like the inside of a cheese larder. There was nothing lavender could do for her. He greeted his friends, fellow boarding school chums, Will Pink and, of course, Harry.

Will had spent time at boarding school in Ireland when

his father's business had fallen apart. His father brought the family over from Sussex to stay on his wealthy uncle's farm. He had only spent two years in Ireland, so his Queen's English had been left unscarred, except for the occasional use of the word 'grand'. Will was horsey-faced and irritating, and Francis loved him.

Will slapped Francis on his back.

'Congratulations, old chap! I think this is the first drink I've had since your stag. Took a while to get over that one.'

Francis and Harry couldn't agree more. It had been a stinker of a hangover. On the Beaufort scale, it would have been a force nine, gusting ten. Had it been any higher, hospitalisation may have been required.

'The next day,' Will continued, 'I threw up all over the wife ... and the cat!'

They all laughed, shaking their heads at the hilarity of their hedonistic night. There would surely be plenty more of them. Harry clinked his glass with Francis. 'Hope you've got new wellies for the farm. You certainly married a cash cow.'

Donnie, meanwhile, was at the bar. His head was splitting. Usually, he loved a good knees-up at a wedding, but to see his sister marry Francis was up there with a death in the family. He noticed his grandmother give him a little wave of her hand, summoning him over.

'Would you mind taking an old girl out for some air?' she asked as he approached her and handed her a whiskey. Nuala giggled. 'Seldom get these in the care home,' she said, knocking it back in one go.

'No wonder if that's how you drink them,' Donnie laughed and wheeled her outside into the evening air.

The moon was full and glowing, casting shimmering threads of light everywhere. The noise of the wedding revellers rumbled inside as Nuala looked up at the brightest star. 'I think that's Venus,' she said, 'named after the Goddess of

Love. Nice to see her shining so brightly tonight ... if not a little ironic,' she chuckled.

Donnie was about to reply when he heard muffled voices through the open window of the men's toilets and instantly recognised his father's gruff voice, talking with Gerard.

'We have all worked hard on the farm, but I'm not getting any younger, and although she doesn't look it, neither is Elizabeth. Kathy has built a smashing little business with her bakery, and now with Francis at her side, it's time to hand over the reins of the farm to them. See what they can make of it.'

Nuala was listening too and looked up at Donnie, her face troubled. Donnie stared back at her vacantly. His body felt weak, and the hand holding his glass lost its grip and shattered on the ground.

No more voices filtered through the window after that, and Donnie and Nuala sat silently for a moment. Nuala felt helpless. She knew her son was making a mistake placing his livelihood in the hands of Francis, and she had no idea how to stop it. Nuala knew the average life expectancy of care home residents was eighteen months. She hoped to buck that trend, but how long would she be around to help pick up the pieces if this went wrong?

As Donnie wheeled her back into the wedding reception, she looked around the room and watched Sheena cartwheeling on the dance floor. Kathy looked so incredibly happy, and behind her, her other grandchild looked like he'd been hit with a sledgehammer. Nuala wondered what her role was here. What was once her farm now belonged to her son, who was now passing it on to his daughter ... and a wolf that had slipped through the door.

Donnie made his way to the bar, pushing Nuala along with him. He watched his father hug Francis and shake his hand. His father moved towards him, not to speak to him; he simply moved in Donnie's direction. Without hesitating, Donnie left Nuala two feet shy of the bar and headed towards his father.

Mickey-Joe's expression suggested a hint of embarrassment when he saw Donnie approach.

'So,' said Donnie, cheerily at first, 'Francis is taking over the farm?'

'Sorry?' replied Mickey-Joe, a little taken aback.

'I heard you talking to Gerard in the toilets. I was outside with Nana.'

'Oh right,' Mickey-Joe said. He hadn't been prepared for this conversation.

'Well, isn't that fantastic?' Donnie gushed.

'Isn't it fantastic?' Mickey-Joe knew Donnie didn't think so but hoped he would go along with it, at least for tonight.

'Is it?'

'It is.'

'Why is he taking over the farm?' *Let's hear it from the horse's mouth*, thought Donnie.

'Let's face it, son, it's not like your heart is in it—you hate farming, and it's time for me to make a decision before I end up like your uncle Pete.'

'You're not *that* old, Dad. What are you going to do? All you know is farming.'

'Oh, I'll still be working on the farm.'

Donnie wondered how his father, with all his life experience, could be such a dismal judge of character.

'He's a moron … and he isn't nice. I thought you needed me.' This wasn't at all how Donnie had wanted to deliver his counterargument. He sounded petulant, which wasn't how he intended to come across. He had envisaged expressing himself in a clever, concise way so that his dad would immediately see his point, slap him on the back in agreement, and thank his lucky stars he had Donnie to guide him away from eegits.

'Of course, I need you.'

'But not on the farm?' Donnie was still going down the same road. He couldn't help it.

Mickey-Joe stopped in his tracks. He didn't want to deal

with this just now. He didn't want to deal with it at all.

'Look, son, your sister and Francis are going to make a go of this. Kathy will need your support ... I mean, for crying out loud, YOU HATE FARMING.'

Several people turned round and stared at Mickey-Joe. He hadn't meant to shout quite so loudly, but Christ, the kid could push his buttons. Donnie's face looked crushed, but even he couldn't disagree that he hated farming. He couldn't bring himself to befriend a calf that would end up in a burger bun. In an attempt to stop people staring and take the sting out of his roar, Mickey-Joe grabbed Donnie by the shoulder.

'Come on, son, this is a wedding. Let's go and get drunk.'

Donnie reluctantly followed his father to the bar, where Nuala was now surrounded by people waiting to chat with her. Harry Beaker sat on a bar stool, exuding superiority. He stuck out his hand and managed to block Donnie as he spoke to Mickey-Joe.

Donnie had met Harry before, and he didn't like him. He liked him even less now. Donnie watched as Harry tried to schmooze his dad. *Someone, please punch this asshole.*

'Mr McNamara, I'm Harry Beaker.'

And what a name, Donnie thought.

'A friend of Francis's.'

No more needs to be said, thought Donnie.

'Francis said you might be looking to invest your money in some other avenues.'

So there it is, thought Donnie.

'I'm backing a new middleware product that integrates back-end and legacy systems.'

Good luck continuing this conversation with Dad. He's now tuned out, his foot is pointing north towards the bar, and he hopes to hell this conversation will end soon.

Mickey-Joe looked perturbed.

'I've got no idea what you're talking about. What money?'

Ha! Thought Donnie. This is what happens when people

think your dead uncle was a multi-millionaire. Sock him one, Dad.

Mickey-Joe was now talking while walking away.

'You're also speaking Double-Dutch. Speak to Donnie. He's the only one that can work the video recorder.'

Harry turned to see a smirk on Donnie's face. He nodded at Mickey-Joe, who now had his back turned to Harry, and tried to leave his stool.

Donnie caught Harry's arm as he stood up.

'Tell me about your product, and I'll be sure to explain it to my father.'

Harry was put out. *Why was he now explaining himself to this imbecile?*

'Essentially, it's a middleware product, far superior to anything on the market,' he mumbled.

Donnie was enjoying this.

'How interesting—what does it do?'

Harry didn't want to stick around.

'Sorry, what's your background?'

Donnie threw him a sarcastic smile. He'd had enough of people like Harry.

'Listen here, you slippery fecker, if you want any investment money, I'm the gatekeeper. So either tell me about it or forget any cash from us. Your call.'

Donnie surprised himself. Maybe it was the whiskey he downed earlier. Perhaps he functioned better half-cut, or maybe whiskey brought out the man in him. A man that Donnie had no idea was there. Either way, he would be ordering another one soon.

Harry was seething. He could not believe he was stooping so low as to try and sell his idea to this little shit.

'It allows systems to talk to one another. The possibilities are endless.'

'I see,' said Donnie, although he didn't.

Harry found himself continuing, even though he didn't want to. No one was interested in middleware, and he was desperate to brag about it to anyone who would listen.

'I've already got a company interested. It's liquid gold.'

Tic thumped down on a barstool beside them and lit a cigarette.

'Who's this?' Tic raised his eyebrows suggestively without meaning to.

Donnie always saw Tic as a welcome interruption.

'Harry Beaker. Harry, this is my friend, Tic.'

Tic inadvertently raised his eyebrows again. He had gotten to the point a long time ago where he was completely unaware he was doing it.

What the fuck? Harry thought. *Was this guy coming on to him or trying to suggest something?*

'Have you got something to say?' Harry asked Tic aggressively.

'No,' replied Tic and raised his eyebrows again.

Harry abruptly pushed his chair back and left, casting a pissed-off but bewildered look at Tic.

Tic shrugged. It happened all the time.

'Sorry,' he said to Donnie.

Donnie didn't mind. It had been a useful conversation and served a purpose, but it couldn't possibly have gone any further without Donnie revealing that he didn't have a clue what Harry was talking about.

Donnie turned to Tic.

'Dad's handing the farm to Kathy and Francis.'

'What? That's not good. What are you going to do? Work on the farm under Francis?' Tic took a long drag on his cigarette and then gave Donnie an involuntary punch on the arm.

'No way,' Donnie said flatly, rubbing his arm.

'Ah well,' Tic said as he exhaled, clicking his jaw to make smoke rings, 'you'll probably end up doing nothing.'

Donnie had to do something. His life was choking him.

'No, it's 1989, Tic. In six months, we'll be entering a new decade, and I'm not going to roll in the same sorry shite in the nineties. It's now or never, Tic. I have to get to LA and become an actor … and this time, I have some funds to do it.' Donnie lowered his voice and leaned over to Tic's ear, 'My uncle left us some money buried in the back garden.'

Donnie knew what he had told Tic was a secret, but he also knew that no one listened to a word Tic said.

'Well, lucky you. I'll miss you,' Tic said and meant it. 'Don't worry, if it doesn't work out, I'll still roll around in the sorry shite with you in the nineties. So, are you a millionaire now?'

'Of course not,' Donnie laughed, 'you knew he wasn't a millionaire. People believe what they want to believe. Anyway, what lunatic would bury a million bucks in the dirt?'

'Still, a little disappointing. It would have been nice to be friends with a millionaire.' Tic's eyebrows shot up as he shouted, 'Fucking peasant!'

Tic composed himself and continued to quiz Donnie, 'What's your Dad going to say about you going to LA to flunk some auditions?'

'He'll disown me.'

'Oh well,' laughed Tic.

'But he won't ever find out,' Donnie said firmly.

CHAPTER TEN

A COUPLE OF NIGHTS LATER

onnie had been plotting since the wedding—devising an exit strategy to get to Hollywood. Once there, he would figure everything else out. Maybe he only needed to get there, and someone would spot him instantly. How had Rob Lowe done it? He was probably just spotted. Donnie conceded that Rob Lowe was further up the spectrum of good-looking, arguably a lot further up. Not that Donnie thought of himself as ugly, but he wasn't Rob Lowe. Maybe he had more talent than Rob Lowe and would soon be apologising to him for taking all the good parts, *'Sorry about that, Rob. I know you wanted it, and you'd have been chosen … if they hadn't auditioned me.'*

Donnie lay on his bed, looking around his bedroom. A small television and video player was on the dresser. Rows of videos flanked both sides of the TV box. He noted several films that Rob Lowe had starred in, *The Outsiders, St Elmo's Fire*, and *About Last Night*—there was no doubt Rob was doing well. However, Donnie also owned numerous John Hughes films, *The Breakfast Club, Weird Science,* and *Ferris Bueller's Day Off,* and he surmised that Rob didn't star in any of those films. Why? He was one of the Brat Pack, surely, he should have been in *The Breakfast Club?* This made Donnie wonder—if the Brat Pack was just a term for a bunch of young actors that made hit movies at the same time, and Rob Lowe was in the Brat Pack, and he hadn't starred in *The Breakfast Club,* could Donnie skulk into the Brat Pack and be hailed as a member, having also not starred in *The Breakfast Club?*

These thoughts were still bouncing around Donnie's mind when he entered the lounge. Neither of his parents looked up from their armchairs, which wasn't unusual. Mickey-Joe was relaxing in his leather chair, a tin of Bulmer's Cider resting in one hand, a copy of *Farmer's Journal* in the other. As usual, Elizabeth was circling the names of horses in the newspaper. Donnie wondered if she might leave them if she won enough money. Would she move to Vegas, gamble her winnings and drink herself into oblivion every night on Jack Daniels and coke? At least then she would be close to him in LA.

Donnie cleared his throat for, what felt like, the tenth time and Mickey-Joe finally looked up, with one eye rather than two, keen to get back to his magazine.

'What brings you here, son?'

Strange question, Donnie thought.

'I live here, Dad.'

'Oh yes,' Mickey-Joe grunted as if it was something he'd been meaning to sort.

Donnie reckoned he had about as much of Mickey-Joe's attention as he would ever get. 'It's about the technology idea that Harry Beaker was on about ... at the wedding.'

'Oh yeh,' Mickey-Joe said distractedly. *This wasn't going to be an exciting conversation.* 'Any good?' he added, just for something to say.

'Nah, total shite, but it got me thinking, and I've been doing a lot of research on this.'

Disappointing—for a moment there, Mickey-Joe thought that was the end of this conversation, but it seemed that, like a predictable dose of the runs after Aunt Ester's cooking, Donnie always had more shit to give.

'I've been developing a computing product in my spare time,' Donnie continued exuberantly.

Mickey-Joe wondered if stabbing himself in the eye would alleviate the tedium of discussing technology.

'It's a new middleware product,' Donnie enthused, oblivious to his father's agony. 'Far superior to anything on the market—I have a gaming company based in California interested in being a beta partner.'

Donnie looked directly at his father, hoping to see some interest, but his father stared back with an expression that Donnie could only read as shock. The kind of shock that looked like he'd received a surprising wallop to the head.

Eventually, Mickey-Joe spoke, 'I have absolutely no idea what you are on about.'

That's what Donnie had been hoping for. Ignorance made his job easier.

'It's this simple. It allows all the back-end and legacy systems to talk to each other. It's liquid gold.'

Mickey-Joe wondered if he'd eaten too much or was about to suffer a heart attack through boredom.

'But I need to go now,' said Donnie.

Thank Christ, thought Mickey-Joe, but mumbled, 'Go where?'

'California,' Donnie said matter-of-factly as if he had said he was nipping to the shop.

'Have you totally lost the run of yourself?' Mickey-Joe asked. *What the fuck did California have to do with anything?* He wondered if Donnie was high.

'Los Angeles, specifically,' explained Donnie, 'where the beta company is based.'

Mickey-Joe looked around the room, and then a thought dawned on him about the last time he'd heard Donnie mention Los Angeles.

'Away to feck. The last time you wanted to go to Los Angeles was to chase some half-wit fantasy of being an actor.'

Donnie pretended to laugh at himself.

'I know, what an eegit,' he said, slapping his forehead. 'It's nothing to do with that, Dad, nothing at all.'

Mickey-Joe wasn't convinced.

'Let's wait till Francis gets back from the honeymoon. He might need you here. We'll talk about it then.'

Donnie's exasperation started to leak.

'We don't have time! Harry Beaker was already talking about the same thing!'

'I thought you said his idea was shite.' This was about as much as Mickey-Joe had collected from the last ten minutes.

'It is. I can do this properly,' Donnie insisted, hoping his idea wasn't falling to shit. 'Harry Beaker is a donkey, a total flute.'

The irony of his son referring to a successful man like Harry Beaker as a flute wasn't lost on Mickey-Joe, but then, his son did know a thing or two about computers. Although he'd failed computer science, maybe Donnie's talents lay elsewhere, and all Mickey-Joe was doing was highlighting his weaknesses. Mickey-Joe looked over to Elizabeth.

'Elizabeth? Are you hearing this? What do you think?'

'I think it's brilliant,' said Elizabeth, who hadn't heard a word.

'Okay, son,' Mickey-Joe relented but did so to end the conversation as quickly as possible.

'If you want to blow your uncle's money on this, that's up to you.'

'It'll get me started and come back tenfold.'

Mickey-Joe laughed sarcastically, 'Maybe we should put some money in, too—if it's as good as you say. Didn't you say it was liquid gold?'

'No, no. I'm doing this myself.'

'Fair enough! It's a lot more solid than all this acting nonsense … that's a one-way ticket to poverty and an early grave.'

Donnie's hackles were up. It didn't take much for that to happen when talking to his father.

'There is such a thing as a successful actor,' he retorted.

Mickey-Joe knew that was right, but he was sure his son would never be one.

'Let's face it, son, it's not like you have any natural ability in that department.'

Donnie clenched his jaw, resisting the urge to argue.

'Liquid gold, you said?' Mickey-Joe was quite sure Donnie had said that.

'Yes, liquid gold,' Donnie replied, delighted that the conversation had moved from actors.

'Well, let's hope so. Don't go wasting your uncle's hard-earned cash on some half-baked idea.'

'I'll probably go tomorrow,' Donnie said, hoping no one would stop him. He needn't have worried because Mickey Joe's eyes were back on his journal and his mother still hadn't engaged. Donnie was convinced he would see her in Vegas.

CHAPTER ELEVEN

THE VERY NEXT DAY, LA

onnie McNamara had arrived—in LA, at least. He walked out of LAX Airport and felt an instant warmth as if he'd walked into a greenhouse. The air not only felt warm; it smelt warm. His feet were sweating in his heavy socks and shoes, so he put his suitcase on the ground and unzipped it, causing a commotion in the thoroughfare trying to get in and out of the airport. Donnie was oblivious to the complaints. He triumphantly found his new rubber flip-flops, pulled off his reeking socks and flip-flopped his way to find a taxi.

The hanging street signs and giant billboards made Donnie feel like he was in a movie. *It's coming*, thought Donnie, *my dream is about to come true*. He felt high. An adrenalin rush zipped through his bloodstream, electrifying his senses. The taxi driver offered him a cigarette as he bundled Donnie's suitcase into the boot. Donnie thanked him and lit up in the back of the cab. Donnie wondered if the taxi driver only offered him one so that he could smoke himself but appreciated it all the same. He took a long drag and blew out the smoke. The smoke caught in the back of his throat, choking him. Thinking he may never breathe again, he held the cigarette as far away from himself as possible before going in for another pull.

'You smoke or what?' asked the taxi driver.

'No,' spluttered Donnie, 'but I thought it was about time I started.'

The driver pulled up on Ocean Avenue.

'Ocean Avenue Apartments, Santa Monica,' he indicated nonchalantly.

Donnie's jaw was hanging open, and he was so distracted he singed his index finger on the cigarette. The taxi driver, whom Donnie now knew as Max, pointed at Donnie's cigarette.

'You must put them out when they get to the butt.'

Max left Donnie on the sidewalk outside whitewashed apartments. Silhouetted palm trees bowed in the gentle breeze, and the beach paraded on for as far as the eye could see. The sun was an enormous golden ball slipping down through a bright orange sky. Everything just screamed 'MOVIE' at Donnie. He felt like he was on set.

Inside the apartment, Donnie set his suitcase down on the bed and looked around his basic apartment: two rooms and a small kitchenette. For Donnie, it was like a palace because he was in LA. Donnie lay down on the bed, his eyes inadvertently shut, and almost immediately, he was in the most blissful, jet-lagged induced sleep he had ever had. He hadn't even taken off his flip-flops.

At four am, he woke with a jolt. The curtains were open, and the lights were still on, but it was dark outside. With utter confusion, he checked his watch. *Fuck*. He was starving; there was nothing to eat in the apartment, and worse, he was wide awake. *So this is jet lag*, thought Donnie.

'I've got jet lag,' he said out loud and smiled, 'because I've just flown to LA,' he was grinning now, 'to become an actor.'

Two hours later, there was less to smile about. Donnie was still awake and was so hungry that he could have eaten his pillow. Instead, he rummaged in his rucksack and found a square of melted chocolate covered in fluff. He picked off what might have been bits of tissue and stuffed the sticky chocolate into his mouth. Jet lag was fucking brutal.

CHAPTER TWELVE

AS SOON AS THE SUN CAME UP

onnie walked outside in his shorts and t-shirt, flicked his shades down over his eyes and inhaled the salty smell of the ocean. Pelicans swooped in the distance as early morning surfers ran down the beach. Donnie ambled the palm tree-lined streets, stopping to admire the pink and purple flowers on silver-barked trees in people's gardens. This place was like another planet—lightyears away from Bellvara.

He desperately needed something to eat. He turned onto the main street and saw a newsstand. As he stopped briefly to peruse a few titles, *Backstage* caught his eye. He flicked through the magazine and, to his delight, saw numerous casting notices listed. He handed a dollar to the newsstand owner and tucked the magazine under his arm. The smell of coffee hung in the air like a tantalising beacon of hope. He followed the aroma into a little cafe, where people drank coffee outside, eating stacks of pancakes and fruit, with dogs at their feet. *Sweet relief,* thought Donnie.

A chirpy waitress appeared with a menu.

'Hey, how are you today? Can I get you some coffee?'

'Cup of tea, please.'

'Excuse me?'

'No, not a bother, coffee would be great … and a full breakfast.'

'What kind of breakfast?'

Panicking, Donnie looked at the menu and stammered, 'Ah, scrambled eggs and pancakes, please!'

'Okay… do you want fruit with that?'

'Sure, why not?'

'You got it.'

Donnie had been mildly stressed by the breakfast order but was also excited by the prospect of having eggs and pancakes for breakfast—just like in the movies.

Donnie took his copy of *Backstage* magazine and studied it. He ran his finger along and saw a notice with today's date, located in Santa Monica. He pulled a map from his pocket and located the address with his finger. Only a few blocks away— this was fate finally stepping in to offer a helping hand. After his fill of scrambled eggs, pancakes, fruit and coffee, he felt like a new man and was ready to take on Hollywood.

He left the cafe in search of a phone box, locating one at the end of the street. The phone booths looked modern but characterless compared to Ireland's vintage green and cream ones. Donnie picked up the receiver and dialled the number on the casting notice.

With a feeling of heady anticipation, he navigated his way down the street, crisscrossing to look into different shop windows, trying to kill time before his first audition.

Finally, it was time to enter the offices for his audition. He looked up at the sign *Melody & Bernstein Casting Agency*. He felt an unwelcome twitch start just under his eyebrow and was unsure if it was nerves or a severe lack of sleep.

Donnie entered the reception and felt immediately cold. The aircon was on full blast, and he wished he'd brought a jacket. Several people sat around perched on chairs, flicking through magazines. Most didn't look up as he approached the girl at reception, climbing over people's legs to do so.

Kira was sitting behind the reception desk and sized Donnie up when he stumbled towards her. Kira had been doing this job for over a year and had become prophetic in knowing who wouldn't get the part. She knew immediately before Donnie opened his mouth that he wouldn't be leaving with a spring in his step. She longed for a magic button on her desk that would cause a trap door to open under the feet of anyone she thought was a waste of time auditioning. How quickly her day would pass then.

Donnie stuck out his hand.

'I'm Donnie McNamara. Pleased to meet you. I'm here for the part of the operator.'

Kira offered her fingers only for the handshake. She looked down at her notes.

'Mmm-hmm. That's right, you called and said there was some mix-up with your agent?'

Donnie's face reddened a little.

'Yes, that's right.'

Kira nodded and pointed to a seat in the furthest corner of the room. Donnie nodded, keen to be away from the girl that seemed to be emitting negative vibes towards him. He sat down and tried in vain not to look at her, keeping his tired, bloodshot eyes focused on the ceiling. His eyelids felt heavy, as if a little man was operating a roller-shutter door behind them. Donnie tried to battle the little man, but he was strong, had a tenacious grip on the shutter, and hauled it down.

Donnie became aware of someone speaking in the distance.

'*You got the part. You got the part.*'

His consciousness began to emerge from its cloak when he heard muffled laughter and the voice again, louder this time.

'*You got the part! You got the part!*'

The laughter was louder and closer, and the voice was so familiar. Then, with a bolt, he woke up, realising it was his voice and everyone in the room was laughing at him. He caught the eye of a bald guy across the room who offered a sympathetic smile.

'Donnie McNamara?' Kira called out to him.

Donnie stood up, a little unbalanced.

'You can go through,' Kira said, expressionless, motioning toward the door.

Donnie gave a big thumbs up to the bald guy, who now wished he hadn't made eye contact. Donnie inhaled deeply, trying desperately to instil some positivity into his mind, and then opened the door.

A slick-looking man, Jay, about forty-five years old, who had the kind of presence that looked as though he would be successful in any walk of life, sat behind a desk next to a younger assistant, Darryl, who looked anxious.

Darryl felt this day would never end. His heart had sung when he heard he would be casting with Jay. Not only was he progressing in his dream job, but he would be spending hours on end with the person he thought about every minute of every day—Jay. Now he had ruined it, and every bone inside him rattled as his mind replayed the moment again and again. He could barely focus.

Yesterday had been an excellent day for Darryl. He had been sharp and efficient, and Jay had been so impressed that he had taken him for a 'bite to eat' at The Galley. They had arrived in his white Porsche 911, and every instinct told Darryl that Jay was trying to impress him. Fairy lights twinkled over their heads as they sat down on barstools.

'We'll have a drink first,' Jay had said. It was a fact, not a question.

He ordered Alabama Slammer cocktails for both of them, and Darryl watched, with a bit of concern, as the barman free-poured his first one. Then there was another, and by the third, Darryl was no longer worried about how much was being poured into his glass. He wasn't a big drinker. Indeed, he hadn't even tried alcohol until fairly recently because he was uneasy about losing control over his mind and saying or doing something stupid. But tonight, he felt confident, happy and proud to sit beside Jay. A waiter showed them to their table—a little leather-benched booth. As Darryl looked through the menu, trying to find something that would be easy to eat, Jay ordered the wine.

The food was slow coming, but Jay was quick to pour the wine. Jay reached over and squeezed his arm. *Oh my God, he was squeezing his arm.* He smiled at him and suddenly felt his mouth water. Then, in one of the most critical moments of his life, his back molars began to float in saliva, and his stomach failed him. The vomit spewed from his mouth over the table and soaked Jay's hand. This was what Darryl was thinking about for the millionth time today.

Jay smiled at Donnie.

'Do you have your side for the bell boy?'

'I must have left it in reception,' Donnie fibbed.

'Have this one,' Jay said, handing Donnie the script.

Donnie stepped forward, trying to scan the script as he spoke, 'Can I tell you a little bit about myself?'

'Sure,' said Jay, although he would have preferred if Donnie didn't. Darryl was miles away with a pained expression on his face.

'I've been in several productions in college. We did plays in the local pub, and everyone in the audience was given Irish stew and a pint. There was also an open-mic night at our community hall, and I did stand-up comedy, but it was off-the-cuff, and, to be honest, I could have been better prepared, but it was a good lesson not to crumble when no one was laughing. We also did an improv night at college, which was mighty, although a lot of people were just acting the maggot, and more recently, I landed the lead role for *Grease*, the musical,' beamed Donnie.

Darryl snapped out of his self-loathing daze and shared a confused look with Jay.

'On Broadway?' asked Jay, suddenly paying attention.

'No,' Donnie muttered, feeling his bubble burst a little, 'at our community hall in Bellvara.'

'Where?'

'County Galway.'

Jay still looked confused.

'Ireland,' Donnie offered.

'Right,' Jay said, as he shared another look with Darryl that said, we've *got a right one here.*

Donnie felt it best to explain in case there was any possibility they did a background check on him.

'Unfortunately … I didn't get to play the part because it was my sister's wedding on the same day. I didn't want to go to the wedding because her husband is an asshole, and obviously, I had landed the lead role—'

Jay cut him off with a snappy smile, 'Let's just get started, will we? Darryl will read for Vivian.'

'Who is being cast for Vivian? Who's our Pretty Woman?' asked Donnie.

'Julia Roberts,' blurted Darryl and then gave Jay an apologetic smile. There had been several of those today.

'Julia Roberts! I loved her in *Mystic Pizza.*'

'Good, good, let's give it a shot then,' Jay urged Donnie, desperate to press on.

Darryl gave Donnie an encouraging nod, but Donnie was still preparing, breathing in, breathing out, and holding his hand up to prevent Darryl from starting. *Let's not fuck this up,* Donnie thought.

Jay felt a bead of sweat trickle down the back of his neck, and his upper lip had become unpleasantly damp. Was it too much booze the night before? It couldn't have been because Darryl had cut the night damn short. It was this guy. He was frustrating him so intensely that he was sweating.

'Donnie, is it?' Jay checked the sheet in front of him to make sure. 'Can we please start? We've got a hectic schedule,' declared Jay, nodding at Darryl to continue.

Darryl read from the script, 'Penthouse, please.'

Donnie did a double take, as instructed in the script.

'Didn't even recognise me, did ya?' Darryl continued.

'No,' replied Donnie, wishing he had more to say.

'Funny what a difference a dress makes. For a moment there, you thought I was a rich person you had to suck up to.'

'For a brief moment,' Donnie sneered.

Darryl looked Donnie up and down, and he did the same. *We're getting totally into this,* thought Donnie. *I am totally believable.*

'But you wouldn't know what that feels like because you always look like a snotty bellboy,' Darryl continued.

Donnie looked up from his script, jumping out of character and asked Darryl, 'Do you think she would call him a snotty bellboy? He's not done so much to deserve that. I mean, it's a bit of a leap.'

Jay sighed.

'That's what's in the script. Please carry on.'

Donnie got back into character.

'I'm not a bellboy, I'm an assistant manager in training. I have Bachelor's degree in Hotel Management. And when I'm managing the hotel, I won't allow any whores on the premises.' Donnie jumped out of character again.

'Oh no, no, no.'

'What's wrong now?' asked Jay through clenched teeth.

'He can't call Julia Roberts a whore!' Donnie protested.

Jay now wanted to throttle Donnie. His voice had become a low whisper.

'He isn't calling Julia Roberts a whore. He's calling her character, Vivian, a whore.'

'I think you might want to rethink that line. Way too harsh!' exclaimed Donnie, shaking his head frantically. *How could they not see this?*

Jay tried to respond without raising his voice, 'We didn't write the script. We do not influence the script. We're here to cast, and you're here to audition as an auditionee. So you have even less say on the script.'

'This,' said Donnie tapping the page with his finger for emphasis, 'is going to lose audiences. No one will want to see Julia Roberts being called a whore.'

'I think this is a draft. They'll likely make more changes,

and then, of course, it's edited after filming, so things get cut,' Darryl offered and instantly regretted it when he saw the look on Jay's face.

Donnie shook his head.

'I hope the rest of the script isn't like this.'

'Okay, Donnie,' said Jay, desperately wanting to wrap it up, 'thank you. You can leave by the same door you came in. Have a great day!'

Donnie smiled graciously, but his heart sank. As the door closed behind him, Darryl let out a little laugh, and Jay's face turned from exasperation to amusement.

'I think we're going to need another drink tonight after this,' stated Jay, to Darryl's surprise. 'That's if you think you can handle it.'

Darryl beamed.

'Only if we can go to a different bar, and I can eat first.'

'Done,' agreed Jay.

Darryl's stomach flipped. Donnie McNamara was completely unaware he had made Darryl's year.

CHAPTER THIRTEEN

AFTER THE AUDITION

Abe Nelson sat at a red Formica table outside Mike's bar. He had been sitting inside, away from the sun's glare and public scrutiny, but the smell of disinfectant used to clean the mess from last night's revellers was catching in his throat. He had walked outside with a stumble in his step and was unsure these days whether it was the first beer of the morning that made his knee collapse or the weight on his shoulders that he heaved around.

Outside was always busier than inside as tourists and passers-by stopped for refreshments in the sunshine. Inside were the people like Abe who just wanted to drink and not have light shed on the darkness of their minds. With sunglasses on, Abe kept his head low. Being recognised was a gauge of his success, and the fact that he rarely signed an autograph these days spoke volumes.

Donnie was wandering down Venice promenade, replaying the audition in his mind and wondering what he could have done better. He couldn't help feeling that the role wasn't right to enable him to shine but accepted that he probably shouldn't have mentioned that there might be something wrong with the script, not at this early stage in his career, anyway. Donnie barely noticed the people whizzing by on roller skates, pretty girls jogging past or the fact that he kept getting in the way of cyclists. He spotted a dive bar ahead and walked towards it. A bit of relaxation and a beer would help gather his thoughts. Although it was early in the afternoon to drink, Donnie consoled himself with the knowledge that it was eight hours later in Ireland.

A Japanese man, Jiro, had just spotted Abe Nelson. Jiro was a pro at recognising stars, and his hobby was taking their picture, but it never crossed his mind to ask. Jiro stuck his camera in Abe's face as Mike, the owner, passed by with a drinks tray. Abe lashed out, but his inaccurate coordination, combined with Jiro's speed and agility, caused him to miss Jiro and punch Mike's tray of drinks. Sticky cocktails and beer sprayed through the air and landed in the faces of two easily offended ladies drinking cranberry juice at a table nearby.

Mike was furious. He had no problem with Abe coming in day after day. He was fond of Abe, but things were getting out of hand.

'Abe, you're barred!' shouted Mike.

Abe was aghast. Barred from Mike's bar was a shit situation.

'What? Forever?' Abe whined.

Mike ran this through his mind, and it didn't seem like a good idea. Perhaps he'd been a little rash.

'No, I'll see you tomorrow.'

Abe stood up with a wobble, and Mike escorted him towards the promenade where Donnie stood, watching the events unfold. When Abe came face to face with Donnie, he looked stunned.

'Steven?' Abe asked Donnie, staring at him intently.

'Donnie.'

'What?'

'Donnie,' Donnie repeated and stuck out his hand towards Abe.

Abe shook his head and muttered, 'You look like someone else.'

'I look like myself too,' Donnie said, eager to make a connection with another human being, but Abe staggered away.

Donnie watched him and felt something click in his brain. He hurried after Abe and gently caught his arm.

'Hey, I do know you. How do I know you?'

Abe shrugged.

'I'm your long-lost cousin. Nope, that's not it. We were on a cruise together in Norway ... Nah, that can't be right. We did aerobics together.'

It was the voice more than anything that suddenly made Donnie realise.

'Oh My God,' gasped Donnie, and Abe knew his cover was blown. 'I don't *know* you, but I do know you. You're Abe Nelson.'

'Thanks for letting me know,' Abe grunted.

'ABE NELSON!' Donnie couldn't help himself.

Abe's day was getting worse.

'Keep it down, will you? I don't want any more fucking cameras stuck in my face ... not that it happens much now anyway.' Abe looked around, a little desperate. 'That's my day trashed. I had planned to spend all day there. Nimble little fucker.'

'Pardon?'

Abe waved his hand. 'Not you, that little asshole.'

Donnie now had no interest in getting a beer at Mike's bar. He was staying with Abe Nelson. This was meant to be.

'It's not the only bar that sells beer. Look, we could go over there!' Donnie pointed to a little beach bar, where families were eating hotdogs, but he could see one man with a bottle of Budweiser in his hand, and that confirmed it as the next stop.

'We?' asked Abe, partly confused and a little concerned.

'I'd like to join you,' Donnie grinned at Abe, which further unnerved him.

'Why?'

'Because I don't know anyone in LA. You're the first person I've had a social conversation with. Please, I'll get you a beer. I mean, it's possible you won't be served.'

Abe thought about this. That was highly possible, it happened all the time, but it didn't happen at Mike's bar, which is why he was there. Perhaps he had no choice but to follow this strange Irish kid over to the beach bar, but he hoped to fuck that he didn't talk much. Abe didn't want to talk.

Donnie couldn't believe his luck. Wait until Tommy the Thesp and Tic heard he was sitting opposite Abe Nelson, drinking beer and shooting the breeze. Abe hadn't said much since they'd had a couple of beers, but perhaps he just needed to warm up. Donnie had told him everything: all about his family and their lack of support, about pretending to be setting up a new software company and about his dream of acting. He decided not to mention the failed audition today. He wanted to end on a high.

Abe stared at him and, for the first time in several hours, lifted his sunglasses away from his face, revealing his trademark blue eyes. Even after years of drinking, they could penetrate, pulling you into his sadness and wisdom, a life of highs and lows, and a soul paddling to stay afloat.

Donnie found Abe's stare a little uncomfortable, especially when he didn't speak, and then finally, after a huge sigh, Abe muttered, 'That's the most ridiculous thing I've ever heard.'

'Why?' asked Donnie, genuinely confused.

'I don't want to be rude to someone who has just bought me a beer.'

Abe wondered if he'd said enough. He wasn't convinced the boy was the full shilling, so he thought he'd better check.

'Are you an idiot?'

'Probably,' said Donnie nonchalantly. He had been accused of it several times throughout his life.

Abe leaned forward, surprising himself that he was continuing the conversation,

'What are you going to do when your parents discover that there is no video game or whatever it is and that you're out here trying your luck at auditions?'

Donnie could see that Abe hadn't fully grasped his plan.

'Obviously, I'm hoping to make it as an actor, and then

they'll believe in me. I mean, it's possible. It could happen overnight. You did it.'

Abe's laugh was laced with irritation.

'You think? You think it happens overnight? Just because you hear of someone one day and didn't know them before doesn't mean it happened overnight. It doesn't happen for *anyone* overnight. Years of rejection, shitty jobs, humiliation, self-doubt … Christ, I even know some actors that killed themselves.' Abe snapped the sunglasses down over his eyes to signal he had had enough of the conversation.

'Oh,' Donnie was regretting his comment. He could feel sweat forming on his brow, and his armpits felt damp.

'And,' Abe continued, 'the work, the preparation, the training—it's not that fucking easy to be an actor. Just from a technical point of view, there's a lot to remember while you're acting.'

'I understand. I didn't mean to show a lack of respect. I have huge respect for you. I want to follow in your footsteps.'

Abe laughed mockingly.

'Why would you aspire to follow in *my* footsteps?'

Before Donnie could stop himself, he mentioned the very thing he was seeking to avoid,

'Well, your footsteps without the incident of taking a piss on the red carpet, maybe.'

To Donnie's relief, after a brief silent stare, Abe laughed hard. Abe was beginning to warm to this kid.

'Direct, I like that.'

'Why did you throw it all away?' Donnie asked, unaware he was overstepping the mark.

'None of your business!' Abe snapped. He remembered immediately why he hated talking to people. A much longer awkward silence followed, and eventually, Abe softened, 'Why don't you be honest with your family? Tell them why you're out here.'

'Because they'll disown me.'

'That's a bit harsh.' Abe was beginning to feel sorry for Donnie.

'That's what I said.'

'So they don't believe in you?' Abe asked.

It was a new, disturbing thought for Donnie. He played it over in his mind.

'No, they don't believe in me.'

'Do you believe in yourself?'

Donnie took a sharp inhale as if mustering inner confidence.

'I see myself making it … but I'm afraid I might not be as talented as I had hoped.'

'Maybe you're talented; maybe you're not. They say the cream always rises to the top, but plenty of people in this business can't act and make millions at it.'

'My Dad says that acting leads to divorce, poverty and an early grave.'

'Has your Dad been following me around? He might have a point. If you want my advice, get a proper job. Why does everyone want to be an actor anyway? You spend your entire life looking for success and recognition, and you end up becoming public property with a price tag on your head … then you get shoved into the bargain bin and can't climb out of it, and you're very quickly shipped off to the charity shop. Seriously, why do *you* want to be an actor?'

Without hesitating, Donnie responded,

'I like being someone else.'

Donnie's words hit Abe like an explanation of his own life. He felt the sadness and familiarity of those words. He momentarily lifted his sunglasses again, raised his beer and clinked it with Donnie's.

'I hear you, kid.'

Abe stood up from the table, staggered sideways and collapsed with a thud on the sand. People stared as Donnie helped him to his feet. With one hand, Donnie fished in his pocket for ten dollars and left it on the table as he supported

Abe's weight back to the promenade.

'Come on. I'll get you home.'

The cab pulled up outside a small craftsman's cottage. The garden was a vibrant spray of peach and yellow rosebushes, and a beautiful lilac tree cascaded over the fence. The blue paint on the front door was blistered, and the curtains were closed. Somewhere in Malibu, there had been a beachfront home that Abe had lived in, entertained in, and raised a family in, but now, this was where he lived.

Donnie helped Abe out of the cab.

'Just leave me here,' Abe insisted. 'Don't come to the door.'

Donnie watched Abe as he weaved towards the gate that led to the front door.

'Fucking idiot!' Abe shouted.

'What?' Donnie called out after him.

Abe looked up, startled, unaware that his thoughts had been spoken. He waved his hand dismissively at Donnie and muttered, 'Not you, me!'

Donnie climbed back into the cab, a little sad for the sorry soul he'd witnessed, but within moments, a huge smile crossed his face. He had just spent the afternoon with Abe Nelson!

CHAPTER FOURTEEN

MINUTES LATER, ABE'S HOUSE

Resting one shoulder on the door, Abe shuffled inside the house as a china cup flew from the living room and smashed on the wall beside him.

'Shit!' Abe shouted and ducked as another cup followed the same trajectory as the first. Abe wondered how she had any china left as he staggered over the broken porcelain at his feet. 'Melanie, it's me! It's Abe.'

Melanie poked her head out from the living room. Her wild green eyes glowered from her dainty face. Her faded blonde hair was sleek and perfect, but her lipstick had missed its destination. 'My brother … my own brother!' Melanie was getting louder, as she did when she repeated herself.

Abe shook his head, unsure where the conversation was headed, but glanced at Melanie's hands to ensure she wasn't holding another cup.

'Murderer!' Melanie spat.

Abe seized his moment and rushed forward, grabbing her delicate hands and trying desperately to regain his balance.

'It's me. It's Abe.'

'Oh, I know it's *you*. I just saw you killing that man.'

She pointed at the television as evidence. 'Pretending to be someone called Jack!' Melanie held her hands up into the air, which Abe couldn't help thinking was for added dramatic value.

'Melanie, It was a TV programme,' Abe explained and sat down before he fell down.

Melanie was unconvinced. 'I'll call the fuzz. Whether you're my brother or not, you can't go around plugging people, honey. It made the news. They'll come looking.'

Abe was losing patience.

'That is the television. It was not the news. It was a TV programme. Jack was a character I was playing, and he killed people. It isn't real.' Abe closed his eyes and hoped Melanie would give up and sit down.

'So you haven't popped anyone?'

Abe's chest heaved.

'No.'

Melanie, relieved, smiled at Abe.

'Well, that's the best news I've heard all day, sweetie.'

Abe opened his eyes and smiled wearily back at Melanie.

Her eyes narrowed as she studied him.

'You are Van Dyked, though?'

Abe rolled his eyes. This was the *here we go again* eye roll. Half of the problem of dealing with Melanie was understanding what she was talking about. She never used to speak like this. It had crept up, along with the disease, with new words being added daily.

'Van Dyke wasn't there,' sighed Abe.

'No, I mean, you've been swimming in the bug juice pond.'

Abe's head started to spin. He closed his eyes and tried to answer her, 'You're making no sense, as usual.'

'You're half in the bag,' Melanie persisted, 'cabbaged … red in the nose … sodden.'

Abe opened his eyes and looked at Melanie, bewildered.

'You're drunk!' Melanie shrieked.

'Oh yep,' Abe nodded, 'just a little.'

He leaned over the edge of the sofa to pick up his guitar, but after one short strum, he slumped sideways and fell asleep.

CHAPTER FIFTEEN

A COUPLE OF NIGHTS LATER

onnie soaked up the electrifying buzz of the newly opened 3rd Street Promenade. Buskers, street performers and outside diners created a holiday atmosphere that made him feel giddy with excitement. He could have sat by the fountain all day, under the shade of jacaranda trees and watched people pass by, but his first stop would be to shop at Santa Monica Palace.

He'd seen the new Levi's ad on television the night before and felt envious of the hunk in the pick-up that stripped down to his undies and used his jeans as a tow-rope. It was time to swap his habitual black trousers, white button-down shirt and Doc Martin shoes for dusty cowboy boots, stonewashed Levi's, a white t-shirt and a leather jacket. He might not have the 'bod' of Nick Kamen or Dan Gauthier, but at least he'd have the same jeans.

Never in his life had he spent so much money on clothes, and never had he felt so cool. The moment of guilt that he felt when he bought the clothes, knowing his funds were going to rapidly run dry, evaporated when he looked in the mirror. It wasn't an imposter reflecting back at him—it was him. *Rob Lowe, I'm coming up right behind you*, he thought as he grinned at his reflection.

Before leaving the cab, he checked himself, overtipped the driver for luck and goodwill and made his way across the road. The whitewashed, old building in front of him had a high, pink flowering hedge and four proud palm trees that enveloped the entrance. Fairy lights adorned the wooden sign that read: *Bar Boulevard*.

Brett, a bouncer that looked like he spent most of his days at Muscle Beach, manned the velvet ropes as Donnie approached. Brett unnecessarily puffed out his chest and took a step closer to the rope as Donnie walked confidently towards the entrance, enjoying the clip-clop of his cowboy boots.

Brett raised his hand, deterring Donnie from advancing further.

'Are you on the guest list?' Brett asked. Brett was a man who loved his job.

Donnie hadn't accounted for this.

'Probably not,' he shrugged, and then it struck him to add, 'but I'll drink a lot and be nice to everyone.'

That's a new one, thought Brett, as he shook his head apathetically at Donnie. He'd heard most of them:

'Do you know who I am?' was one he liked because he would always respond with,

'If you don't know who you are, I can't let you in here.'

'Can't you just add me to the guest list?' was one he had heard last night from an inebriated but wily Scotsman, and Brett thought it novel enough to let him in.

'I'm with Bruce Willis' never worked, and one excessively tall moron had declared,

'I am Tom Cruise.'

Occasionally though, when Brett was getting to the end of the month and had run out of cash, a hundred-dollar bill did the trick nicely—but when he was flush, rules were rules.

Donnie's brain was in overdrive. How was he going to get in? By the imperious look on Brett's face, not easily. This was Donnie's chance to mingle, join the fray, and maybe even launch his career. He'd spent a fortune on incredibly trendy, new clothes, and Brett didn't even care. If Donnie was going to get a chance to network and brush shoulders with Hollywood movers and shakers, he needed to get inside. Donnie felt his heart thump in his chest.

Just beyond the entrance, a rock band, Alabama 3, were hanging out, smoking something that didn't smell like tobacco to Donnie. They looked like the real deal, skinny and cool. Larry Love, the lead singer, watched the angst on Donnie's face as Brett widened his stance and dismissed him. Then, Larry called out to Brett with his raspy voice and toothy grin.

'Hey, let a brother in!'

Brett immediately stepped aside, like a password had been uttered.

'I'm sorry,' Brett muttered, 'I had no idea he was your brother.'

Larry lay a hand on Brett's shoulder. 'We're all brothers.'

Brett nodded as if he understood, but he did not.

Starstruck, though he had no idea who they were, Donnie passed the velvet ropes and attempted a confident swagger towards Alabama 3.

'Thanks so much! Who are you guys?' Donnie spouted, suddenly realising he may have committed a social faux pas.

Rock Freebase, the lead guitarist, was uncomfortable with this Bambi-eyed kid staring at him.

'Fans scare the shit out of me sometimes,' he said as he leaned further away from Donnie.

Harpo Strangelove, the harmonica player, who looked more like John Lennon than John Lennon himself, shook Donnie's hand. 'He can't be a fan, Rock, if he doesn't know who we are. Hi, I'm Harpo, and this is Rock and Larry,' he said, motioning to the other band members.

'Donnie … McNamara.' Donnie immediately wished he hadn't added his second name.

'Do you want some skunk milk?' Harpo asked, mildly amused.

'I don't know what it is, but I'll get you guys some at the bar!' Donnie declared, delighted with his new friends.

Larry laughed.

'Good to meet you, brother. I'm Larry. We're a band— Alabama 3, but we're not from Alabama; we're from Brixton.'

'Brixton?'

'Yeh, Brixton ... London,' Larry added, wondering why he needed to.

'I'm from Ireland.'

'No shit,' Larry laughed again.

'I'm out here to be an actor,' Donnie offered before acknowledging that no one had asked.

'Course you are,' Rock replied, wanting to head inside and find someone more intellectual to talk to. 'We're in fucking Hollywood.'

'We've been in a couple of films,' volunteered Harpo.

Rock wondered how much grass Harpo had smoked to want to converse with this guy.

'Yeh,' Larry added, exhaling thick smoke, 'typecast as the drug-fuelled, alcoholic musicians.'

'If the cap fits,' laughed Harpo.

'Really?' Donnie was in his element. 'Are you playing here tonight?'

'We sure are,' Larry grinned again, always looking like he knew something that no one else did.

'Right,' nodded Donnie, 'well, let me get you some drinks ... some skunk milk.'

'It's okay,' chuckled Harpo, 'it's on the rider.'

Donnie followed them into Bar Boulevard, feeling like the Gods were shining on him tonight. Larry put his sunglasses back on and headed for the stage.

Donnie waited for the barmaid to look up to order his drinks. When she finally did, Donnie was blown away. Never had he seen a girl so pretty. She nodded at him to indicate he could order, but Donnie couldn't talk. She was the epitome of cool. Her short blonde hair sat in perfect, shimmering waves. Her grey eyes sparkled, and she wore a casual black top that exposed one sun-kissed shoulder.

'Hi, what can I get you?' she asked.

'A pint of Harp and three sk ... skunk milks, please.' Donnie was disgusted with himself. He had never stuttered like this in his life.

'Excuse me?'

'Sorry, must be the accent.'

She smiled, making her even more beautiful. Her teeth could have modelled for a toothpaste advert.

'Okay, but I don't know what Harp or skunk milk is.'

'Harp is a lager.'

'A lager?'

'You know, a beer, I guess. We drink it in Ireland. Maybe you don't have it. I have no idea what a skunk milk is, either. It's what Alabama 3 are drinking.'

'I see …' she smiled again, and Donnie felt his legs go weak. 'Well, that could be a pretty potent concoction of anything.'

'To hell with the beer!' Donnie was trying to be as cool as he knew how. 'Let's do four of them then.'

'Four of what?'

'Four pretty potent concoctions of anything.'

'Okay,' she laughed, 'your call.'

Donnie watched her every move as she expertly poured bottle after bottle into a cocktail shaker and filled four beautiful drinks with layers of orange and red, like a sunset in a glass.

'Careful now, they're pretty potent.'

Donnie sighed and looked straight into her eyes, wanting to get lost there. He wondered if she was related to Meg Ryan. She looked away, not shy but coy. He desperately wanted to continue talking to her, feeling the pull of her magnetism and energy.

'Are you an actress?'

'Because you're in a Hollywood bar, right? No, I'm a singer, but mostly I organise bands.'

Donnie could see she had other customers to serve and was beginning to pull away. But he didn't want the conversation to end.

'What do you sing?'

'Songs,' she answered, flashing him a smile as she breezed

over to serve someone else.

How incredibly cool, thought Donnie. He wondered if this was love at first sight. He inwardly berated himself. Not love, not yet ... he knew nothing about her, but she was intoxicating, and he wanted more.

With more than a bit of spillage, Donnie carried the drinks over to Alabama 3, who were setting up on stage. Larry winked at Donnie and downed the cocktail in one.

Donnie returned to the bar as Larry, with a cowboy hat and shades on, belted out their first number, *Hello, I'm Johnny Cash*.

From the shadows, a crowd appeared in front of the stage. Donnie was keen to join them as the music pounded a terrific beat, but the girl was smiling at him from behind the bar, and if she was in the vicinity, he was going nowhere.

'They're amazing!' Donnie tried to be heard without leaning too far over the bar.

'They are.'

'I'm Donnie, by the way.'

'Hello, Donnie, by the way.'

'No, it's just Donnie—not Donnie, by the way.'

She smiled again.

'Just Donnie.'

Donnie was too entranced to notice that she hadn't introduced herself.

'Maybe you'll dance with me?'

'Not while I'm working.'

'Maybe you could dance with me some other time?' He wasn't going to let go for as long as she was still smiling at him.

'Maybe I could.'

'Maybe tomorrow?'

'Busy tomorrow.'

'All of tomorrow?'

She dazzled him with another smile and went off to serve a group of girls at the end of the bar. It seemed to take forever, not because she was slow but because he was desperate to seal a date, and those girls were ordering all kinds of awkward shots and cocktails. He stared down at them a little too hard because one of them gave him the finger.

Finally, she was back at his end of the bar.

'All of tomorrow?' Donnie persisted.

'You don't give up, do you?'

He wasn't sure if it was a compliment or if he was creeping her out. She turned away again, took some beers out of the cooler, then leaned over the bar and said,

'If you're around at six-thirty tomorrow morning, I'll be surfing at Santa Monica beach, left-hand side of the pier.'

Surfing. That could be problematic, Donnie thought.

'Can you surf?' she asked, and Donnie was sure she was reading the fear on his face.

Donnie thought about his answer.

'Em … I have surfed.'

She moved away again as Donnie was left playing out the traumatising memory in his mind of a trip to Mayo. Two people holidaying from Devon had been surfing on the beach, and he had foolishly asked if he could give it a lash. Without any instruction, he had taken the board straight into the Atlantic rollers. The sea sucked him up and then pinned him down, barely coming up for air, before getting pummelled again by the next monstrous wave. The sea had been a cruel mistress to Donnie, disorientating and teasing him by allowing a brief, choking breath before plunging him back into the icy abyss. When he had finally surfaced, the surfboard clattered down on his head for good measure.

But if life-threatening batterings from the ocean were what it took to meet up, he'd be there. Donnie knocked his drink back and smiled at her.

'You're not likely to be up at six-thirty if you have too many of those.'

'I'll be there,' Donnie replied, knowing that nothing would stop him, least of all a hangover.

Larry was singing a new song, *Peace in the Valley*, and Donnie turned his attention back towards the stage. The song was like poetry delivered in rock 'n' roll. Larry had the audience in his hands. Larry beckoned a figure out from the darkness behind him.

'Summer Taylor, everyone!'

To Donnie's amazement, there she was, on stage with Larry. Her name was Summer. Of course, it was. What else could she possibly be called? Heaven?

Summer sang with a voice so incredible that Donnie thought he might burst with pride, even though he'd only met her tonight.

Donnie couldn't control himself. He leapt around like a lunatic to her singing, lost in the madness of love, lust and a damn good song. People whirled by him as he bounced into the air, arms swinging in a poor attempt to copy some of Larry's signature moves. Drinks were catapulted out of people's hands as he danced on, impervious to the chaos he was causing. Summer noticed Brett making his way towards Donnie, his jaw set, ready to eject the unruly. Brett glanced up at Summer on stage because even his job couldn't detract him from watching her magic. Summer pointed at Donnie and shook her head at Brett. Like a loyal guard dog, Brett stopped in his tracks and backed off, leaving Donnie in a state of blissful oblivion.

It wasn't long before Donnie was helped into a cab by Harpo and Summer. Still high on Summer and music, he hadn't stopped grinning, but his vision had tripled. There were three Summers, and he wasn't sure which one she was.

'Wow. There's three of you ... three Summers.'

Harpo smirked mischievously at Summer.

'I think it was our fault. It usually is.'

He shut the cab door as Donnie's face pressed against the window, watching all of his Summers disappear behind him.

CHAPTER SIXTEEN

SIX O'CLOCK THE NEXT MORNING

The alarm blaring woke Donnie with a fright, and once he realised what country he was in and who he was, the pain in his head started to kick in. His mouth felt like he'd licked the bottom of a budgie cage, and his eyes were tight as if they didn't fit their sockets. He scrambled up from the bed in his underpants and kicked last night's clothes out of the way as he made a beeline for the sink, finding a tiny glass that required filling six times before he could rehydrate. Donnie groaned. If it had been any other day, he would be taking himself straight back to bed, but he was meeting her this morning. He was meeting Summer.

His balance in the shower was problematic every time he closed his eyes, so he turned the water from hot to cold, hoping to shock his body from the hangover's grip. Gritting his teeth, he endured the sharpness of the stabbing cold water against his skin.

Donnie made his way to the beach, wearing a pair of neon yellow shorts, a navy t-shirt, and shades to conceal his bloodshot eyes and protect them from the glare of the sun. He consoled himself with the fact that the worst of his hangover was over, and it would be upwards from here, which was preferable to waking up feeling fine only to be knocked into hell at midday.

Donnie scanned the shops beside the beach and spotted a surf hut. He sauntered in and was greeted by a dude in floral board shorts, long sun-bleached hair and a propensity to say the word 'man' after everything.

'Hey man, I'm Noah. What's happening?'

He surprised Donnie by giving him a high five.

'Hey,' said Donnie, unsure how to continue, 'I'm looking to hire a surfboard.'

'Sure thing, man. What are you looking for?'

Donnie frantically scanned the hut and pointed at the nearest board. It was blue and small.

'That one,' he said hopefully.

'You sure, man? You done much surfing?' Noah could suss a novice pretty quickly.

'You know. A bit ... man,' Donnie replied, hoping his use of the word 'man' would conceal his embellishment.

'Okay, man, what about this one?' Noah pointed to a yellow Mini Mal.

'Yes, that's perfect—looks like a bit of bastard to carry, though.'

Noah laughed, wondering if this guy was super funny or a total dunce. He lifted the board and handed it to Donnie, who tried to balance it without knocking everything in the shop over.

'You need a wet suit?' Noah asked.

'Ha, ha ... very good, teasing the Irishman. Yes, that's right, it's cold in Ireland.'

Noah had no idea what he was talking about, so he shrugged.

'How long do you want the board for?'

'Oh, I'll bring it back in a couple of hours.'

'Okay, man, it's five bucks.'

Noah scanned the ocean as Donnie fished in his pocket for his wallet.

'Bit of an onshore break,' Noah announced.

'Yeh, onshore break,' Donnie agreed, although he had no idea what Noah was referring to.

Donnie carried his surfboard under his arm and deter-minedly marched towards the sea. Bending down, he dug a hole in the sand, buried his wallet, checked if anyone was watching him, and then placed his flip-flops as his marker on top of the sand. He noticed other surfers running in wetsuits towards the water. *How soft are these people?* Donnie wondered. *Why would you possibly need a wetsuit in California?*

Donnie waded into the water, immediately feeling like he was being attacked by a million needles. *Fuck me. It's freezing,* he thought. *Why? Why is it cold? This is the Pacific Ocean, not the Atlantic.*

Suddenly, a voice behind him shouted,

'Hey, where's your wetsuit?'

He turned to see her. Summer. She looked fit and fabulous, and Donnie wondered if there was any point to this charade.

Summer laughed encouragingly.

'Come on, tough Irish guy.'

She lay on her surfboard and paddled out like a pro. Donnie did his best to copy her, lagging far behind and getting thrown off several times as he tried to venture past the break. He had to dig deep, knowing she was just within reach. Eventually, he was sitting on his board alongside her, shivering and exhausted.

There was a short silence as Donnie couldn't speak until he regained his breath.

'So, there's no sharks, is there?' he asked, hoping he hadn't asked a stupid question.

'Sharks?' Summer raised an eyebrow at him.

'Yes, I mean, there's none around here? None in Santa Monica?'

He was sure he was making a fool of himself, but his intense fear of those sea monsters pushed him to ask the question.

Summer frowned.

'Best not to think about it.'

It wasn't the answer Donnie was expecting, and now she filled him with panic.

'What do you mean? *Are* there sharks?'

'Sure,' she answered readily, 'but there hasn't been an attack here since January.'

'What!' Donnie was hoping to God she was winding him up. He would rather have seemed gullible than end his life in the mouth of a sea beast.

'Put it this way ... I wouldn't have chosen *that* surfboard.'

Now he was sure she was teasing him.

'Why?'

'It's yellow.'

'What's wrong with yellow?' Donnie's anxiety rose again.

'Yum yum yellow! Sharks love yellow.'

'Very funny,' he said, praying it was.

'No, it's a statistical fact. Sharks go for yellow.'

That was it. He may or may not have screamed, '*FUCK!*' but the word bounced through his skull as he paddled as fast as he could for shore, whipping the water to a foam. So this was how it was going to end. Some fucking dude in a surf hut, who clearly hated the Irish, had given him a shark-signalling surfboard. A monster would rise from below and seize him with terrifying multiple rows of killer teeth. He would be dangled above water just long enough to see his dream of Summer wiped out in a pool of his own blood as the heinous shark would drag him under the water, and he would become just another fucking statistic.

The leash touched his leg in the water, and Donnie knew his fate was sealed.

He screamed, 'SHARK!' and tumbled off the board, only to be pinned down by a crashing wave. He scrambled to the surface, petrified by what lay beneath his struggling legs. Then, just as air filled his lungs, another wave grabbed him in its relentless jaws, turning him upside down and inside out before catapulting him head-first onto the beach. He lay there, coughing, winded, dazed and feeling incredibly lucky to have narrowly escaped certain death.

Summer crouched down beside him.

'Hey, are you okay?'

'Did it get anyone?' Donnie asked, amazed to be talking at all.

Summer threw her head back and laughed, leaving Donnie to wonder how anything could be amusing at a time like this. She gave his back a rub which felt amazing, and now that he was out of the biting cold grip of the sea, the colour came back to his face, and he could feel the pneumatic drill of his heartbeat slowly return to normal.

'Do you want me to get you some water?' Summer asked.

Donnie waved his hand at Summer, trying to play down the incident.

'No, I'm grand now. I'm alive. Thanks be to God.'

Summer smiled curiously at him.

'Okay then, I'm gonna go back out and catch a few, and if you're still here, we could grab breakfast.'

'You're going back out?' Donnie was aghast.

'There's no shark,' she assured him, choking on a little laugh. 'I don't think anyway.'

'Mind yourself!' Donnie called after her as she ran back into the spray and ploughed through the waves.

Donnie eased himself to his feet and looked around for his flip-flops. But, unfortunately, they weren't where he had left them. He skimmed the beach with his eyes, and as he turned around, he noticed them tumbling together in a wave thrusting on the shore. With an exasperated sigh, Donnie waded into the sea, recovered his flip-flops and then dived into the breaker, embarking on a fool's mission to find his wallet. Shaking and beaten, he trudged out of the ocean only to see his wallet lying sodden on the sand. Before the wave could suck it up again, he pounced on it and slogged up the beach to retrieve his surfboard.

Donnie wobbled back to the surf hut, dangling the surfboard awkwardly under his arm.

Noah was sunning himself in a deck chair outside the shop, which further riled Donnie.

Deliberately, Donnie stood directly in front of Noah,

blocking his sun.

'Hey, Man,' Noah said, pulling his sunglasses down onto his nose, 'that was quick.'

'Were you trying to kill me?' Donnie narrowed his eyes at Noah.

'No way, did you get slammed?' Noah was genuinely empathetic.

'Slammed? I almost got fucking eaten! What's with the yellow board, you fucking dope? That was a suicide mission!' Donnie dumped the board next to Noah, who picked it up, a little perplexed.

Noah called out after him,

'Have a nice day, man!'

Donnie walked back towards the sea and searched the waves for Summer. He saw her as she effortlessly sprang up on her surfboard and rode the wave towards him. He couldn't fathom how the sea was her playmate but seemed hell-bent on assassinating him. He waved at her but couldn't tell if she had seen him. Finally, he lay back on the sand, his hangover cured by water and intense fear, and closed his eyes, grateful for solid ground.

HE WASN'T SURE how long he had been asleep when Summer approached him, hair tousled, wearing shorts and a t-shirt. He jumped up, the ass of his shorts still damp from the salt water, and walked with her along the beach and up to the boardwalk.

Summer ordered an omelette at the cafe and a coffee. Donnie decided it was best to ask for the same. His idea of a proper breakfast was sausages, bacon, black pudding, white pudding, a couple of fried eggs, and a round of toast, but he hadn't so much as seen sausages or pudding on the breakfast menu since he got here. So he made a mental note to ask his mother to post him some, along with some tea bags. Today had been a day of extremes: escaping death and breakfasting with Summer.

'So, have you always lived in LA?' Donnie asked as he

shifted in his seat, trying to get comfortable in his wet shorts.

'I grew up in a small town in Nevada. It was okay, but I always felt different to everyone there, you know, like a misfit. I started singing and knew it was what I wanted to do, so I came to LA, following a dream, I guess.'

'I can't imagine you ever being a misfit.' Donnie wasn't trying to compliment her; he could only envisage that she would have been the most popular girl in class, boys falling at her feet and girls crowding around her, hoping her magic would rub off on them.

Summer smiled gently.

'My Mom and Dad were hippies and joined The Manson Family cult. I was born there surrounded by a truckload of drugs, murders, thefts … stuff like that. My mom ran away with me, and because of all that, I had trouble fitting in. What about you?'

Donnie stared at her, his jaw hanging open. He had been about to tell her that he had been a misfit too, that his life had not been what he wanted it to be—but how could he? In her eyes, he had been blessed. What kind of ungrateful, snivelling human being would she think he was? He had no idea what to say, so he shook his head and muttered,

'I'm so sorry. That's brutal.'

Summer burst out laughing.

'I'm kidding. We weren't with The Manson Family. I had bucked teeth and acne growing up. It wasn't the best start.'

Donnie felt like an ass, although a wave of relief came over him that he might be able to complain about his own life rather than grudgingly count his blessings compared to someone who had endured the horrors of a cult upbringing.

'Well, I wasn't in a cult either … unless you count the Catholic church!' he laughed, but Summer didn't get it. Donnie deduced she wasn't Catholic. 'I grew up in the west of Ireland. My family has a farm, and it's not my thing.'

'Like surfing?'

'Exactly! Not being interested in farming where I come from is like being a nudist in the Arctic. It just doesn't make sense to them. I always wanted to act, and no one got that at all. They would have been more likely to encourage me to join the Manson Family than pursue a career in acting ... so here I am, against the odds, in LA ... following a dream.'

'Wow. It's tough when family doesn't support you, but you know what? I always think it's the ones who really have to fight to prove themselves that come out on top. Don't you think?'

'I never really thought of it that way, but sure, that makes sense.'

'So you might end up on the big screen, and I'll be looking for your autograph.'

Donnie laughed, soaking up the comment.

'Sure, the big screen would be great, but I suppose I just wanted to change my life.'

Summer saw something in Donnie. Something rare, and then it struck her—it was an honesty, a laying bare of personality that she had never encountered before. Most people she knew in LA were over-confident; whatever insecurity lurked on the inside, they masked with zealous ambition and usually a bucket full of bullshit.

'Did coming here change your life then?' she asked.

'Well, it's been more than I could have hoped for so far. Yesterday I was drinking beer with Abe Nelson. One of my all-time heroes, and I think he may even have liked me.'

Summer looked at Donnie in surprise.

'Abe Nelson? He had some crash. What was he thinking? At the film premiere of all places. I felt sorry for him. Something must have gone very wrong in his life. He had it all.'

'Maybe he just needed the toilet ... I don't know. He didn't say, but he's alive and well in Venice Beach—alive, anyway. It was surreal to meet him, and then ... I met you.' Donnie couldn't help himself. He knew he should play it cool, but he couldn't. He was smitten, and if he shot himself in the foot, at least he would always remember this breakfast with Summer.

Summer had been flattered many times by guys. Flattered, disappointed, loved, left, adored and ignored. She wasn't sure, but something about Donnie was real.

'And how did I make such an impression?'

'Are you kidding?' Donnie was sure she already knew the answer to that. 'I think you must make an impression wherever you go. You're the coolest girl I've ever met.'

Summer put her fork down and looked at Donnie. His face immediately reddened. He swallowed hard, hoping to God he hadn't said too much. He looked back at her and grinned, 'And you saved me from a shark.'

'There was no shark.'

Donnie raised his eyebrows, amazed by her bravery.

Summer checked her watch.

'I'm sorry. I have to go.'

Fuck it. I should have kept my big mouth shut, thought Donnie. *She's running for the hills.*

'Can I call you?' Donnie blurted.

'I don't just give out my number,' Summer replied more curtly than she meant to, but she barely knew him, and she'd been stalked by unwanted suitors before. They were impossible to shake off, so the best option was to move town, but she liked LA and didn't want to move. Although, she wondered if she was building her defences too high, and her gut feeling was that Donnie was decent and kind. But, then, Ted Bundy was reportedly charming.

She winked at Donnie.

'For all I know, you could be a serial killer.'

'I'm not,' Donnie assured her, 'but they probably all say that. I'm staying at Ocean View Apartments, room twenty-two. It has a phone. You know, you have to phone the apartments and ask for room twenty-two, and they put you through.'

Summer giggled, thinking he was being funny. She smiled

at Donnie as she got up from the table.

'Good luck, Donnie. Don't give up!'

'Thanks,' said Donnie, and under his breath, he muttered, 'I won't.'

Summer dug into the pocket of her shorts for some money.

'No, I've got this,' Donnie insisted.

'Thank you, that's kind.'

Donnie reached into his wallet and pulled out sodden dollars.

'Did your wallet go surfing with you?' Summer grinned.

'I think it went on its own adventure.'

He watched her as she walked away, willing her to turn around. She did and dazzled him with a smile, so bright Donnie thought his heart would explode.

Donnie grinned the whole way back to his apartment. If there had been music, he would have danced, but as soon as he was back in his apartment, he was already staring at the phone, yearning for it to ring. He peeled off his shorts, grabbed a towel and headed for the shower.

Feeling refreshed, he walked towards his bed and saw the red light flashing on the phone on the bedside table. *Oh, Hallelujah!* He leapt through the air and pressed the button for his message, nervous and hopeful of its content. But, instead of the sweet voice of Summer, a familiar and loathsome voice boomed around the room.

'Aloha, Donnie, Francis here.'

Two weeks in Hawaii, and Francis already thought he was local. What an asshole, thought Donnie.

'Your Dad thought Kathy and I should swing past LA on our way home from our honeymoon. Gives us a few extra days, I suppose, but he wants us to meet your … beater partner.'

'Beta partner,' Donnie corrected the answering machine in a croaked whisper.

'I guess he's checking up on you. See you tomorrow lunchtime!' Francis quipped as the long beep punctuated the end of the call.

Donnie stared at the phone.

'Shite!' he said out loud. He lay down on the bed and stared at the ceiling. *How in God's name was he going to dig himself out of this hole?*

CHAPTER SEVENTEEN

LUNCHTIME THAT DAY: 24 HOURS BEFORE FRANCIS & KATHY'S ARRIVAL

onnie walked up Abe's garden path, carrying a brown paper bag under his arm stuffed full of cans of beer. Melanie was kneeling by the rose bushes, pruning dead heads and quietly singing Tammy Wynette's, *Stand by Your Man*. Donnie approached her tentatively, knowing that his visit may be unwelcome, but needs must, and Donnie was desperate.

Melanie squinted at Donnie in the sun. She looked taken aback. 'Steven!' she squealed.

'No, Donnie,' he smiled reassuringly, hoping it would help.

'You're trying to confuse me,' Melanie shielded the sun from her eyes, trying to get a better look.

'No, I'm really not. I'm Donnie. I came to call on Abe.'

Melanie's hand shook a little as she continued to prune the roses. Donnie knelt beside her and took the secateurs from her hand.

'Here, let me help with that.' He clipped the rose and smiled at her again.

'You know Abe?' she asked, her voice low and cautious.

'Yes,' Donnie said, wondering if *know* was a little strong.

'Are you dangerous?' she asked, her voice now stern.

'I wouldn't say so. No,' he chuckled, handing her back the secateurs.

'Are you walking heavy?'

'Am I what?'

'Are you packing?'

'Packing what?'

Melanie was exasperated now. 'Are you carrying a gun?'

'Not likely!' laughed Donnie.

Melanie seemed surprised and threw him a look that Donnie could only read as pity.

'If you're here to see Abe, I'd bring some heat. He shoots first and asks questions later,' she said firmly.

'Okay,' Donnie thought he'd better tread carefully, 'he's here, though?'

Melanie pulled herself to her feet and placed the secateurs on the ground.

'Oh, he's here, it's your decision, but we better leave those there. We don't want an accident.'

No secateurs, thought Donnie, *but he was meant to bring a gun*. This made no sense at all. Confused, he followed Melanie into the house.

Abe was asleep on a brown leather sofa, his guitar on his chest and scattered empty beer bottles at his feet. Donnie looked around the room. Apart from the beer bottles, it was tidy enough. A cherrywood bookcase, overflowing with books, stood against the back wall. A cerise pink, velvet chaise long sat under the window, and gold-framed watercolours filled every available wall space. There were no film posters, no awards lining the shelves and no sign of the life Donnie knew Abe must have led.

Melanie stood behind Donnie and peered over his shoulder at Abe. He looked peaceful, the torment erased from his face, his once dark hair now more silvery-grey. His expensive shirt was torn at the pocket and worn at the cuffs.

'Doesn't he look so innocent when he's sleeping?' Melanie said wistfully. 'You'd never know, would you?'

'Know what?' Donnie asked.

'That he seriously needs some brake fluid.'

'Some what?' Donnie wasn't sure if he was going to understand anything she said.

Melanie seemed to think the same because she stepped back from Donnie and studied him before interrogating him,

'Are you a bit of a window licker?'

'No! What? Why does he need brake fluid?'

'Brake fluid … Psych meds,' Melanie was losing patience with this idiot. 'He's a murderer!'

'He's an actor,' Donnie asserted.

'He's probably that too, for all we know,' sighed Melanie.

Abe opened his eyes, suddenly aware that Melanie was talking to someone other than herself. He saw Donnie standing in front of him and sat bolt upright.

'What the hell are you doing in my house?' he barked.

Melanie shook her head at Donnie.

'I told you, you should have been strapped.'

Donnie knelt, bringing himself down lower than Abe, in a bid to show humility.

'I'm sorry, Abe. I really need your help.'

'What could be so important that you have to come to my house?' Abe was angry now and wished he hadn't been drinking with a weird stranger who was now blatantly stalking him.

Melanie sat down in the chair next to Abe and, to Donnie's gratitude, tried to calm him.

'Isn't he a dead ringer for Steven, Abe?'

Abe softened a fraction but still looked tense, like the jittery look an alcoholic gets at closing time, knowing he's finished all the booze at home.

'Yeh, he is,' Abe finally answered.

'He seems like a good kid,' Melanie offered. 'A bit sappy, maybe.'

Donnie nodded and then wondered why he was agreeing with her.

'Maybe someone is after him!' she added, with a touch of unwarranted excitement.

Donnie gave Melanie an appreciative look and tried to explain,

'Someone is after me, and I do need your help!'

Abe sighed and rolled his eyes. An eye roll that said, *my life is fucking nuts.* He looked back at Donnie. 'I don't know why I am always surrounded by crazy people.'

Donnie thought now would be an appropriate time to offer a welcome gift. So he opened the brown bag and handed Abe the beers.

'That's good of you, ' Melanie quipped, 'he's out of redneck wine.'

Abe relaxed once beer was in his hand.

'Who's after you?' he asked, not particularly caring because he was sure there was nothing he could do to assist, even if he had the motivation to do so.

'My brother-in-law,' Donnie was relieved he was finally getting somewhere.

'Ah,' sighed Melanie with a knowing look in her eye, 'the assassin is often known to the victim.'

Donnie nodded, again wondering why he kept agreeing with Melanie.

'On the upside, my brother-in-law isn't that bright. He's—'

Before Donnie could finish, Melanie interrupted,

'A bit of a fuck-knuckle?'

'Sure,' Donnie, once again, concurred with Melanie.

'That's enough, Melanie!' Abe was getting frustrated. He gulped back his beer as Melanie put her hand out to take one from Donnie. 'Sorry, Melanie, no beer for you,' Abe said, waving her hand away before turning back to Donnie. 'Tell me about this fuck-knuckle brother-in-law of yours then.' Abe's annoyance had turned to curiosity, wondering how on earth Donnie thought he could help.

Donnie sat on the sofa next to Abe and was relieved that he didn't seem to mind.

'His great-grandfather used to be the landlord. I don't know of any actual evidence that his family were that bad when it came to the famine, but they're still, well, you know …'

'I've no idea what you're talking about,' Abe closed his eyes to escape momentarily. 'What's this got to do with the Irish famine?'

'Nothing, really. I've no doubt they burned a few houses, kicked out a good few decent tenants and left them to starve to death. I mean, it wouldn't surprise me.'

'Are you worried he's going to burn your house down?' asked Melanie, on the edge of her seat.

'No, no, that's not the problem,' Donnie replied, wishing he hadn't taken this tangent. 'He's coming to LA. He wants to meet the partner for my fictitious computer idea, and I can't … I cannot let him go back to my Dad and tell him I'm out here to become an actor.'

'So you're the actor!' Melanie butted in.

Ignoring Melanie, Abe studied Donnie. He had to admit, he kinda liked this kid, but he was living in some fantasy land, and Abe was fearful he was about to be catapulted into it.

'How do you think I can get you out of this shit storm you've created for yourself?'

'I thought maybe … maybe you could pretend to be the beta partner.'

A silence filled the room before Abe belly-laughed. It was a laugh that went on far too long for Donnie's comfort. Something else had to be said. Abe wasn't taking him seriously.

'You're one of the best actors in the world!' Donnie enthused.

'That, I am not.'

Donnie was desperate. Flattery was getting him nowhere, even though he believed it was true. With abandoned pathetic eyes, he pleaded with Abe,

'And I only know two people in LA. You're my only hope. Please, Abe, please!'

Abe sucked in his breath,

'For fuck's sake,' he muttered, aware that he was being

pulled into Donnie's delusional shit-storm.

'Is that a yes?' Donnie was scared to check. It had definitely sounded like a resigned 'yes'.

CHAPTER EIGHTEEN

THE DAY FRANCIS AND KATHY ARRIVED

Donnie had been up at sunrise and had gone for a walk to clear his head. He sat for a while on the rocks, listening to the hypnotic thud of the waves and breathing the salt air into his lungs. The sky was swirls of blue and yellow as the orange sun peeped up over the horizon. With only a few early morning strollers and dog walkers on the beach, Donnie enjoyed nature's melody of sounds. He watched the black silhouettes of pelicans flapping together on the rocks, screeching like a crowd of excitable women blethering at a coffee morning. Beyond the crashing breakers, some swooped and dived at breakneck speed to catch a hearty breakfast.

Donnie was dreading the arrival of Francis. Not that he was ever pleased to see Francis, but today his entire plan could unravel and take him back to his boring life where no one would ever know what he could have accomplished. No one, other than the locals of Bellvara, would ever know his name, and Abe, after a couple more years of drinking, may not even remember he was there. Summer would be a distant memory, just like his dreams of stardom.

But at this moment, as he watched the waves crash to shore, spending their energy on the sands of Santa Monica beach, he noticed an older lady—hard to say how old—she may have been sixty, or she may have had a very hard paper-round and only been in her early fifties. She was pushing a trolley along the promenade stuffed to the brim with checkered bags containing all she owned in the world. It would have been a sorry sight, but the woman, dressed in a thick coat that Donnie deemed too heavy for Los Angeles, was smiling. She was watching the sun come up, and Donnie could hear the faint murmur of her raspy singing. He watched as she thumped down on the beach like a sack of spuds, raised her arms, and breathed in the same salt air Donnie was enjoying. It made Donnie realise that perhaps this woman was just grateful to be alive. He could have dwelled on the message he thought he might be receiving from God, Jesus, or just the woman herself, but he decided not to. He had too much to do. Instead, he would go home, shower and book a restaurant for lunch, thinking that dinner allowed far too much time for Abe to be twisted by the time they arrived—and Donnie was worried about how heavily this plan relied on Abe not being banjaxed by lunchtime.

FRANCIS AND KATHY had a five-hour flight ahead of them to LAX from Maui. Kathy had imagined that Hawaii would be beautiful: powder white beaches, swaying palms and turquoise waters. But she didn't know that Maui would truly feel like paradise: the scents of jasmine and moringa, the ever-changing light, the baby Northern Cardinal bird with its fluffy red coat that ate crumbs from their balcony, and the heavenly fragrance of the plumeria lei that had been placed over her head on arrival. It was an obvious destination for honeymooners that electrified the senses and made visitors want to adorn themselves in flowers, from their hair to their shirts, to mimic the beauty around them.

Kathy could have spent days dancing on beaches, sipping coconut cocktails and plunging into the breakers, but Francis became easily bored— he was deaf to the sound of the ocean, blind to the feast of colours and indifferent to the seductive scents of the island. By the eleventh day, he was distant, moody and dark, and Kathy could not understand why.

On the last morning, she woke and quietly climbed from the bed, noticing the rose petals shaken from the bedclothes onto the floor the night before. She made her way to the balcony, where she hoped the paradise outside would save her from wondering if she actually knew the man she had married.

Her stomach was in knots, and her mind chattered with self-doubt. But when Francis woke, his form was light and cheery, as if she had imagined the last two torturous days of their honeymoon. He cracked jokes, complimented and minded her on the journey, and by the time they arrived at the apartment block, she had filed his cruelty away to the back of her mind where she would quickly forget the memory even existed.

Francis and Kathy had booked themselves into the same apartment block as Donnie, and he arranged to meet them directly at the restaurant because he wanted to get lunch out of the way, reassure them all was well with his project, and then, hopefully, no one would mention it again. Perhaps if he made it all sound boring enough, they would zone out, not ask too many questions, and Francis would fuck off back to Ireland.

Francis was beyond curious as to what Donnie was up to. Francis had carved out many manoeuvres to achieve his objective. He had married Kathy, and the ensuing inheritance would save his manor house and ensure he could live the life he was accustomed to. He was, at last, financially secure without anyone suspecting that his own family fortune had long since evaporated. However, Francis was very concerned that his wife was either lying to him or an entire village had been wrong about the inheritance the McNamara family would receive. The fact that Donnie was out in LA investing in some computer venture led Francis to believe that much more loot was flying around than his wife was letting on. By marrying her, he thought he had gained her trust, and it would only be a matter of time before his hands were firmly in the family till, but she seemed more guarded than he had anticipated. Francis was acutely aware that he was being left in the dark on financial matters. Meeting Donnie was about to shed some light.

DONNIE HAD CHOSEN a stunning rooftop restaurant, thinking the sea view might detract from the conversation. He scanned the restaurant for Abe but couldn't see him until a smartly dressed man near the back wall raised a hand. Donnie looked a little closer and, finally recognising Abe, walked over.

'Great disguise!'

'Yes, I had to dig out my old prosthetic nose. Change the nose, and the whole face looks different. Sunglasses help too.'

Donnie noticed that it wasn't just Abe's face that had changed. He had washed, shaved, and wore a crease-free shirt and clean blue jeans. He looked like a new man. Maybe even a sober man. Donnie observed the glass of white wine in his hand.

'Second glass today, so I should plateau nicely around lunch and can up the ante later,' Abe laughed. He had a self-deprecating laugh that was endearing and sad at the same time.

'Well, nothing wrong with a few,' Donnie knew that his idea of a few and Abe's opinion of a few may be radically different. He looked at his watch. 'They'll be here any minute.'

Abe nodded. He felt a little nervous. It had been a long time since he had acted. It had been even longer since anyone had asked for his help.

'What's fuck-knuckle's name again?'

'Francis ... and my sister's name is Kathy.'

Francis and Kathy appeared at the front of the restaurant. Donnie stood and gave them a beckoning wave. Kathy was behind Francis, bronzed and seemingly happy, her summer skirt billowing as she walked. Francis strutted towards Donnie, wearing navy shorts and a white shirt, checking out everything and everyone. He maintained his superior air and stared too long at the girl in the low-cut red top with the boob job. Kathy noticed her as well and knew it was a boob job. *Skinny girls haven't got boobs that big. Plastic surgery seems an unfair advantage*, she thought. *Leave something for the girls who struggle with weight.* The girl in the red top with the boob job stared back at Kathy. Kathy looked away, embarrassed, and Donnie wondered why they were both so preoccupied with the girl in the low-cut red top with the boob job. She certainly wasn't the only boob job in the restaurant, but Donnie wished she was seated a little closer to them as she could have been another helpful distraction.

'Hello, Donnie!' Kathy hugged him as Francis and Donnie nodded to one another.

Abe stood up, and Donnie introduced him.

'This is Abe Rockefeller.'

'My pleasure!' Abe exclaimed, charming Kathy as he kissed her cheek. He shook Francis's hand and gave him a hard stare as he endured his crushing handshake. Abe knew you could tell a lot by a person's handshake, and this vice-like grip told him that Francis was a dickhead.

'Related to *the* Rockefellers?' asked Francis in a hopeful tone.

'Yes,' confirmed Abe, 'and I've heard a lot about your impressive family.'

Francis eagerly pulled up his chair.

'I thought you looked familiar.'

'You do look familiar,' agreed Kathy.

Donnie was relying on Kathy's inability to remember a film she watched yesterday and hoped that Francis was more interested in wealthy surnames than celebrities.

Abe changed the subject quickly.

'I've ordered some champagne to celebrate!'

Right on cue, a waiter delivered four glasses and champagne in an ice bucket.

'Celebrate?' quizzed Francis, eyeing the champagne and checking the label.

'Donnie and I are going to make millions together!' Abe raised his eyebrows at Francis.

'Millions?' Francis pulled his chair closer.

'You heard. Millions!' Donnie repeated, feeling slightly anxious that Abe might be taking this a step too far. He had given him a good brief the night before, and already it was clear that Abe had no intention of following it. He was in full improvisation mode, which Donnie assumed was dangerous ground.

'What is it exactly that Donnie and his computer technology, software, whatever you call it, is doing for your company?'

Abe swung back in his chair. Something he daren't attempt with a few more wines inside him.

'We're a video games company. Donnie is providing a middleware product that essentially acts as the glue to hold everything together for our latest game.' Abe had no idea what the words coming out of his mouth meant. He was following his script, which he had hoped he wouldn't have to do.

Francis looked lost, but Kathy smiled. Kathy often smiled when she didn't understand something.

'That sounds lovely. What's the name of your latest game?'

Abe hadn't accounted for that question—and from the flicker of tension on Donnie's face, neither had he.

'*Dwarfland*,' blurted Donnie.

'*Dwarfland*?' Francis and Kathy repeated in unison.

'That's right, *Dwarfland*,' continued Abe, giving Donnie a sideways glance. *Fucking Dwarfland*, thought Abe, wondering, not for the first time, if Donnie was one beer short of a six-pack. 'Lot of money in dwarves,' he laughed hard enough to make himself believable. He picked up the bottle of champagne and filled their glasses. If there was ever a situation where booze didn't lighten up the atmosphere or entirely lose the thread of a conversation, Abe didn't know of it.

'So tell me a little bit about it,' said Francis, picking up his glass.

'Blah blah blah *Dwarfland*,' Abe said and rolled his eyes. It was the kind of eye roll that said, *I've had it up to my tits with this guy, and I can't be fucked talking to him anymore.*

Donnie's mouth opened and closed. He knew Abe was losing

patience and was now hanging by a thread. *It could all come tumbling down about now*, he thought.

'Pardon?' asked Francis, although he had heard perfectly well. Abe leaned in and grinned at Francis as he enthused,

'Let's not get bogged down in boring minutia. There's plenty of time for shop chat. Now it's time to celebrate the ingenious technology Donnie has created. Combined with our games, we're going for world domination!'

He clinked Francis's glass with his own. Then, taking the bait, Francis grinned back at Abe and drank his champagne. Donnie heaved a sigh of relief. It was a stellar performance.

CHAPTER NINETEEN

LATER THAT AFTERNOON

Kathy was feeling a little bit tipsy. Champagne had that effect on her. At the wedding, she had kept herself to one glass and then moved on to wine because her history with champagne had been less than great. On occasions previously, when she had drunk champagne, she had wet herself in the back of a taxi in Limerick, got arrested in Dublin for 'breach of the peace' and had been thrown out of a disco in Salthill (which was tricky to achieve) for removing most of her clothes whilst singing Tina Turner's *Private Dancer*. It wasn't the drink for her, and she'd had at least four glasses today. At least this time, she could head for the safety of her bed for a nap: no cops, no pile of clothes on the dance floor, and no requirement for incontinence pants.

She got out of the taxi at the apartment and found the heat was making matters worse.

'I'm going to lie down. Can you bring me some fizzy water, please, Francis?'

'Where from?' shrugged Francis.

'I've some Perrier in my room,' Donnie offered.

'Francis will get it. Won't you, Fran?' she said as she tottered off through the main doors of the apartment block.

Donnie unlocked his door as Francis followed him. The presence of Francis directly behind him felt like a predatory animal—one wrong move and Francis could pounce, rip the head off his dreams and gnaw on his soul. A red light flashed on his answering machine, causing Donnie's stomach to flip.

'You've got a message,' said Francis, pointing to the machine.

'I see that,' Donnie replied, trying to fob him off. He didn't want Francis to know anything about anything.

'Aren't you going to check it?'

'I will, yeah,' Donnie replied nonchalantly as he walked over to the fridge and pulled out a bottle of Perrier.

Francis pressed play on the machine.

Donnie jumped when he heard Summer's voice in his room.

'Hey Donnie, it's Summer. I'm going to be at Bar Boulevard tonight. I'm not working, so meet me there around eight if you're free and have recovered from your shark attack.' The sound of her wickedly cool laugh filled the room.

Donnie stared in disbelief at Francis, his emotions torn between anger for the invasion of privacy and the exhilaration that Summer had called and wanted to meet.

'Hey, what the hell are you at?' he yelled at Francis.

'Checking your messages for you,' Francis said with a smile. 'Who's Summer?'

'She's a friend.'

'Wow,' Francis raised his eyebrow, 'Donnie's got a friend.'

Donnie handed him the water.

'Here, bring this to Kathy.'

'So, it's Bar Boulevard tonight?' Francis smirked.

Donnie shook his head.

'No, no, I might go for an hour or so if you guys are having a rest.'

'Kathy needs a rest,' agreed Francis. 'Too much champagne and flying makes her puffy. Did you notice?'

'No, can't say I did,' Donnie said, ushering Francis out the door.

Francis paused in the doorway. 'You know, this project might work. How much are you investing?'

'I can't discuss that,' Donnie replied, hoping it would suffice as an answer.

'Don't be ridiculous,' Francis replied, 'I'm family. This affects us all.'

'I'm using some of my inheritance money. It should cover everything until the deal goes through with Abe.'

'I see. Did you receive the same amount as Kathy, or did your uncle play favourites?'

'What? Uncle Pete loved all of us. All the children got the same.' Donnie had no idea where this conversation was going.

'So you got ... ?'

'Plenty,' Donnie retorted, 'as did Kathy and Sheena. Why don't you speak to Kathy about this?'

Francis let out a low laugh.

'Of course, I've spoken to Kathy about it. We share everything. I just wanted to make sure you hadn't been hard done by. You know, Kathy and I could help you with your investment in *Dwarfland.*'

'That's so thoughtful of you,' Donnie said sarcastically, 'but I would speak to Kathy directly about that if I needed any help, and as it turns out, I don't.'

Donnie pushed the door further over, hoping to embarrass Francis into leaving.

With a pompous tone, Francis continued,

'You're a dark horse. I didn't think you'd have the capability to pull something like this off. I always found you to be socially incompetent.'

'I see,' replied Donnie, unperturbed, 'well, you're not a dark horse. I've always found you to be a complete arsehole, and you *are* a complete arsehole.' He gave the door a final push, and Francis stumbled into the corridor.

Donnie heaved a sigh of relief. He walked over to the answering machine and replayed the message, feeling a euphoria that even Francis couldn't dampen. Hoping his good fortune was on a roll, he decided to focus on auditions, so he picked up *Backstage* magazine and circled a few more possibilities. Under each of them, in bold print, it read, *Apply through agents only.*

Donnie sighed and lay back on the bed. He knew he needed an agent, but how could he get one when he didn't have any work to show them, and how could he get work without an agent? *Catch fucking twenty-two,* he thought. Donnie rolled over on the bed and picked up the phone, dialling the ad's number.

'Hello?' said Donnie, impersonating a posh English accent, which he decided was better than attempting an American one. 'Yes, this is Wilson Peters. I'm from De Niro, Williams and Hanks. We've got a rising star here. He's versatile, good-looking, and extremely talented. I'd like to put him forward for an audition with you ... His name? Donnie McNamara. He's Irish. You'll love him.'

Donnie hung up the phone with a satisfied smile and then dialled the next number. The stars were finally aligning.

CHAPTER TWENTY

LATER THAT NIGHT

Donnie felt so high on adrenalin that he glided up to the velvet ropes, guarded by Brett, outside Bar Boulevard. Brett, considerably taller and wider than Donnie, smirked down at him.

'You again? I hope you're not planning to jump around like a lunatic tonight?'

Flustered, Donnie shook his head—there was no way Donnie could let Brett come between him and his date with Summer.

'I'm only yanking your chain,' sniggered Brett. 'Summer told me you might be coming.' He unclipped the velvet rope to let Donnie pass.

'She's here?' Donnie was still in disbelief.

'Yeh, she's here!' Brett pointed towards the bar as if Donnie didn't know where to go.

Donnie strolled into Bar Boulevard, a purple haze of cigar smoke and the smell of Bourbon filtered through the air. The candlelit tables were filled with suited execs and beautiful-looking girls. Donnie spotted Summer straight away, chatting to the barman and drinking from a bottle of beer. She looked stunning, wearing ripped faded jeans and a lilac blouse. Her beauty was natural. She was her name: Summer.

Donnie wasn't sure how to approach her, but he had to do something other than stand a few feet away, gawping at her. He decided to use his acting skills to conjure up some confidence. He strode over and squeezed her arm tighter than he intended.

'Hi,' she said, 'glad you made it.'

'Thanks for asking me. Can I get you a drink?'

'Sure.'

Summer tapped the bottle of beer as Donnie pulled up a couple of bar stools for them.

Here he was, sitting at a bar on a date ... Was it a date? It felt like a date ... with Summer. Life couldn't be much better.

The barman that Summer had been talking to still lingered, looking Donnie up and down, sizing up his competition.

Summer realised he had been left hanging when Donnie arrived.

'Sorry, Duke, this is Donnie. Donnie, this is Duke.'

'Pleasure to meet you, Duke,' Donnie said, 'could we have a couple of beers, please?'

Duke stared at Donnie, grunted something incomprehensible, and finally reached into the fridge for their beers.

'So, have you got any auditions coming up?' Summer asked Donnie, her grey eyes sparkling in the candlelight.

'I've got two coming up. No major roles, but if I can get some small roles, I'll work my way up.'

She leaned forward, and Donnie could feel the warmth of her breath on his face. It smelt minty and fresh, and her lips were close enough to kiss. He felt the need to pull back slightly, worried he might involuntarily plant his mouth on hers.

'I'm sure you will. Are you all prepared?' she asked.

'I do this thing where I close my eyes and imagine everything going my way,' Donnie explained, but he wasn't sure if he should be admitting this.

'Like the hippies?' she asked, laughing.

'I suppose so.'

Donnie had never compared himself to a hippie and wasn't sure he wanted to. The ones around Bellvara were what they called 'crusties'—less floral and more unwashed, but probably smoked equal amounts of pot.

'I'm not a hippie, though,' Donnie felt the need to clarify. 'I could never grow my hair long, and I'm not sure my face would know how to grow a beard. What I mean is … I imagine that I already am where I want to be. Sometimes it works; I'm standing here with you.'

Donnie couldn't tell if he was coming across as romantic or cheesy, but she smiled when he said it, and that had to be a good sign.

'What about you and your singing?' he asked. 'Have you got any gigs coming up?'

'Nothing this week, but I take all the jobs I can get and keep persevering. Never give up.'

'Me too. I'm not going to give up.'

She clinked her bottle of beer with his, and her eyes were on him, frightening the life out of him and mesmerising him simultaneously. In the silence, he fought for the courage to say it.

'Do you want to go out with me?' he whispered.

'Sorry?' she asked, puzzled.

Christ, he was going to have to repeat it.

'Do you want to go out with me?'

Summer seemed confused and looked around the bar.

'I am out with you.'

'No, what I mean is … do you want to *go out* with me? Be my girlfriend.'

Summer smiled so broadly that Donnie wasn't sure if she was about to laugh in his face or agree. She reached over and squeezed his hand.

'You are so sweet. I don't think anyone has asked me like that since high school.'

Donnie smiled back, fully aware she still hadn't answered his question. Should he take that as a 'no' or ask again to be sure? He certainly didn't want a situation where Summer was now his girlfriend, and he was completely unaware of it.

He leaned in a little closer, and just as he did so, a large hand gripped his shoulder. He whirled around on his stool to see Francis. This was possibly the best night of Donnie's life to date, and Francis appearing behind him was about as welcome as shit in a swimming pool.

'Aren't you going to introduce me?' Francis put his arm around Summer, making Donnie want to punch him in the face. 'I'm Francis, Donnie's brother-in-law,' Francis said, leaning in to kiss Summer.

Donnie was horrified. This incredible dream was turning into a nightmare. His voice box was paralysed, along with his facial expression of dread.

Eventually, in an attempt to save Summer from his creepy gaze, Donnie croaked,

'What are you doing here, Francis? Where's Kathy?'

'She's still sleeping. Jet lag or champagne over-pour, who knows? I was wide awake, though, so I took up your invitation to join you this evening.'

Summer looked questioningly at Donnie. Donnie did his best to smile.

'Sorry, Summer, this is my brother-in-law, Francis.' The words felt like grit in his mouth.

'Yes, he just said that,' Summer looked from Francis to Donnie. 'You didn't say you had family coming out?'

'I didn't know until today, and I didn't think Francis would be able to join us.' Donnie hardened his stare at Francis. 'I thought you'd be jet-lagged.'

Francis laughed.

'It's only a three-hour time difference between here and Hawaii, so I think I'll manage. Takes more than jet lag to keep me down.' He looked at Summer and then leeringly added, 'If you know what I mean?'

Summer recoiled and looked the other way. *Francis may well be the chink in Donnie's armour,* she thought. Not that Francis was Donnie's fault, but he made Summer's skin crawl.

'Barman!' Francis shouted with a click of fingers, making Summer's blood boil. She hoped Duke wouldn't serve him, but unfortunately, he hadn't noticed the finger click.

'A bottle of champagne and three glasses! We're celebrating.'

'Good for you,' Duke said nonchalantly, wanting to add, *'who gives a shit.'*

'We're celebrating?' asked Summer, feeling her evening with Donnie had been hijacked.

The only person feeling that more was Donnie.

'Donnie is,' Francis said, waving an arm in Donnie's direction. He didn't give a toss about Donnie, but it was a perfect excuse to drink champagne and impress Summer. Duke poured their glasses, only smiling at Summer and shuffled off.

Summer still wasn't sure what they were celebrating.

'The start of his new career? Meeting Abe Nelson?' she asked.

Donnie's face turned pale.

'Abe Nelson? No, Donnie, have you been telling stories again?' Francis couldn't have been more condescending if he tried. '*He* doesn't know Abe Nelson.'

'I do know Abe Nelson. He's a great guy.' Donnie was sick of Francis talking about him as if he wasn't there, and whilst he did not want to unravel his lies, he wanted to shove it right back at Francis.

Francis burst out laughing, and Donnie felt the heat rise into his face. He had to keep his cool, but his heart thumped like a battle drum.

Francis stopped laughing and spoke as if he thought both Summer and Donnie were morons and barely understood English.

'I ordered some champagne because Donnie's computer project, or whatever it is, looks like it might actually work and even be lucrative. Hard to believe, I know. Nothing to do with tall tales about Abe Nelson. This is why we need to check up on you, Donnie. You live in a fantasy world.'

This couldn't be going any worse, Donnie thought. He saw Summer look utterly confused and wondered how he would navigate his story without his whole new world crashing in on him.

'What computer project?' Summer asked, her back stiffening.

'It's nothing. I don't want to bore you,' Donnie said, silently praying that would suffice.

'You're not boring me.'

Goddamn her curious mind. Donnie hoped that if he just smiled, the conversation would stop. There was a moment of silence which alerted Francis to something being amiss.

'He's working with a video games company on their game, *Dwarfland,*' Francis said, narrowing his eyes.

'Really? That's fantastic. Why didn't you say?' Summer asked, genuinely perplexed.

Donnie felt his head poking slightly above the hole he was in and tried to close off the conversation.

'I thought you'd find it dull. It's only the early stages.' He thought diversion would be his best hope of reprieve. 'Francis, Summer is a singer.'

'Are you? That's nice.'

Francis couldn't care less and was keen to continue the original thread and get to the bottom of what was making Donnie look like he was sweating with nerves.

'Donnie's project isn't really in the early stages. He's being modest, which I have to say, is unlike him. Did you think he was just out here on *vacation*?' Francis affected an American accent which made him sound even more patronising.

And then she said it,

'No, he's an actor. He's out here doing auditions.'

Donnie's inner rage turned to panic, and he thought he might well throw up. Nevertheless, he managed to avoid Francis's sharp stare.

'No, he isn't,' Francis replied, but his bullshit antenna was up.

'Why did you tell me you were out here to be an actor?' Summer asked, feeling wary.

Donnie attempted a small laugh.

'I don't think I said that.'

Summer's jaw dropped. She felt a familiar fog of deception all around her.

'Yes, yes you did. That has been the basis of our conversation.'

In desperation, Donnie began to ramble,

'I think I said acting is fun, and I've done a bit … if you can call hanging out with people in the care home acting.' He winked at her, but she failed to notice.

'But you said—'

Donnie had to cut her off before she continued,

'That I enjoyed a bit here and there, and I'm out here developing software with a video games company.' Donnie looked at her pleadingly, willing her to stop talking and hoping that she would pick up his vibe and that he would explain everything later, but Summer was too rattled to pick up any vibe.

With her face reddening, she slowly put her glass of champagne down on the bar, picked up her handbag and walked out.

Donnie raced after her, but she held her head high and kept walking. He saw the back of her head as she jumped into a cab, ignoring Donnie as he shouted her name.

Donnie's heart heaved. In less than ten minutes, Francis had obliterated what may have been his entire future. Of course, he would never know, but he was convinced he wouldn't get another chance like that again. A girl who liked him for who he was.

Francis cursing behind him made him jump.

'Fucking *Dwarfland*? I can't believe I got sucked in.'

'What are you on about?' Donnie asked, but his eyes still followed Summer's cab rambling down the boulevard towards rows of green lights, pulling her further and further away.

'I should have known it was bullshit.'

'No, it isn't,' Donnie insisted.

Francis was exasperated. 'Okay then, Donnie. Let's go to the company's offices tomorrow and meet all the geeks working on *Dwarfland*, shall we?'

Donnie stared straight ahead, his dreams tumbling down around him.

'And who the hell was that guy we met today?' demanded Francis.

Donnie spoke in a quiet monotone as if nothing mattered now, 'Abe Nelson.'

'Jesus Christ!' Francis began to wonder if Donnie was mentally insane.

'It *was* Abe Nelson.'

'Abe Nelson hasn't got a nose like that, and anyway, why would Abe Nelson ever want to hang out with you?'

Donnie stayed silent.

'So you're out here to be an actor? That's hilarious!' Francis snorted. However, Francis didn't find it funny that the promise of making millions, which he could have muscled in on, was bullshit.

'Why is it hilarious?' Donnie was sick of his bullying.

'Because you can't act. You're a tool. Always were. Still are.'

'You believed my story about *Dwarfland*. That was acting.'

Francis thought for a moment. There may yet be an opportunity for him. Not the millions he had hoped for but some kind of consolation from the incompetent little bollox.

'I tell you what I'll do,' Francis said, throwing a supercilious smile at Donnie, asserting control, 'you carry on with your pointless, pathetic attempts at becoming an actor, and I won't say a word to Kathy or your family.'

Donnie turned and eyed Francis with suspicion. *Where was he going with this?*

'Why?'

'Because I will tell them I am helping you with your computer project. I'll get some extra funds from your Dad.'

'No, no. I don't need more money. Why would you do that?'

'I quite fancy some time out here,' Francis replied, relishing the idea. 'Beats working on the farm. You got that right. I can have a little holiday to myself, and Kathy can go home and help your Dad on the farm.'

This made no sense to Donnie.

'You're just back from honeymoon. Why would you need another holiday? Why would you want my sister to go home on her own?'

'We're married now. I'm not going to get much me time. So make hay while the sun shines … and the sun is definitely shining in California.'

'You're an asshole.'

Donnie didn't think he could despise Francis more.

'So,' Francis continued, ignoring Donnie's comment, 'I can either tell the family about your lies about *Dwarfland* or stay out here and pretend to help you. Your call.'

Donnie felt doomed. The idea of Francis staying in California and having this over him was excruciating, but to leave now with everything at stake and his family hating him for what he had done was too much to bear. Donnie looked at the ground and muttered,

'If I land a really good role, you'll let me explain to my family in the way I want to?'

Francis couldn't believe the simpleton's optimism.

'Sure, Donnie, I'll let you tell them whatever you want.'

Donnie composed himself and looked Francis straight in the eye.

'It was Abe Nelson.'

CHAPTER TWENTY-ONE

THE FOLLOWING MORNING

F rancis's snoring woke Kathy early. She decided not to wake him and quietly dressed in a long white skirt, pink t-shirt and flip-flops. She picked up her purse and sunglasses and headed into the bright sunlight. When Kathy reached the beach, she removed her flip-flops. The sand was calming and cool under her feet. She strolled closer to the ocean, soaking up the relaxing sounds of the waves lapping on the shore. A couple were sitting on the beach with a little girl adding shells to the sandcastle her father had built for her. Kathy smiled as she passed them, closed her eyes and imagined a beautiful life ahead, filled with love and children of her own. But her smile faded to a frown as her mind bounced back to the last days of their honeymoon. They had been lying in a hammock together, the Pacific breeze fluttering the palm trees above them. What had been a blissful, paradisiacal moment soured quickly when they started talking. Kathy tried to remember each word of the conversation to analyse further what he had said and how he had said it. She closed her eyes as she walked on the sand, hearing his voice in her head above the gentle beat of the waves.

'So the five grand you got from your uncle, is it some kind of first instalment, or is there some sort of hold up with the rest of his estate, or what? Francis spoke flippantly as if trying to conceal that he wasn't concerned by the answer to his question.

At first, Kathy thought he was pulling her leg. She laughed and then said,

'Isn't it wonderful? Think of what I can do with the bakery. I can get proper equipment, marketing, packaging, and maybe a logo. I'd love a logo!'

Francis had sat up, almost knocking them both from the hammock. His voice changed to a higher pitch.

'When is the rest coming?'

Kathy stared back at him, steadying herself on the hammock.

'What are you talking about?'

'What did your father get? What did Donnie get?' Francis interrogated her.

'What?' Kathy was at a loss for words, unsure why he was asking these questions.

'He was a multi-millionaire!' Francis raised his voice.

Kathy suddenly realised she had fallen for Francis's prank and laughed loudly, but when Francis heaved himself out of the hammock and walked off, her heart raced, and a pain shot through her chest. With shaky hands, she lowered herself to the ground. All the time she had known Francis, he had never spoken of money. She knew that he had come from a very wealthy background and probably never needed to think about money, so why was he being so aggressive about the inheritance? Did he actually believe she was going to inherit millions? Kathy had felt sick at the thought—this couldn't be why Francis wooed her. He had plenty of his own money.

Kathy tucked her thoughts away in a folder in her brain marked *paranoid* and tried to enjoy the rest of her walk, focusing on all the good times she and Francis had shared. They far outweighed the last two days of the honeymoon. She felt the sun warm on her face as she sauntered back up the beach. *I'm incredibly lucky,* she thought and repeated it over and over again in her head until she arrived back at the apartment.

Francis was already up and dressed when she breezed back in the door, rosy-faced from the sun and salt air.

'Where were you?' Francis asked in a tone that made the flush in Kathy's face disappear.

'I went out for a walk. You were fast asleep—I didn't want to wake you.'

'You could've left a note or something. I was worried. I had no idea where you were.'

'I'm sorry,' Kathy said, sitting on the bed next to him as he put on his shoes. 'Well, we're pretty much packed for the trip home. Do you want some breakfast before we go?'

Francis put his arm around her.

'I'm sorry, but I'm not going with you. Donnie and I had a chat last night, and he's asked if I can stay on for a bit and help with *Dwarfland*.'

'Oh? What help does he need?'

'He needs *my* help, Kathy. It's a big project, and he's on his own out here. It's a big responsibility, and I want to make sure your father is happy that he's getting the support he needs and, of course, watch the finances for him. You know what he's like.'

Kathy felt her stomach lurch.

'Right, so I'm going back to Ireland on my own?'

Francis groaned.

'It's just a flight, Kathy, and I won't be long behind you.'

Kathy had not seen this one coming, and she couldn't fight her feelings of suspicion. She just didn't know what she was suspicious of.

'How long?' she asked.

'I'm not sure yet. Come on, we've just had two great weeks in Hawaii, and we've the rest of our lives ahead. Donnie needs my help. You know that.'

Kathy could not imagine Donnie asking for Francis's help. Something just wasn't right, and the idea of a lonely flight home filled her with dread. There was something about arriving back in Ireland after her honeymoon alone that Kathy knew was awkward and wrong.

'What exactly are you going to be doing out here?' she asked, trying to make her voice light.

Francis said nothing. He only stared at her.

DONNIE WOKE UP as if from a horrific nightmare, only to recognise it as his new reality. He pushed his face back into the pillow, seeking solace that wouldn't come. He stared at the ceiling, wondering how it had come to this: from cloud nine to falling arseways into the slurry pit.

He got up, made himself a coffee, and played Summer's answering machine message like some kind of self-torture. He didn't even have her number to call and explain. He would have to get it somehow or go back to Bar Boulevard when he was sure Francis couldn't follow him. He would find her, apologise and tell her the truth, which he had been doing all along.

There was a knock at the door. Donnie looked ahead and imagined Francis's smug face behind it. He stormed up and flung open the door. Kathy's concerned face looked back at him.

'Sorry, did I wake you?'

'No, not at all,' Donnie replied, ushering her into the room.

Kathy shuffled in and sat down with a feigned, happy sigh.

'Well, I am so glad that you and Francis are finally hitting it off.'

Donnie did a double-take but nodded, knowing he could blow his cover again.

'It's really good of him to stay and help you with *Dwarfland*, but I'm going to miss him … away from me so soon!' She gave a little laugh that Donnie immediately recognised as one she used to cover up any emotional turmoil.

'Everything okay, Kath?' he asked, hoping it wouldn't lead to any more challenging questions about *Dwarfland*.

Kathy enthusiastically nodded and smiled, but Donnie wasn't convinced.

'Do you want to go for a coffee?' he asked, thinking she might open up over a cuppa.

'No, I have to get going. Francis said he's moving into your apartment. Makes sense, I guess, but I never thought I'd see the day,' Kathy said, and Donnie thought he might collapse.

She stopped before she reached the door. 'What is it exactly that he is helping you with? What he knows about computers you could write on a postage stamp.'

Donnie grimaced. He had to think fast on his feet.

'I think Dad might have put him up to it. Keeping an eye on me ... and he's quite good at charming people, might be able to open a few more doors.'

'Of course, that's it, that makes sense.' Kathy hugged him and then walked towards the door before muttering, 'Mum and Dad are going to be so proud of you ... and Francis.'

Although *Dwarfland* was entirely fictional, Donnie felt irked that Francis was stealing the glory. Was there no end to his pilfering of Donnie's life?

CHAPTER TWENTY-TWO

THE NEXT AUDITION

Living in a confined apartment, indeed any space, with Francis was hideous, as Donnie knew it would be. Every self-promoting statement and tyrannical criticism made Donnie fantasise about different ways misfortune might befall Francis. Donnie wasn't a hater and didn't intend to wish him dead, but he did like to imagine a scandalous fall from grace and, on darker days, his funeral, which no one attended.

There were numerous other problems cohabiting with Francis: he took longer in the bathroom than Kathy, he physically took up too much space, he observed Donnie's everyday activities with sinister scrutiny, and his laugh grated in Donnie's ears like a constipated opera singer. He was the worst possible flatmate Donnie could have conjured up, and he wondered what he had or hadn't done in life to deserve this. Donnie also failed to understand why Francis would want to be there, following him around and going out till all hours without Kathy. Donnie's suspicions about Francis's faithfulness grew daily, concluding that if there were no obvious good traits about Francis, why would he assume that he possessed any loyalty? Donnie pushed these thoughts aside because to catch Francis up to no good would mean that he would have to tell Kathy, and if he told Kathy about Francis, Francis would blab to the whole family about Donnie's deceit. He was trapped in a vile, vicious cycle.

Donnie had been back to Bar Boulevard four times, twice followed by Francis, and so twice he had to abort his mission.

The other two times, Summer was nowhere to be seen, and neither Brett nor Duke had been working, so he couldn't ask for Summer's number. But, today, after his audition, he was going there again. He was convinced she would be there this time. Finally, he would get her number, explain himself and just maybe, this river of shite might abate.

Auditions had been hard to come by, let alone land decent roles, so he had taken a punt at a reconstruction documentary about murders in LA. At least once he got the part, he could say he was working and start to build a new showreel. He did have a showreel, but in hindsight, he decided not to use it as he felt that Tic's video skills and commentary hindered his footage of performing at the care home.

Donnie walked into reception, where a pretty and welcoming girl sat behind a desk. Donnie was glad she was not like the last receptionist, who had knocked him off his stride from the get-go.

'And how are you today, Donnie?' she asked sweetly.

'Feeling pretty good, thanks. You?'

'Mmm-hmm,' she replied, and Donnie wondered if she realised that wasn't an answer.

'You can go straight through,' she smiled, pointing toward a door with frosted glass and a bit of paper stuck to it that read, *Auditions in Progress*.

She called out after him,

'Good luck!'

Donnie smiled back at her, thinking what a difference a touch of kindness made. It gave him a little flush of optimism.

The sign on the door gave Donnie butterflies in his stomach. Documentary or not, he found he had to pinch himself that he was entering another audition … in Los Angeles.

He opened the door to a trendy-looking woman and a beaming man beside her. The woman had cropped, angled hair and a reasonably austere manner that Donnie found a touch intimidating. The man was upbeat and dressed casually in jeans and a black t-shirt, but he still managed to look suave.

In complete contrast to the people in it, the room was airless and stuffy, and the carpet looked and smelt like a million cats had pissed on it.

The woman surveyed Donnie through her heavily framed glasses, which magnified her steely, grey eyes.

'Hi, I'm Misty, the Producer. This is Levi, the Director, and you are?'

Donnie instantly hankered for a cooler name, and then it occurred to him that they might have adopted these names, and perhaps their real names were something like Mary and Leonard. He reckoned they were on to something, though, and scanned his brain for a name that sounded more alluring than 'Donnie'.

'What's your name?' Misty repeated affably, wondering if Donnie was suffering from a bad dose of the jitters.

'Well, I was just wondering that myself,' Donnie replied, 'what about Wrangler or Hazy?'

'Excuse me?' Misty stared at him, bewildered.

'I'm Donnie McNamara,' Donnie explained, 'but hearing your names, I think I might change mine.'

Misty looked unsettled, but Levi was more easily amused and burst out laughing when Donnie said this.

'Okay, Donnie or Wrangler,' he said, pointing to the camera that focused on Donnie from a tripod next to the desk, 'if you could say your name to the camera and the part you are auditioning for, please.'

Donnie could see that Levi fitted the role of Director, but also thought he could be equally at ease as a positive thinking guru, prancing about the stage, telling an audience that they were in charge of their own destiny and instructing everyone to use words like '*I can,*' rather than '*I can't.*' Donnie fully endorsed this new mode of thought and practised it, but it had occurred to him that the fact that he was an out-of-work actor, sharing an apartment with the person he disliked most on the planet, suggested it might not be working.

'Donnie?' asked Levi, checking again to see if he was hearing him. 'If you could take a seat and say your name and the part you are auditioning for to the camera, please.'

Donnie stared at the camera, like a prisoner for a mugshot, and spoke as slowly and clearly as he could.

'I'm Donnie McNamara, and I'll take any part I can get,' he said, pulling at his shirt. It felt tight across his chest, and he wished he'd worn something looser.

Misty looked at Levi with the slightest hint of a smile. Donnie couldn't work out if she was warming to him or if the smile had something sarcastic to say.

'Okay,' Levi grinned a little too much for a person making a documentary on murderers, 'so you know this a docu-style crime drama, based on recent murders in LA.'

Docu-style crime drama? That had a much better ring to it, thought Donnie. He could imagine himself shoving it in Francis's face—

'*Hey, Francis, I landed myself the lead role in a docu-style crime drama. So away to fuck now, please.*'

'Okay, Donnie ... so, from your accent, you don't sound like you're from LA. Have you been in LA long?'

'I'm from Ireland, but I always dreamt of coming to LA, and now I'm finally here, living that dream.' Donnie thought Levi would appreciate the point about living dreams as he still had him pegged as a positivity guru. 'You've got to give everything your best shot, be ready to strike when the iron is hot,' he continued, 'and I've been here a while now. I mostly hang out with Abe Nelson in Santa Monica, and I love going to Bar Boulevard. There's a girl I like there—'

Feeling this could go on for some time, Levi interrupted him,

'Yes, that's a neat place, all right. Okay, Donnie, give it all you've got!' Levi punched the air with enthusiasm.

Donnie wasn't quite sure what he was meant to be doing. Nobody had given him anything to read.

'Yes, well, I can play any of the victims,' he offered,

immediately realising how pathetic that sounded, so he added, 'in fairness, I can play any of the murderers too.'

Misty studied him, unsure what to make of this babbling mess in front of her. Was he simple or in character? There was an uncanny familiarity about him, however. A likeness she couldn't place. Then it struck her. She looked from Donnie to the pile of photographs on the desk and started sifting through them frantically. Eventually, she found what she was looking for, and with a disturbed expression, she said,

'You do look strangely like one of the murderers.'

Misty then handed a photo to Levi, who raised his eyebrows. Donnie looked from one to the other before she held it up for him to see, with an accusing look in her eye.

'Great!' exclaimed Donnie. 'I'll play him then.' *Finally*, thought Donnie, *I'm getting a break.*

Misty seemed baffled. She leaned forward across the desk and spoke more sternly,

'Do you have your copy of the script for the audition? It would have been sent to your agent.'

'Ah …' said Donnie, realising where things may have gone wrong, 'I don't have it, I'm afraid. They mustn't have posted it to me in time.'

'No problem, no problem,' said Levi, handing Donnie the script.

Misty looked back at her notes.

'Wait a minute. Donnie McNamara … It says here that you are represented by De Niro, Williams and Hanks. I've not heard of them.'

Donnie laughed.

'Everyone … I mean, literally, *everyone* has heard of them.'

Misty's brow furrowed, creating two pointed peaks of skin at the top of her nose.

'*They* are your agents?'

Donnie shrugged. *Was there any need to get into this? Why couldn't they get on with the audition? He was clearly a dead ringer for the murderer.*

'Agents, mentors, whatever,' he shrugged.

Misty leaned back in her chair, like a psychiatric therapist and clasped her hands together. Donnie wasn't sure if she was downing tools, relaxing or about to pray.

'So, you are telling me that Robert De Niro, I'm guessing Robin Williams and Tom Hanks are mentoring you?'

Donnie could see this line of questioning was taking him further away from his audition, so he thought he'd better explain,

'Yes, I mean, they are probably not aware of it, but they've been my biggest inspiration. De Niro is a glaring choice for obvious reasons. I still don't understand why he didn't win the Oscar for *Taxi Driver.*' Levi nodded in agreement, which encouraged Donnie to continue. 'Williams is a comedy genius. I loved *Mork and Mindy,* but have you seen *Good Morning Vietnam*?'

'Yes,' said Misty and Levi in unison.

Donnie attempted to mimic Robin Williams,

'*Goooood Morning Vietnam! Hey, this is not a test. This is rock and roll. Time to rock it from the Delta to the DMZ. Is that me, or does that sound like an Elvis Presley movie? Viva*—'

'What are you doing?' Misty interrupted.

'Hang on,' Donnie was on a roll, 'I haven't got to the, '*Oh, My God, it's early*' bit yet.'

'There's no need. We know the film.' Levi was now beginning to look as uneasy as Misty.

'You see my point,' Donnie concluded on Robin Williams, 'he's hilarious. He'll be a household name, mark my words … and Tom Hanks is only getting started. I think he'll be one of the most—'

Misty couldn't handle any more of it. When she finally interrupted, her lips were tight, and she spoke so softly that Donnie had to lean in to hear her.

'No one is disputing the talent of Robert De Niro, Robin Williams or Tom Hanks. We're here to see what you can do.'

Donnie felt she was missing the point.

'Of course, but they're worth mentioning. If it wasn't for them, I wouldn't be here.'

Levi thought they must have crossed wires.

'Oh … did they suggest you become an actor? Do you know them?'

'No,' Donnie laughed, 'but if you know them. I'd love to meet them.'

Misty was so freaked out by Donnie that she wanted to get as far away from him as possible.

'Let's leave it there. We have a lot more people to see today. Thank you for coming in. We'll be in touch.'

She stood up in case there was any ambiguity about what she meant.

'But I haven't read any lines yet.' Donnie was beginning to wonder if he had a bit of an unexplained personality clash with Misty.

'That's okay,' smiled Levi, 'we have a physical match. We'll call you.'

Donnie gave them the thumbs up and flashed them a smile as he left, but inside, he felt hollow because it was his face they were interested in, not his acting ability. He didn't even get a chance to show them what he could do.

He quietly shut the door, which seemed to creep Misty out even more.

She turned to Levi.

'What the hell was that? Do you think he is this guy?' She tapped the mugshot of the murderer in front of her, her eyes widening. 'Levi, he's a dead ringer for him. I'm telling you, it's him, Odie Sauer!'

'It could be him,' Levi replied, his concern rising. 'From what they say about profiling, killers like to get close to their crimes after the event. It is possible. Let's send the footage to the police, and as a precaution, we should maybe warn the agents of De Niro, Williams and Hanks.'

CHAPTER TWENTY-THREE

LATER THAT EVENING

Donnie had wandered around, not wanting to eat, not wanting to drink or talk to anyone, making time hard to kill. He sure as hell wasn't going back to the apartment because however low he was feeling, Francis would manage to slay any hint of hope he had left in his soul. He would amble aimlessly until it was time to go to Bar Boulevard. Sorting things out with Summer would give him the lift he needed, and he desperately wanted to see her. Something had to go his way today.

His last audition had depressed him. He felt he'd let himself down, perhaps talked too much about himself, but he acknowledged that he would no doubt fare better if he could get his hands on the script before the audition. Not so easy when it would be posted to a fictional Wilson Peters at the fantasy agency of De Niro, Williams and Hanks. Finding a legitimate agent that might put him forward for an audition would require time Donnie didn't have.

Finally, he was heading to Bar Boulevard. He managed to pass Brett with a cheery salute and was detained no further at the velvet ropes. It was early enough to be here, so the bar was pretty quiet, and then he spotted her ... cutting lemons behind the bar. She looked up as he walked in and quickly returned to her lemons. She let her hair fall over her eyes, reverting to a childhood belief that if she couldn't see him, he couldn't see her.

Donnie felt his mouth go dry. He cleared his throat louder

than he had intended. She still didn't look up. He reached the
bar on shaky legs.

'Summer, I owe you an apology.'

'Yeah,' she said, cutting the next lemon with more vigour.

Summer was fed up. As far as she was concerned, she had
met them all: the womanisers, the men who pretended they
weren't married, the control freaks, the dull and boring, the
narcissists, the addicts, and the downright lazy. She thought
Donnie had been different, but he was just a liar, plain and
simple—liar.

'It's a complicated story. I am out here to be an actor, and
everything I told you was legit —the truth!'

She wasn't responding, and she had no intention of answering.

The barman, Duke, walked behind the bar and stood beside
Summer.

'Everything okay?' he asked.

'Yes, thanks,' replied Donnie, although the question had
been directed at Summer.

Donnie waited for Duke to move away before continuing,
but he didn't.

'I don't know if you noticed, but my brother-in-law Francis
is an asshole,' Donnie persisted.

Duke snorted, but Summer said nothing.

'And I couldn't tell him or any member of my family that I
wanted to be an actor, so I had to tell them a lie against every
fibre of my body.' Donnie realised he was pushing reality a
bit but continued regardless, 'You know what it's like when
people don't believe in you. You know.'

Summer looked up but still didn't speak.

'I had a chance to get out here, and I took it, and Francis
suddenly appeared, and I didn't get a chance to explain to you.'

Summer was softening, but Duke still stood with his arms
folded like her henchman.

Donnie sensed a change in her demeanour and kept pressing.

'Why would I meet you and tell you a pack of lies? I liked

you—I still like you. I asked you out. Why would I do that if
I was telling you a pack of lies?'

'I think we all know the answer to that,' said Duke, looking
to Summer for agreement.

'I didn't know what to make of it,' Summer said softly.
'Nothing made any sense.'

'Exactly!' Donnie could see a hint of belief in her eyes. 'Would
it not make more sense that I was telling you the truth and
lying to that tool? He has been a pain in the hole all my life.
Seriously, I could not believe he showed up that night. I'm still
coming to terms with him marrying my sister. If you don't
want to see me, that's fine, but please don't let it be because
of that gobshite.'

She smiled at Donnie, and he felt instantly happy for the
first time since he last saw her.

'I'm really sorry,' Donnie continued, 'I haven't and would
never lie to you.'

Summer walked out from behind the bar and stood beside
Donnie. Duke finally got the hint and stacked some glasses.

Summer leaned on the bar with the other hand across
her middle as if she was still trying to protect herself from a
potential threat.

'I heard you were looking for me before. I've had enough
assholes in my life, and it just floored me that you might be
another. I began to worry about my ability to judge character.'

Donnie reached out and touched her arm.

'I'm not an asshole. Just an eegit, an idiot,' Donnie laughed
and then realised there might be some truth to his joke.

'Idiot is better. I have to go back to work. Are you hanging
around till later? I get off at ten-thirty.'

'Sure,' Donnie replied, leaning in a little closer. He wasn't
sure whether to kiss her. He decided against it. The door had
just opened, and he didn't want it flung shut in his face again.
He grinned at her and whispered, 'I am not going anywhere.'

Without warning, two police officers burst into the bar and

approached Donnie with purposeful strides.

The first officer stood directly in front of him.

'Odie Sauer?' he questioned.

'Pardon?' Donnie replied.

'What is your name?' asked the officer.

'Donnie McNamara.'

The two officers shared a look before the first one nodded and said,

'That's right, Donnie McNamara, Odie Sauer, any more names?'

'What? No,' replied Donnie, baffled.

'Can you come with us, please.' It was an instruction, not a question.

'No, thank you,' replied Donnie. He had no intention of leaving Summer and going anywhere with them.

'We need to ask you some questions.'

'Questions about what?' Donnie asked, wondering if he had broken some American law he was unaware of.

'If you could come with us?' The officer spoke more forcefully.

'No, thank you!' Donnie repeated defiantly.

'You need to come with us, or we'll have to arrest you.'

'What's going on, Officer?' Summer asked, feeling extremely uneasy.

'We're investigating a homicide.'

The officer's words landed like a grenade. Summer recoiled as Donnie, flummoxed, protested his innocence.

'I swear, I have no idea what he's talking about,' Donnie protested. 'Come on, for feck's sake.'

Donnie's language caused the officer to pounce, shoving Donnie up against the bar and forcefully grabbing his arms behind his back.

'What the fuck? I haven't done anything. I'm Irish. I'm an actor!'

The cops attempted to drag Donnie from the bar. He felt the

need to resist. If he went with him, his life as he knew it could be over. Here, in Bar Boulevard, he was safe. Summer was his witness. Summer knew him. He knocked himself sideways into a bar stool and fell to the ground.

'I'm not going anywhere!' he yelled. 'You've got the wrong person!'

But Summer was now twenty feet away, in tears, and being consoled by Duke. His arm was protectively around her shoulders, a victorious smile curled at the corner of his mouth. Donnie writhed on the ground for about four seconds before being lifted into the air by an officer on either side and ejected from Bar Boulevard. His feet barely touched the floor as he was hauled towards the police car.

CHAPTER TWENTY-FOUR

JUST BEFORE MIDNIGHT

Abe played his guitar with a belly full of beer and a couple of glasses of Scotch to anaesthetise his chattering mind. Melanie had gone to bed hours ago, although she could be up any moment because distinguishing between day and night had become confusing for her. There had been many occasions when she left the house to go somewhere in the middle of the night and had been bewildered why it was dark at two in the afternoon.

These were Abe's loneliest times, the end of an evening after Melanie was in bed. As much as she frustrated him these days, she was company, and she was still Melanie, although he had no idea how long that would last.

Abe strummed on his guitar in his usual night-time form and even muttered a few words that could have been singing if he tried a bit harder. He always thought life would move forwards in an upward direction, with perhaps a few setbacks, but he wasn't expecting to get older and have so much less than before. Obstacles in life were meant to teach you a lesson and move you to the next level, but Abe felt like he had tumbled backwards in waves of remorse to the point that his old life was a dream that he had never lived.

DONNIE HAD BEEN waiting torturously for two ass-numbing hours in an empty room. The walls were painted a depressing beige colour, with matching floor tiles—an airless box designed to make a person go insane. Donnie had run through every scenario in his mind as to what the outcome of his predicament might be. But, as each minute ticked by slower than in the outside world, the worst-case scenario seemed more likely to occur, as he envisaged a decade-long diet of porridge and fame for all the wrong reasons.

When someone finally appeared, it was neither of the officers that he had already had the misfortune of meeting. Instead, it was a bulbous, overbearing man with a sweaty moustache and brown suit. Donnie felt like he was in a stereotypical detective movie, except it was much darker than that—this was his life.

As he didn't introduce himself, Donnie imagined the man's name was Detective Dryshite.

Detective Dryshite closed the door behind him and leaned against it as if to emphasise that Donnie wouldn't be using the exit any time soon. He then stared at Donnie for an excruciatingly long time before asking,

'What is your full name?'

'Donnie Michael Christopher McNamara,' Donnie replied, answering the same question he'd been asked ten times already that night.

'What's your address in Ireland?'

'Cloonabuck, Bellvara, County Galway.'

'Zip code?'

'No such thing.'

'What?' asked Detective Dryshite.

'We don't have zip codes. The postman knows everyone. You could probably send a letter to Donnie McNamara, somewhere in the west of Ireland, and it would get there. Unless you live in Dublin, and then you might have to be a little more specific.'

'Do you think this is funny?' Detective Dryshite wasn't in the mood for discussing the postal service in Ireland.

'No, I just want to go home. My arse is killing me, and I

haven't done anything wrong. As I told the two clowns that arrested me, you've got the wrong person. To say you've ruined my night would be an understatement.'

Donnie could hear himself speaking but didn't seem to have any control over the words that tumbled out. He wondered if he'd just added another decade to his sentence but, to his utter amazement, he saw the flicker of a smile under Detective Dryshite's moustache.

'Resisting arrest, insulting two police officers ... you're not off to the best start in Los Angeles. We know who you are. We know you are not Odie Sauer, but I just wanted to confirm everything I had in the report.'

'So I can go?'

Detective Dryshite stood aside, opened the door and motioned for Donnie to leave the beige box. Donnie walked slowly towards the door, wondering if this was some test he was about to fail and just as he reached the doorway, Detective Dryshite grabbed his shoulder and muttered into his ear,

'The two clowns will take you home.'

The clowns were going to take him to his apartment in Santa Monica, but the last thing Donnie needed was Francis spotting him getting out of a cop car. So Donnie asked them if they would drop him at his friend's house; the only friend Donnie had in LA was Abe.

He gave the officers the address, and they pulled up outside. The older clown pointed at the house.

'This one?'

'Yes, thanks.'

'Isn't that where Abe Nelson lives?'

'Yes, he's my friend,' Donnie muttered, hoping that would satisfy them.

The two officers looked at each other, and the older one said,

'Come on, we'll walk you to the door. Explain it was a misunderstanding.'

'No, really, there's no need. I can explain myself.'

'We'll come with you,' insisted the officer.

The two officers flanked Donnie on either side as the older one pressed the doorbell.

Nobody answered, but the strumming of a guitar could be heard inside. The officer pressed again, for longer this time. Finally, there was movement, followed by the sound of something falling over and smashing and a muffled, '*Fuck sake,*' before footsteps were heard shuffling to the front door. Abe opened the door in his boxers and a *Laurel & Hardy* t-shirt. He looked shocked to see the police and then more vexed when he saw Donnie standing between them.

'What's going on?' Abe demanded.

'Sorry to trouble you, Mr Nelson. Your friend, Donnie, hasn't had a great night. A case of mistaken identity. We just wanted to make sure he got here safe.'

Donnie gave Abe a little wave and smiled apologetically.

'Why is he here?' Abe asked, exasperated as he rubbed the long stubble on his face.

'He said he wanted to come here,' the older officer said, smiling. He was already delighting in the story he had for his wife when he knocked off for the night, and he wondered if he should seize the opportunity to ask for an autograph.

Before he could get a pen out, Abe pulled Donnie in the door, thanked the officers and briskly shut the door behind them.

'Thanks, Abe!' Donnie put his arms out to hug Abe.

Abe swatted his arms away.

'Thank me for nothing. I feel like punching you.'

'Please don't. I've had a really shit day.'

'I've had a really shit few years!' Abe bellowed, and Donnie was unsure whether to follow him into the lounge. He wondered if giving Francis ammunition might have been preferable to facing Abe's wrath.

Abe threw himself down on the sofa while Donnie looked around aimlessly.

'Sit!' Abe instructed.

Donnie perched himself on the edge of the armchair.

Abe poured himself a Jack Daniels.

'We need to chat about boundaries.'

'Sure, boundaries, cool,' Donnie replied, thinking the situation might not be as bad as he had anticipated.

The room was dark, with only a small lamp on. Abe was happier in the low light—it mirrored his mind and dimmed his vices. If he searched his soul, he was almost glad Donnie was there. He'd greatly missed company, someone to share his thoughts with and help him through the dark hours.

Abe talked openly but not coherently about subjects Donnie could not contribute to. Ex-wives were a complete mystery to Donnie. He would have counted himself lucky to have one wife, as that would have meant that at least someone liked him enough to marry him in the first place, but Donnie had to concede that he didn't relish the idea of being married to Abe's ex, Crystal.

'I was away a lot, working,' Abe explained, 'and I couldn't wait to get back to her. We would open a couple of bottles of wine and stay up talking till morning. Making love, talking.' He waved a hand at Donnie as if Donnie knew precisely what he was talking about. Abe re-filled his glass and rambled on, 'Life was good. The work was good. My home life was normal. Normal … and there's fuck all wrong with normal!' He shouted this as though he was berating himself.

Donnie chuckled.

'Normal? You were a Hollywood star living in Malibu. Where I'm from, that's totally alien.'

Abe nodded, half-listening. He wanted to pour his guts out and would prefer to do so without interruption.

'But after a while, I don't know, a few years maybe, she wasn't there when I got back, and when she did arrive home, we didn't stay up till dawn anymore. Sure, there was the odd chat over a glass of wine, but I didn't realise somewhere there had been a turn in the road, and we both went different ways.

And then my head got turned. I had loved Crystal so much that I thought I was immune to infidelity, but when we drifted, the cracks appeared, and I let Sophie in. Big mistake!'

Donnie saw the tear in Abe's eye and wasn't sure if he should go over and comfort him. He decided against it. Abe didn't seem like the kind of guy who wanted a cuddle on the sofa from another man. So instead, he tried to think of something to say, something profound that might ease his pain or make him see his troubles in a different light.

'It can happen,' Donnie said, wishing something better had come to mind.

'It did fucking happen,' Abe looked at Donnie with a hint of annoyance, and Donnie wasn't sure why. 'It fucking happened, all right. I'm saying that my marriage wasn't over, but things weren't great before I smashed it to pieces. If we'd talked and sorted out whatever was missing, maybe this wouldn't have happened.'

Donnie scratched his chin.

'Abe, I'm no expert on relationships. I'm not an expert on anything, but from what you've told me, your ex has done some pretty vile things to get her revenge. Would you really want to be married to someone like that anyway?'

Abe sat bolt upright as if Donnie had given him an epiphany.

'You're goddamn right, I don't!' he roared, staggering over to grab Donnie's shoulder. 'Thank you, Donnie. Sometimes it's hard to see the wood for the trees.'

Donnie was glad to be able to help, although he thought his comment was blindingly obvious. Abe leaned back on the sofa, shut his eyes, and let out a contented sigh.

'Y'know Abe, there's currents for cakes and raisins for everything,' Donnie kept talking, thinking he was on a counselling roll.

'What are you talking about?'

'Well, you thought your life was great, but something was missing. Sometimes everything has to collapse to rebuild better—raisins, reasons for everything. And sometimes you need a friend to talk to.'

Donnie looked over to Abe for some acknowledgement of the wisdom he was spouting, but Abe was fast asleep. Donnie leaned back in the armchair and tried to get comfortable.

DONNIE WOKE THE FOLLOWING morning in the same upright position in the armchair. An empty bottle of Jack Daniels was on the table, but there was no sign of Abe. He got up, and the welcome smell of bacon and eggs filtered up his nostrils. He followed the aroma to the kitchen and found Abe cooking breakfast and humming to himself.

'Good morning!' Abe cheerfully greeted Donnie. 'Breakfast?'

'Yes, please.'

Donnie sat down at the kitchen table as Melanie floated into the kitchen in a silk dressing gown, her hair in perfect curls. If Donnie didn't know Abe, it was Melanie who looked like she had once been a Hollywood star.

'What are you headbangers up to? Partying without me?' she asked as she sat at the table as if Donnie being there was nothing unusual.

'Breakfast, Melanie,' Abe suggested.

'Pancakes?' she asked hopefully as she saw Abe piling bacon on a plate.

'No.'

'Damnit! No pancakes. Maybe I'll go back to bed.'

'You've never liked pancakes. You have bacon and eggs every Saturday.'

'I do? Okay then.'

She sat down and waited for Abe to pass her plate.

Abe sat down and joined them. There was a familial feel to the three of them, passing condiments and chatting.

'Got any auditions coming up?' Abe asked Donnie.

'Two tomorrow.'

'For?'

'Nothing major, but I don't seem to be getting the parts for 'nothing major' either.'

'Well,' Abe said encouragingly, 'tides can turn.'

'They can turn both ways, and a storm can always get worse,' Melanie stated, negating Abe's optimism.

'True, Melanie,' continued Abe, 'but Donnie is out of work and got arrested last night for murder, so let's hope his low ebb is over.'

'Who did you murder?' demanded Melanie. She put her knife and fork down and glared at Donnie.

'I wasn't *arrested*. I was questioned, and I didn't murder anyone. I just looked like the guy. I have a common face.'

'Everyone says they didn't do it,' Melanie said, shrugging.

Abe winked at Donnie and whispered, 'She thinks I shoot people because of the television.'

'I can hear, you know!' Melanie shot a look at Abe.

They finished breakfast, and Donnie didn't want to leave and go back to the apartment with Francis. He hadn't felt this at home in a long time.

'I'd better get going,' he said, hoping someone would argue.

'Okay then,' Abe said, and it wasn't until Donnie got to the door that he added, 'you know, you can stay any time.'

A feeling of belonging swelled in Donnie, like finding a family he fitted with more than his own.

CHAPTER TWENTY-FIVE

THE NEXT DAY

onnie was finally back in his apartment after a good night's
sleep, and to his delight, there was no sign of Francis.
Donnie had been there all night and all morning, and if
it wasn't for the fact that Francis's belongings were strewn
across the floor and empty shopping bags were scattered all
over the place, he might have thought he'd fecked off back to
Ireland. Whatever was causing his absence, Donnie didn't care,
especially since he had two auditions today. Two auditions
that might change his life. He was brimming with positivity
and thought that today was the day the tide would turn for
him. He would get a role and go back to Bar Boulevard later
and explain to Summer that he wasn't a murderer. *First a
liar, then a murderer.* He thought the latter might be a more
challenging hurdle to get over.

His next audition was in a meeting room in some obscure
offices downtown. It didn't scream 'studio' to Donnie, but he
was running out of options with no agent, no showreel and no
credits to his name. He was relying solely on someone spotting
his talent. He was already sweating when he arrived at the
audition. It was a sweltering hot day, and he'd been walking
around for ages trying to find the right door.

When Donnie finally entered the audition, which was as
obscure as its location, he met Oliver Cantmore, who had a
Bichon Frise dog on his lap, colour-coordinated in the same
red t-shirt. Oliver was so skinny that Donnie wondered if

this filmmaker was so broke he couldn't eat. His cheekbones protruded from his face like razor blades, and his brown eyes were flat and soulless. His vision was regularly impaired by his hair falling over his eyes.

Working the camera was Vicky. Vicky had an upper-class English accent but played down her roots by wearing ripped black jeans and a *Siouxsie and the Banshees* t-shirt. She had piercings on every conceivable surface of her skin, and her jet-black hair looked unnatural and was hair-sprayed to point north, south, east and west. Oliver and Vicky were an incongruous pair, and Donnie couldn't imagine where or how they could have met. Oliver introduced himself, Vicky, and the dog as 'Wilbur'.

'As you know,' said Oliver, as he ran his fingers through his floppy hair, 'it's a unique, breaking-the-boundaries comedy. We're looking for lots of improvisation from our actors, so I'll get straight to the point. Are you funny?'

Donnie knew the answer Oliver wanted was obvious.

'I'm hilarious.'

Oliver had eyes that darted around the room as if he had spent a long time locked up and was looking for a means of escape.

'This might be my first short film—'

'Short film?' repeated Donnie hoping that Oliver had meant to say, *feature* film.

'Yes, *groundbreaking* short film. I've been around the block many, many times, so I know funny when I see it.'

Donnie couldn't see anything funny about Oliver. If he'd been asked to describe him, *devoid of humour* would have fitted well. He had failed to see a smile crack his lips since entering the room.

Oliver prodded Donnie further,

'Can you make people laugh?'

Donnie thought about it for a moment.

'Probably not.'

Vicky made some sort of choking noise behind the camera.

'Okay,' Oliver thought Donnie was trying to be funny, 'tell me something funny that happened to you recently.'

Donnie racked his brains but could think of nothing. He didn't want to revisit the mistaken identity of a murderer, as not enough time had passed for Donnie to find it amusing himself.

'Why don't you make the script funny, and then you won't need the actors to improvise?' Donnie suggested.

It wasn't a suggestion that went down well, as Oliver looked at him with contempt.

'Because that would miss the whole point of what we are creating. Can you answer the question, please? Something funny that happened to you?'

Donnie looked around the room for inspiration, but his eyes kept getting drawn back to the dog on Oliver's lap. The dog eye-balled him back. Donnie was convinced the dog had some form of hypnotic power as he found himself propelled back to Ireland, laying bare a story he thought had been deleted from his mind long ago.

Donnie had walked into the living room where his little sister, Sheena, stood, hiding something behind her, a guilty smile on her face. Her arms were outstretched, partially obscuring the Sacred Heart above the fireplace. Donnie walked behind her to see their collie dog, Meg, wagging her tail. Her front paws were adorned with neon pink leg-warmers, she had yellow plastic beads around her neck, and a visor with multi-coloured flashing lights on her head.

'She doesn't mind,' Sheena had insisted.

Donnie leaned down to remove the visor as Sheena pushed him back.

'Don't! You'll ruin her outfit.'

Elizabeth then appeared in the lounge and sighed when she saw Meg.

'Donnie, what is going on here?'

'Well, obviously, I didn't dress up the dog.' Donnie nodded towards Sheena.

'I didn't dress up the dog!' Sheena protested and then threw Donnie an impish look.

Elizabeth walked back out of the lounge and muttered, 'Look at the fecking state of the place.'

Sheena skipped over to the record player in the corner of the room. She picked out a single and put it on. Phil Collins began to sing *In the Air Tonight*. Sheena clapped at Meg, and the dog jumped up on her hind legs, visor flashing, as Sheena held her paws.

'She loves dancing with me!' Sheena laughed as she waltzed the dog around the room.

Donnie loved Meg. She was a friendly, patient family pet but not a tremendous amount of use on the farm, given that she was scared of cattle and refused to work them. Even sheep could send her bolting in the opposite direction. The dog that earned all the farm glory was Nip—so-called because that was what she did. Nip wasn't so friendly but followed Mickey-Joe like a shadow, obeying his every command. Sometimes Mickey-Joe didn't even need to utter instructions because Nip knew instinctively where he wanted the cattle, giving Mickey-Joe justification to insist that the dog was telepathic.

As Phil Collins upped the ante of what was in the air tonight, Nip entered the room, a little muddy from a hard day's graft. She wasn't usually in the lounge. As a lone wolf, she preferred her spot at the backdoor, ready to chomp down on the ankle of any unwanted visitor. Donnie clapped at Nip, wanting to join his sister's fun with Meg. Nip didn't respond. Donnie got down on all fours and shook his bottom as if soliciting the dog to dance to Phil. Nip ignored him. He closed in on Nip and barked like a dog, making Sheena laugh, but Nip remained unamused. Donnie then proceeded to sniff the dog as if pretending to be another dog might break the ice, but nothing. Sheena was his audience, however, and she found this hilarious. On all fours, Donnie continued to walk around the room sniffing Nip, and one thing led to another, and Donnie, continuing the humour, caught hold of Nip's tail and sniffed her backside. Nip's teeth sank into Donnie's ear as Phil reached his drum crescendo.

Mickey-Joe rushed into the room, hearing Sheena's high-pitched scream over Donnie's low wail and Phil's drums. Donnie clutched his ear, blood pouring through his fingers as Nip bounded towards Mickey-Joe, wagging her tail and rolling over onto her back for a tummy tickle.

'What, in the name of God, is going on in here?' barked Mickey-Joe.

'Nip bit Donnie!' Sheena shouted, her voice a fusion of amusement and hysteria.

'It's okay, just a bit of blood.' Donnie knew where he was in the pecking order in relation to Nip and expected no sympathy from his father.

'What did you do to her?' Mickey-Joe demanded, patting the dog's head.

'She bit me. I didn't bite her,' Donnie protested.

'You must have done something?'

'No, no, nothing at all—must have just given her a fright.' Sheena helpfully added,

'He was sniffing her backside.'

Mickey-Joe looked at Donnie incredulously as Elizabeth entered the room.

'Oh my God!' she shrieked.

'I'm all right.' Donnie tried to reassure her.

'You're getting blood all over my carpet!' she roared back at him.

Donnie had gotten a little annoyed at this stage.

'I think it might need stitches.'

'Cop on! It's just a bit of blood!' Mickey-Joe shouted as he turned and walked out of the room, shaking his head, with Nip at his heels. 'Come on, Nip.'

Donnie snapped out of his memory and looked back at the shocked faces of Oliver and Vicky, realising that somehow he was on all fours on the floor, re-enacting the dog debacle.

He smiled up at them sheepishly.

'You've got to agree. The name Nip is a bit of a fucking understatement.'

Within moments, Donnie found himself propelled into the hallway with a shove from Oliver. He wondered how such a lightweight could push him with such force whilst still holding on to his precious dog. Oliver's voice boomed across the corridor,

'You sick fuck!'

Donnie scrambled to his feet and ran down the corridor, searching for the nearest exit. Once outside, Donnie consoled himself with the fact that he didn't want to work with Vicky or Oliver, and he definitely didn't want to be involved with their amateur project—it could easily have created repercussions for his career in the years to come.

He had another audition that day on the Warner Brothers Studio lot. It was for a featured extra, but … it was on the *Warner Brothers Studio lot,* and Donnie was beside himself with excitement.

He arrived at a security gate and handed over his passport and meeting information. Shortly after, an upbeat young guy called Chris picked him up in what seemed to be a golf cart. Chris was tanned and fit with blonde highlights through his hair. His eyes were a striking blue, and he could have been a male model if he wasn't so short. Donnie reckoned Chris would be exaggerating if he said he measured five foot four.

Chris seemed to love his job, and Donnie was almost willing to trade his dream of being an actor for Chris's job, hurtling around the studio lot—right in the thick of it.

'What time is your audition?' Chris asked in a southern drawl.

'About another forty-five minutes,' replied Donnie, checking his watch.

'Whatcha auditioning for?'

'*Robin Hood,*' Donnie answered, unable to stop smiling and then thought he'd better add, 'Not Robin Hood himself but a part in the film *Robin Hood: Prince of Thieves*.'

'Fantastic! Well, if you've time, I can give you a short tour if you like?'

Donnie was beyond elated. Chris showed him street sets used in *The Dukes of Hazzard* and passed by the water tower with the large WB logo on the front of it. Donnie was having so much fun that he almost forgot about his audition.

Chris pointed over to stage sixteen.

'That's stage sixteen, the biggest in America,' he quipped. 'I'm sure you've seen *The Goonies*?'

'Have I *seen* it? I begged anyone going to Galway to drop me at the cinema for two weeks running. I saw it four times at the cinema and about twenty on the video I got that Christmas!'

'Well, that's where they filmed the scene where the kids land in the cavern and see one-eyed Willie's ship!'

Chris was as enthusiastic as Donnie. Clearly, the magic never wore off.

'And,' continued Chris, 'over there is stage twelve. That's where the vampire cave scenes in *The Lost Boys* were filmed.'

Donnie was so overwhelmed that he could only speak in a whisper.

'*The Lost Boys* is my number one favourite film of ALL time.'

Chris grinned.

'Mine too.'

Donnie couldn't help but quote,

'*You'll never grow old, Michael, and you'll never die, but you must feed!*'

Chris laughed.

'Right, let's get you to your audition. I don't want to hold up the next Kiefer Sutherland.'

Donnie was so happy that his eyes welled up. He looked away, hoping his new friend, Chris, didn't notice.

With a high five, Chris bade him good luck, and Donnie had such a good vibe that he was in the right place—he felt a premonition that he *was* going to be the next Kiefer Sutherland or at least star beside him. He could almost feel the Oscar clutched in his grateful hand.

'Thanks so much,' gushed Donnie, 'you must love your job.'

'Oh, I do, but the hours are brutal,' Chris revealed, 'but, sure, it's only for now.'

Donnie suddenly became acutely aware that Chris's voice had changed from a southern drawl to a pronounced Dublin accent.

'I'm an actor too. Waiting for my big break,' Chris divulged.

'What? Really?'

'Sure, who isn't out here?'

'Right. Is that a Dublin accent I hear?' Donnie asked.

'Sure is … that's my real one. I try out a different accent every day—to practice, you know. So how was today's southern drawl?'

'Convincing,' Donnie replied, but he couldn't bring himself to smile.

Chris winked at Donnie.

'See you after!' he shouted, trundling away in his buggy.

Donnie felt his stomach sink, suddenly realising that he was only one of the millions trying to achieve the same goal, where only the chosen few would succeed.

He closed his eyes before entering the audition and tried to bring back the joy he had felt before Chris's bombshell comment.

'Fuck it, this is it,' he muttered to himself. 'This time, aim high. Go big, or go home!'

He knocked on the door, and a young woman's radiant voice called back,

'Come in!'

She stood up and shook his hand when Donnie came through the door.

'Hi, I'm Heather. You must be Donnie. Take a seat.'

Heather had a kind face and a gentle demeanour. Being young, she was not hardened by the burdens of life or the ruthless industry in which she was paving her career.

'So, you understand it's a featured extra role—you would be playing a peasant with one speaking line, and then you'll be part of the crowd.'

'Yes, I understand. I have to start somewhere.'

'You're absolutely right, but it will be an amazing movie. We have already cast Kevin Costner as Robin Hood, and it looks like, as of today, we have attached Sean Connery.' Heather's passion for the project was evident.

Donnie felt comfortable chatting with Heather. She was making this much easier for him. 'That's so exciting!' he replied. 'Hang on a minute, Sean Connery?'

'Yes,' beamed Heather.

'Do you have a side with some of his scenes on it that I can read?' Donnie was going big.

Heather hesitated, unsure.

'What for?'

Donnie raised his eyebrows at Heather.

'Well, Heather, think about how much money you could save the production if you hired me instead of Connery. I do a massive Connery impersonation. It's my party trick. You see, the Scottish accent is not so different from the Irish and well, I know people would know I wasn't Connery, but it's the accent he's known for. That's why people love him.'

Donnie stood up and lifted his chair behind the desk beside Heather's. He turned to face her, doing his best to convey Connery's character of Malone in *The Untouchables*, re-enacting the scene in the church with Kevin Costner. Heather was taken aback and not sure what to do about this intrusion of space. Then Donnie spoke in a voice that sounded like Connery but categorically was not Connery,

'*You wanna know how to get Capone? They pull a knife, you pull a gun. He sends one of yours to the hospital, you send one of his to the morgue! That's the Chicago way! And that's how you get Capone.*'

Heather laughed, thinking this must be a joke and then looked nervous when she realised Donnie was serious. She had been told to get straight down to the audition with featured extras and not to engage in too much small talk. She was beginning to see why. She fidgeted with the papers in front of her as Donnie took his chair back to the right side of the desk. Heather let out an inadvertent sigh of relief.

'I think you're missing the point,' she said gently, 'they want to hire Sean Connery. They've been in talks with his agent for ages.'

'That is my point,' persisted Donnie, 'I am so much easier to hire. It's a 'yes' from me. No talks required. I don't even have an agent!'

Heather's tone was beginning to sour.

'Connery is playing the King. You're too young to play the King.'

Donnie saw a glimmer of hope.

'Nothing make-up couldn't fix. Come on, what do you say?'

'No, I can't do that,' Heather's patience was fraying. 'I'm here to audition you for a peasant in the crowd.'

Donnie could now see he was losing her. One last try. He reverted to his Connery accent.

'I know that Heather, but who wants to be a peasant when they can be King? Somewhere in your bag is the rest of the script. Just a little peek at Connery's scenes? Just give me a chance, please, Heather.'

Heather felt she only had herself to blame for mentioning Connery in the first place, but it was time to end this.

'I'm afraid not. I admire your ambition, but we'll have to leave it there. Thanks for coming in.'

'But we haven't even done the scene for the peasant in the crowd?' Donnie objected.

'You just said you didn't want it.'

'I was only trying to aim high. It's always worth a try, isn't it?' Donnie was desperate.

'U-huh,' mumbled Heather, 'let's do the line then.'

'Make way for the King!' Donnie shouted as Heather scribbled something in her notepad.

'Can I try it a different way?' Donnie asked.

'Sure.'

'Make way for the King!' Donnie's second effort was identical to his first.

'That was great. Okay, thank you, Donnie. It was great to meet you,' Heather said as she stood up to open the door for Donnie.

Knowing he had flunked the audition, Donnie did his best to give her a confident smile as he scurried out the door.

CHAPTER TWENTY-SIX

FIVE MINUTES AFTER THE AUDITION

Donnie felt devastated. He realised he'd overcooked it—if he had just stuck with the part she was offering, he could have been filming with Kevin Costner and Sean Connery. He hated himself at that moment, and his face turned scarlet every time he replayed the last half hour in his mind.

'What's up, buddy? How d'you go?' Chris hailed from halfway down the lot.

Donnie shrugged as Chris pulled his cart up beside him.

'Not your day?' Chris pushed.

'I fucked up. I did a Connery impersonation.'

Chris chuckled.

'Everyone has to be able to do that. Hey, did you see him in *The Untouchables*? He's deadly.' Chris then repeated the line Donnie had used in the audition but with more authenticity, *'They pull a knife, you pull a gun. He sends one of yours to the hospital, you send one of his to the morgue! That's the Chicago way!'*

'Yes, it's a great film, all right.'

'It's fierce competitive out here. You don't see that from back home. You think you come here, and boom, you're noticed! But us mad few will keep on trucking, won't we?' Chris conceded.

'Sure,' Donnie agreed, wishing Chris would offer something more positive. 'How long have you been out here?'

'Let's see, now … five years this year,' Chris said, smiling as if that in itself was an achievement.

'Right, I see. So you've had a few parts then?'

Chris sucked in his breath before responding as if he was about to divulge a series of accomplishments.

'Well, I'm a bit of a serial extra, and I've been in a couple of student films, but my big claim to fame is that I was almost a stand-in for Michael J. Fox on *Teenwolf*. Same height, y'see?'

'Almost a stand-in?' Donnie asked, confused.

'Yeh,' Chris said wistfully, 'there were two of us, and Michael didn't need much help with stand-ins, so I just sat around drinking a lot of coffee and eating doughnuts.' Chris howled with laughter. 'Ah well,' continued Chris, 'God loves a trier, eh?'

Donnie tried to muster a smile as Chris high-fived him again.

'Best of luck, buddy! Hope to see you on the big screen someday, or I might catch you at the next extras audition!'

Donnie stared after Chris. How could he remain so sunny and cheerful when he had all the facts: this was a pointless waste of time, a lottery, a fool's dream, and it became disturbingly apparent to Donnie that he was the fool—at least Chris had a cool job.

The day had turned humid, and Donnie felt the air choke him the whole way home—his claustrophobia was fuelled by his anxiety. How was he going to make it in this industry? If he persevered for ten years, would he become like Chris, proud to be a stand-in on a movie? It was a far cry from an Oscar acceptance speech. He remembered, as a child, standing on top of the back wall of the yard and telling his mother he was going to fly. He had leapt from the wall, willing himself forward as he flapped his arms frantically and landed in a crumpled heap on the grass. His mother had encouraged him and even got a hay bale from the shed, giving him a chance to land on something less likely to break his bones. Each time he returned to the kitchen and declared that he was making progress and landing just a bit further away, she would smile and say,

'Keep trying!'

He remembered the flush of excitement and determination when he told her, 'I will do it. I will fly!'

Several hours later, he was getting grumpy and frustrated but, nonetheless, still determined. His mother called him inside for dinner, and he refused. His next jump might be the one where he would soar across the fields. With one hand on her hip, his mother had insisted that he come in for dinner this instant, and when he refused again, she said,

'Donnie, you will never be able to fly. No one can. It's impossible. Come in for dinner!'

His feelings that day mirrored the disillusionment he felt travelling back from his auditions. Donnie had never climbed the back wall in the yard again, and he had a feeling that today he had reached the end of the road with auditions. His dream of being an actor and winning an Oscar felt silly and naive, like the idea of sitting on a cloud or finding the end of a rainbow.

MELANIE ANSWERED THE door to Donnie and ushered him towards the backyard, where Abe was stretched out on a lounger under the shade of an orange tree. On his chest was a dog-eared notebook, and his can of beer was placed in a yucca plant pot beside him.

'Well, how did you get on?' Abe sat up and took a swig of his beer.

Donnie shook his head and looked up at the sky as if watching his ambition float away above his head.

'I was no good, Abe. I don't think this is for me. They hated me.'

Abe waved his hand dismissively.

'Come on, now. It can't have been *that* bad!'

'I cannot act. I certainly can't audition. I can't even be a peasant in the crowd.'

'Who wants to be a peasant?' retorted Melanie.

'I can't even be a murderer when I look just like the guy,' Donnie whined.

Melanie couldn't understand what his problem was.

'Honey, why would you want to be a murderer?'

Donnie continued, 'I have lied to my family. I had to lie to Summer. I've been arrested in front of Summer. I wanted to prove myself, and I have—I have proved that I am nothing but a failure.'

Donnie looked up, hoping Abe or Melanie would argue the point, but they didn't.

'And then, I'm being coerced by my brother-in-law, who I think is probably doing the dirt on my sister, and I can't even tell my sister because then he'll rat on me.'

He sat down on the lounger beside Abe and let out a huge sigh. Finally, he was done with it. If he couldn't get a part in anything, the Oscars might as well be in another dimension.

'Thank you, though, for everything you've done,' he said, tears forming in his eyes. 'I'm so glad I met you and Melanie.'

Melanie beamed and adjusted her hair.

'You finished?' asked Abe.

'Yeah, I'm not going to get within an ass's roar of my dream. I can see that now.'

Melanie sat down beside Donnie and took his hand in hers.

'It's the dreamers and crazy ones who make the most of their life,' she said. 'Do you want to be a plodder? A steady ship?'

Donnie didn't want to be boring. He knew that much, but the steady ship admittedly looked more attractive. He turned and gave Melanie wry smile.

'I just don't think I can do it.'

'Say you can, you can. Say you can't, you can't!' declared Melanie.

Abe felt sympathy for Donnie, but he'd been where Donnie was before. This was one of the junctions where most people turned around and threw the towel in, not just in acting but with anything in life. Too many knocks and people tend to retreat, frantically waving the white flag to prevent having to bear another rejection. This was the point where Abe knew you had to keep going.

'Where do you think you are going wrong?' Abe asked.

Donnie hadn't considered that he had been going wrong anywhere. He saw it as a lack of ability, perhaps some unpleasant external forces, or maybe he didn't deserve to succeed.

'I don't know, but I have to go back to Ireland and tell the truth to my family. It's all just been a stupid notion,' Donnie moaned.

'Maybe, but perhaps you need to brush up on your auditioning techniques. Maybe you're coming across as too desperate.'

'I am desperate!' Donnie spouted.

Abe clapped his hands to snap Donnie out of his downward trajectory.

'Okay, well, if you want to return to Ireland, that's fine, but I'm happy to work with you on an audition I lined up for you.'

Donnie's heart skipped a beat as he gaped at Abe.

'You did? How?'

'Nah, never mind. If you're a failure, you won't want it. You've given up now.'

It was the bolt of lightning Donnie needed. He suddenly felt like a hurricane had blown away the negativity cloud sitting over his head.

'No, no, I haven't given up. What audition, Abe?'

'I mentioned your name to George. He said he'd see you.'

'George?'

'Yeh, George, George Lawless,' Abe said, smiling. 'I still have some friends in the industry, you know.'

Donnie's mouth was hanging open.

'Why are you laying your reputation on the line for me?'

'My reputation? Don't make me laugh!' Abe replied. 'I pissed that away. George is a good friend. He's offered me stuff in the past, but I don't want to get back on that bucking bronco again.'

Donnie's stomach was in bits.

'What if I fuck it up?'

'Going by what you've told me, it's a strong possibility.'

'I don't want to let you down,' Donnie persisted, almost talking himself out of the best news he had ever received.

'So don't. Look, try not to fuck it up, but it's on you, not me, so do it for yourself.' Abe had a faraway look in his eye. 'My son Steven wanted to be an actor, and I didn't help him. I thought it was for his own good. You have to be made of stern stuff for this industry and cope with rejection without falling apart. Steven was sensitive, and I didn't want him to endure that pain. What I saw as protecting him, he saw as controlling and stifling.'

'I'm sorry,' Donnie said because he didn't know what else to say.

Abe shrugged. These thoughts were constantly with him.

'Maybe you're too sensitive for this industry. Whatever … that's for you to work out. Here are the details.'

Abe pulled out a piece of paper that was folded inside his notebook, then picked up a few pages of a script from the table beside him and handed them to Donnie.

Donnie looked at the pages with a huge grin. He jumped up from his seat and hugged Abe, who reluctantly hugged him back. Melanie joined in and wrapped her arms around both of them.

'You're the best friend I ever had!' Donnie exclaimed through new tears of joy.

Relenting, Abe replied,

'This world is so full of bullshit, you're probably mine.'

CHAPTER TWENTY-SEVEN

THE BIGGEST AUDITION
OF DONNIE'S LIFE

The yellow cab rattled along Sunset Boulevard, and Donnie sat in the back with Abe. He wondered if, just a few months ago, he would have believed that he would be going to an audition for a George Lawless movie in a taxi with Abe Nelson. Sometimes, he thought, life can drag by for years where nothing changes, and then it can change forever in one day.

He looked up at a billboard advertising the film *Dead Poets' Society*, showing Robin Williams being carried on the shoulders by a bunch of school kids.

Donnie nudged Abe.

'*Dead Poets Society*—I want to see that! Robin Williams is in it.'

'You like Robin Williams?' asked Abe.

'He's my favourite actor ... I mean, except for you. He's a comedy genius. Have you seen *Good Morning Vietnam*?' Donnie didn't wait for Abe to answer. '*Hey, this is not a test. This is rock and roll—*'

Abe put his hand on Donnie's arm to silence him.

'I've seen it, and Robin Williams is one of my favourite actors, too. He's a force of nature. I always wanted to work with him.'

Donnie sucked in his breath.

'Why don't you? Go back! Star in another film!'

'That ship has sailed,' Abe said bluntly, looking out the other window.

'You must still have some ambitions? You haven't won an Oscar yet,' Donnie quipped.

'Thanks for pointing that out. Winning an Oscar was never my dream.'

Donnie doubted this.

'Sure, why wouldn't you want to get to the top of your game?'

Abe threw Donnie a withering look as the cab pulled up outside The Sunset Towers Hotel. Donnie paid the driver and scrambled from the car, high on excitement. Abe followed slowly behind as Donnie marvelled at the iconic art deco building, standing proud on Sunset Strip.

'John Wayne stayed here!' Donnie proclaimed.

'Sure,' nodded Abe, 'all the big names—Marilyn Monroe, Liz Taylor, Frank Sinatra. It's almost as important a landmark as the Hollywood sign.'

'Wow! Have you stayed here?'

'Sure.'

Donnie followed Abe through the lobby and onto the terrace, feeling like he was following the footsteps of Hollywood legends. Abe knew where he was going. He'd been here more times than he could remember, lunches, meetings, drinks, parties that went on until dawn. Several years had passed since he was last there, but it looked and felt the same—there was something gloriously nostalgic about being back—like a part of him still belonged here. Abe and Donnie took a table near the pool and looked out over the haze-shrouded cityscape of LA.

So surreal, thought Donnie. A cool breeze swept in, and a couple of bikini-clad beauties swam in the pool.

A smartly dressed waiter approached.

'What can I get you?'

'A beer for me and a water for my friend,' Abe said cheerfully, sunglasses on.

'Certainly, Mr Nelson.'

Abe almost jumped. It had been so long since he had been recognised. But, then again, it had been an age since he had frequented anywhere other than a dive bar.

Donnie looked at the script clutched in his hand, and his nerves kicked in. He stood up and paced the terrace.

'Sit down,' instructed Abe.

'Just psyching myself up,' Donnie mumbled, his hands shaking.

'You're psyched enough. Take a seat.' Abe was sure Donnie's nerves eliminated his filter, and he needed a filter today.

Donnie sat down, rigid with fear. He stared at the scene on paper, which blurred on the page.

'You were doing fine just a minute ago,' Abe reassured him, patting his arm. 'You know the scene. Remember, even though it's a comedy, it has to be authentic. Picture yourself in the situation. Picture winning back the girl of your dreams. Can you do that?'

'Summer ...' Donnie replied in a melancholic croak.

Ralph, a young, eager PA, strutted towards them.

'Donnie McNamara?'

Before Donnie could answer, Ralph spotted Abe.

'You look a lot like Abe Nelson.'

'Is that so?' smiled Abe.

Ralph smiled back. 'It's a compliment.'

'Is it? Good to know. I am Abe Nelson.'

'You're funny!' Ralph half-laughed.

'Maybe so,' persisted Abe, getting a little annoyed, 'I'm still Abe Nelson.'

Ralph wasn't convinced and wasn't going to be made a mockery out of.

'Okay then, Donnie, if you could follow me, Mr Lawless will see you now.'

Donnie stood up to follow Ralph and whispered over his shoulder to Abe.

'I think I'm going to shit myself.'

Abe put his head in his hands and hoped for the best.

George Lawless was casting for his new film with his Casting Director, Barbara Beatty and a young camera assistant, Lucy. George was old school and liked to make quick decisions, which was probably why he was always assigned Barbara, who was a stickler—pedantic and slow. George remembered the old days of casting when he thoroughly enjoyed watching the young hopefuls in anticipation of finding a star and then drinking until dawn with the rest of the team when the job was in the bag. He couldn't see Barbara as a drinking buddy. George had long since decided that Barbara was an atmosphere vacuum. She was the hand that held the pin against his colourful balloon, and when it popped, she would hang in the shadows smirking while George would try to salvage the scattering of his enthusiasm.

George examined the headshot of Donnie.

'What do you think, Barbara—handsome?' Although George had spent decades living in LA, he still spoke with a hint of an Irish accent.

'Geeky,' Barbara responded dryly. Her mouth curled down at the corners, giving the appearance of a constant grimace. George had often mused that the wind had changed at some point throughout Barbara's life and had left her smile upside-down.

George turned to Lucy, who was adjusting her tripod. 'What about you, Lucy,' he asked, showing her the headshot, 'do you think he's handsome?'

'Yes,' smiled Lucy, 'he has friendly eyes and a warm smile. There's character there, not just good looks. He'll be interesting, I think.'

'Thank you, Lucy, for your constructive input,' replied George as he turned and gave Barbara a smug smile.

'So,' Barbara continued, 'this one has no experience whatsoever. Nothing.'

'That's right,' agreed George, 'should be fun.'

'Or pointless,' Barbara added.

'Everyone's got to start somewhere.'

'Not in your films, they don't,' argued Barbara.

'I'll have to correct you there, Barbara. Many of my films have been the making of previously unknown actors. We've already cast Romi Miller, so we can afford to launch new talent.'

'Have you told Romi that?' asked Barbara in an attempt to suck up George's enthusiasm.

George was relieved to hear a knock on the door. Sitting next to Barbara was like teetering on the edge of an unpleasant weather front. George wanted to prove her wrong. He was about to see a new star. He could feel it.

Donnie entered the room as confidently as he could. He was smiling but felt light-headed the minute he saw George Lawless. The presence of the man filled the room. He was a legend, all right. This was the fucking scariest moment of Donnie's life, far scarier than almost being chomped by a Great White.

George stood up. At well over six feet, this made matters worse.

'Hello, Donnie, I'm George. Pleased to meet you.'

Donnie shook his hand and hoped his lips weren't quivering.

'This is Barbara, our Casting Director,' George continued. 'Barbara will be reading for you today, and beside Barbara is Lucy, who will be filming you.'

Lucy gave Donnie a welcome smile and a little wave which compensated for the indifferent nod he received from Barbara.

'Good to meet you all. Thanks for reading for me, Barbara.' Donnie shook her hand, too, but it felt cold and limp, like the expression on her face.

'Take a seat,' George motioned behind Donnie.

Donnie sat down and completely missed the seat, falling on his backside on the floor. 'Fuck,' Donnie said under his breath, but it was loud enough for both George and Barbara to hear. He scrambled to his feet and placed his butt firmly on the chair with a flustered smile.

'So, Donnie,' continued George as if nothing had happened, 'it's a comedy. It's light—it's fun. You're from Ireland, which is perfect. All the best people are … no offence, Barbara.'

Barbara rolled her eyes. It was the kind of eye-roll that said *same old regurgitated jokes.*

'So let's stick with your natural accent,' George affirmed.

Donnie tried to lighten up and spoke in his best American accent, 'There was no need for me to be practising my *tomatoes, vitamins, basil* and *vacation* words then.'

George and Lucy laughed, but Barbara didn't.

'How long have you been in LA?' asked George, happy to converse with a fellow Irishman.

Donnie's filter was gone. 'Long enough to drink skunk milk, lose the best girl I ever met and be terrified of going home.'

'Skunk milk? I tried that once. Felt like I was on the moon. Gravity hurt like hell when I came back to Earth.' George shook his head with a sigh, momentarily reminiscing over those crazy days.

'Mine wasn't really skunk milk,' Donnie confessed. 'It was just a concoction of everything behind the bar.'

Barbara had no idea why she was listening to such utter drivel, but on it went.

'Ha!' George thumped his desk with his hand. 'I've been there too!' He looked at Barbara in an attempt to break her silence. 'You must have done that, Barbara?'

'No, I'm tee-total.'

There was a silence during which Donnie noticed George wink at him. He didn't know whether to wink back, but Barbara stared in his direction, so he thought better of it.

'Okay, let's get on with the scene then. Barbara, take it away,' George instructed heartily.

Finally, thought Barbara. She cleared her throat and delivered her line like a seasoned pro, which made Donnie wonder if she had secretly harboured a dream of being an actress.

'I've had a crush on you since I was ten.'

Donnie was so focused on Barbara that he forgot where he was and blurted out,

'I wasn't even born then.'

George burst out laughing, Lucy attempted to remain composed, but Barbara showed no sign of being amused.

'That's not in the script. I'll start again. I've had a crush on you since I was ten.'

Donnie responded, 'You know how I felt about you. It's your fault I'm trapped with a neurotic malfunctioning moron.'

'Your girlfriend?' Barbara asked.

'No, me. I have to live with myself every day.'

'I miss you,' Barbara said, and Donnie tried to envisage someone else saying it.

'I miss you too. I miss everything about you. Even your breath in the morning and the way you drive. Why didn't you stay?' Donnie was on a roll now.

'Because you told me big fat lies and then lied about telling me big fat lies, and then didn't apologise for lying, nor did you apologise for lying about lying.'

Barbara's words hung in the air, and Donnie swallowed hard before delivering his next line. 'I know, and I'm sorry. I'm so sorry for everything.' Fat tears rolled down Donnie's face, and without warning, he free-wheeled into a full breakdown, muttering under his breath, 'You fucking stupid, thick, useless, gobshite.'

Lucy zoomed in on Donnie's tortured expression.

Donnie looked to George, apology written large across his face. George grinned, but Barbara did not.

CHAPTER TWENTY-EIGHT

MINUTES AFTER THE AUDITION

Donnie rushed back to the terrace, his face burning with humiliation. He felt sick in the pit of his stomach, and his legs felt weak, as if they were detached from his hips as he walked.

Abe saw his distress and immediately knew. Maybe it had been a bad idea. Maybe the kid couldn't act, and this constant rejection would damage him forever. Perhaps he had subjected Donnie to the very thing he had protected his son, Steven, from.

'Well?' Abe asked nervously.

'Desperate. A fucking car crash!' Donnie hovered beside Abe, not wanting to sit down.

'You didn't shit yourself?' Abe certainly hoped that wasn't the problem.

'No,' Donnie shook his head, 'I cried and cursed. It barely resembled my preparation for the role. They didn't ask me to do the second scene. I made a complete balls of it.'

This was one big fuck up, thought Abe.

MEANWHILE, GEORGE WAS still grinning at Barbara.

'Well, I think he's perfect, Barbara.'

'Are you being funny?' Barbara was never sure if George was being funny, but this time, surely he must be.

George smiled, aware that he would have a battle convincing her.

'He came into the room in character. All that chat about vitamins and basil and being terrified to go home ... I liked that. He's given the character a kind of Tourettes, and I think we should use that.'

Barbara frowned. Every inch of her was unconvinced.

'He's darkly hilarious, Barbara. People are going to love this guy. Lucy, what do you think?'

'Awesome!' Lucy enthused.

George folded over his notebook to emphasise that he was doing no more work for the day, and the decision was made.

Barbara elongated her neck, as she did when she wanted to put someone in their place. She was well aware that George was the Director, but she was here to keep him in check.

'You must be joking, George. We have four more auditions today and six tomorrow. If we can't find someone better than Donnie McNamara, this film is in big trouble.'

George laughed, which further exasperated Barbara.

DONNIE SAT IN the back of the taxi with Abe in silence. He knew he'd blown it.

'I'm sorry, Abe,' Donnie eventually said.

'What are you sorry for? It's an audition. You have to keep going. Look at it as practice. This was a long shot, so don't let it get you down.' Abe spoke flatly, finding it hard not to show his disappointment. He gave Donnie a gentle punch on the arm. 'Look, let's get a take-out tonight. Come and stay with us again.'

'Thanks, Abe, I'd love that. I need to go to the apartment and pick up some things. If you could drop me there, I'll head over to your house after.'

Donnie didn't want to express to Abe that he felt worse than ever before—that he had so little left in his motivation tank, and his bottle of belief had evaporated. Perhaps tomorrow would be a new day, and Donnie would battle on, but increasingly he felt incapable of succeeding.

Seeing Francis today would likely kick Donnie deeper into his black hole of depression, but he needed clothes from the apartment.

DONNIE OPENED THE door as Francis wandered around the apartment with just a towel, drinking a cocktail.

'Ah, Donnie! Care for a cocktail after all your hard work in the movie business? Oh, by the way, your grandmother died.'

Donnie felt a blow to the stomach.

'What?'

'Your grandmother. She's just died … sorry for your loss,' Francis said without any emotion in his voice.

Donnie reached for the doorframe to balance himself and tried to blink back the tears trickling from the corner of his eyes.

'What? When?'

'I just got a phone call from Kathy,' Francis said, sitting on the bed. 'Of course, you'll need to go to the funeral, but I thought it would make sense if I held the fort while you were gone.'

'Hold what fucking fort, Francis?'

'The fort you created. It needs minding, but don't worry, I'll be here, and when you get found out, they'll think you had me duped as well. So if you want to tell them that you've lied to them, I'll come with you to the funeral. It's your call.'

'When did she die?'

'Kathy just called, so it was recently, wasn't it?'

Donnie walked backwards out of the apartment, his body shaking and let the door click shut. He took a deep breath and headed back out onto the street.

He hailed yet another taxi and hoped the driver wasn't in a chatty mood. His only choice was to go to Abe's house, yet it was the last place he wanted to go. The driver wasn't talkative, and the silence only heightened Donnie's grief as he swiped at every tear that soaked his face.

By the time he pressed the doorbell at Abe's house, he was inconsolable. Melanie opened the door. She reached out and pulled Donnie into her arms.

'Oh, you poor dear, what's happened?' she asked and then called out to Abe, 'Abe, we have a leaker!'

Donnie followed her into the living room, where Abe was playing his guitar and drinking beer with the curtains shut. He stopped strumming the minute he saw the wretched sight of Donnie in front of him.

'Jesus Christ ... you can't let this get to you. It's just an audition.'

'I'm sorry, I'm sorry,' Donnie mumbled. Donnie wished he could pull himself together, stop the tears and speak coherently, but his body ignored his plea and continued to erupt heavy sobs.

Melanie pushed him into a chair.

'Now, now,' she soothed, 'heavy hearts, like heavy clouds in the sky, are best relieved by the letting out of a little water.'

Donnie couldn't grasp what she was saying but nodded anyway. He tried to speak, but the words wouldn't come out. His mouth was forcing itself shut to prevent a wail from escaping. He took a sharp intake of breath as Melanie and Abe looked at each other with concern. Then, finally, Donnie opened his mouth, exhaled and managed to whisper, 'My grandmother has died.'

Melanie jumped up and put her arms around Donnie in a strangling embrace and tried in vain to soothe him.

'I am sorry, Donnie. You were obviously close,' said Abe.

CHAPTER TWENTY-NINE

TRAVELLING HOME

Donnie was back at LAX, dejected and depressed. The last time he had been at this airport, he was bursting with hope and the promise of a new world, and now he was heading home to bury his grandmother. She had been someone who had, without judgement, encouraged him in life and applauded his differences. He had never thanked her for that. He had wanted to return, let her share his success, and reassure her that her enthusiasm was not misplaced.

Instead, his ally was gone, and he had to face the music for his deceit to his family, and he would, once again, be the family disappointment.

The cost of his flights alone without anything to show for it would shame the family. He could have coped with that—had he not disappointed Abe and entirely ballsed things up with Summer. Instead, he had glimpsed his dream in a tangible form and then swallowed a grenade of failure, cased in humiliation, blowing his possibilities to pieces.

His journey back was bleak, with fitful bursts of sleep and waking with sorrow in his heart. Being there when someone close to you dies was one thing; travelling back for their funeral seemed far worse. His plane arrived late, causing him to miss his bus, so he had two hours to kill in Dublin. He was exhausted but weak with hunger, realising he had not eaten anything since yesterday because his appetite was no longer communicating with his brain. He headed straight for Grafton

Street and felt reassured by the sight of an American diner—a massive burger would be the only comfort he would get today. He polished off the burger and extra chips but immediately felt worse. His stomach was behaving like a petrol car that had just been filled with diesel.

Donnie wasn't dressed for the rain when he arrived. Having seen nothing but sunshine for quite some time, he hadn't accounted for the weather in his wardrobe. He ran towards the bus as the rain attacked sideways, drenching him. Large slops of water dripped from his hair as he squelched aboard the bus to Bellvara.

He claimed a seat next to a window at the back of the bus, hoping to avoid conversation with any other passenger. He stared at the glass, rather than out of it, and watched to see how long each raindrop would cling to the window before falling to its demise in a stream along the rubber seal. He fixated on one, willing it to hold on longer than the others, but it didn't. Donnie wondered to himself what was the point in trying in life when the laws of physics, nature, and the universe, were stacked against him? Like the raindrop, he would fall into a stream with all the masses of society and be carried somewhere he didn't want to go. Thinking of his grandmother, he surmised that life was merely a slow meandering path to death. Donnie wasn't used to feeling this low. He was the sort of person who could shrug off most of life's unpleasant curveballs, but today he wanted to close his eyes and wake up in another person's skin.

The bus felt damp and rattled and bumped through Dublin, weaving scarily through traffic and pedestrians, and every light seemed to go red on approach. Donnie still couldn't shake the digging feeling in his stomach. He wasn't sure if it was the fast food or his body deciding to eat itself, completely fed up with its host.

The bus shook in the wind as it accelerated on the outskirts of Dublin. The fields outside the window were fudged with mist, giving Donnie the feeling that he was entering some kind of abyss. His thoughts wandered to his life before. The life he was going back to. He felt his eyes sting with tiredness, and his eyelids close tightly in reflex. He was back in his grandmother's care home. The vanilla air freshener, mixed with mothballs and the clinical smell of disinfectant, clung to his nostrils. He could see his grandmother in her chair with the old-fashioned doilies on the arm, sitting beside Maureen with a yellow blanket over her knees. Her face, lined by laughter and loss, always held a beautiful smile. Donnie wondered how anyone would hang around this world for so long, especially when five of those years had been spent with several residents who sat catatonically staring into space.

Donnie smiled as he remembered Tic filming their rehearsals at the care home. He would be steady enough for a few seconds before the inevitable, involuntary reaction—followed by swearing.

'Oh, it's charades!' Flo would rise excitedly and then have to grab the arm of her chair for balance. Flo would readily forget that her body lived in the ageing present. Living in memory and not reality was incredibly confusing for Flo, and she would get cross when she didn't know what was going on, or why people would talk to her as if she was stupid.

'No, it's our play, remember?' Tommy the Thesp would remind her, unable to mask his frustration.

'Of course she remembers!' Maureen would say. 'Don't you, Flo?'

'Of course I do,' Flo would agree, not entirely sure what she was meant to remember.

'It's just like charades,' his Grandmother had said, 'so you do whatever you want, Flo.'

DONNIE OPENED HIS eyes as the bus came hurtling down the hill towards Bellvara, the castle presiding over the bay, still seeming to protect its people from invasion. The sea shone silver and reflected the last of the sun's rays so brightly that Donnie had to shield his eyes. Donnie felt a wave of happiness overcome him, a feeling of going home that he had never felt before, but then he had never been away this long. The ominous dark clouds of his mind lifted, and he started humming the words of one of his grandmother's favourite songs, *The Galway Shawl*, usually sung after closing time.

Donnie stopped his mumbled singing when he realised two young female backpackers were tittering behind him.

The sky turned a deep purple with a scattering of pink, wispy clouds. The horizon was burnt yellow as the sun bade her nightly farewell. For the first time, Donnie noticed that no two sunsets ever looked the same here. Tommy the Thesp greeted him from the bus. Donnie hadn't arranged to meet Tommy and wondered whether Tommy had been hanging around the square looking for someone to talk to.

'Hey, Donnie! I'm sorry for your loss. She was a great character.' Before Donnie could respond, Tommy continued, 'So what's the craic? How's Tinseltown?' Tommy's eyes danced. He was in his usual hyperactive state.

'Oh, mighty,' Donnie said, 'lots to tell you, Tommy, but you know yourself, I'm not really in the mood for the craic just now. I just want to get home.'

Tommy thumped him hard on his back and motioned towards his car.

'I'll give you a lift up the road,' he said, grabbing Donnie's suitcase and slinging it in the boot of the car before Donnie could argue. 'I've got some news, though, if you can handle that,' Tommy gushed.

Donnie was glad the attention on him was diverted for now. 'Sure.'

'This is massive news!' Tommy held Donnie's gaze before letting him in the car, creating a long pause for maximum effect.

'What then?' Donnie asked as he climbed into the passenger seat.

'I got a part in Eastenders! I'm off to London, Donnie. I'm on my way!'

'Eastenders! You did? Jesus! That *is* massive! How?' Donnie's stomach heaved, and his eyes started to burn with tears.

'Got lucky, I guess. Did a fierce audition, and my face fitted, I suppose. Who's arguing, though, right? I got the fucking part.'

A few meandering sheep on the road caused Tommy to slow the car on the single-track road. Donnie no longer had the engine revs to drown out the gulping noise in his throat. He coughed loudly, hoping his voice wouldn't crack as he tried to continue the conversation.

'What's the part?'

'An Irish immigrant—alcoholic. We'll not say anything about stereotypes or being type-cast. I don't care about type as long as I'm cast!' Tommy screeched with laughter, and Donnie did his best to agree.

'Well, I'm really happy for you,' Donnie said, and he was. He was just miserable for himself on every level.

'Thanks. It's a small part, but I'm hoping, you know, to keep my character's story going. Make an impression. It's all about making an impression, isn't it?'

Donnie nodded without smiling. Indeed it was all about making an impression. He desperately needed to change the subject.

'Have you seen any of them from the care home? How are they all? Maureen must be in bits. She loved my Nana.'

'Haven't seen them,' Tommy shrugged and then added, 'although I heard Flo died too before your grandmother.'

'Oh, did she?'

'Yeh, it was only a matter of time. She was barely here. Although, I bet she would have been pleased about my Eastenders role!'

Donnie nodded on auto-pilot again, feeling a pang of loss over Flo as well. It was like the exodus of a generation, one by one, filing out of this world and leaving them all behind.

Tommy's car pulled up outside the gate at the bottom of the driveway to Donnie's family farm.

'I'll leave you here,' Tommy said. 'Of course, I'll try and get up to the house later and make it to the Mass, but make sure you have time to go for a pint with me before I hit the big smoke. I need to catch up on all the craic. We're busy people now, Donnie!'

Donnie got out of the car and lifted his suitcase from the boot. Tommy the Thesp tooted his horn all the way up the road. With a heavy sigh, Donnie trudged down the driveway. This wasn't the homecoming he had envisaged.

The front door of the house opened, and Meg, the collie, was first through it, scrambling to greet him. Donnie appreciated the welcome. Mickey-Joe appeared at the door, his expression switching from fret to relief. Donnie couldn't help noticing that his father seemed to have aged in the short time he had been away.

Mickey-Joe stepped out, squinting in the evening sun and opened his arms to his son. 'Thanks be to God, you're here, son.'

Donnie was rigid but let his father pull him into his chest and hug him. His father held him by the shoulders, and Donnie could see that he had been crying. Donnie knew no one, including his father, was immune to grief, but there was a vulnerability about him that unnerved Donnie.

Sheena ran down the stairs towards the door, shouting his name. Donnie's heart swelled; he had not realised how much he had missed her. Then, like a cannonball of love, she jumped into his arms and buried her face in his jacket.

'Ah, Sheena. I missed you.'

Sheena beamed back at him. 'No, you didn't, but you're home now. Did you bring me a present?'

'Of course! Give me a chance, though.'

Donnie turned to his father. 'Is she here now?' he asked.

'Yes, son, she's in the lounge with your mother, Kathy and a few others.'

Donnie entered the lounge to see his grandmother laid out in her coffin. Chairs were placed around the room with people sitting, drinking tea and coffee and chatting. The chatting stopped when he entered the room. He blessed himself and wasn't sure whether to walk over and hug his mum first or kiss his grandmother, but Kathy appeared beside him and threw her arms around him. Donnie leaned his head on his sister's shoulder and cried. His mother stood up and hugged him too.

'She wouldn't want you to be sad, Donnie. She wouldn't want that at all,' Elizabeth said, wiping her own tears.

Donnie slowly approached his grandmother and looked at her in the coffin. Her face looked waxen and vacant, and Donnie knew she was not lying in that box. She had gone somewhere else, leaving her old, useless body behind. Perhaps she was flying through spring meadows, singing her favourite songs and finally regaining a physical youthfulness to match her spirit. There was solace in seeing her soul wasn't there.

People came and went all day and night. Candles were lit, and prayers were softly murmured. Donnie shook people's hands in an exhausted trance. It was like a replay of Uncle Pete's funeral, with the same faces, the same words, and the same sadness.

Donnie had always associated funerals with rain. The sadder the funeral, the more drenched the mourners, but the day they buried Nuala, the sun was bright, and the sky was a vivid blue. Kathy had got up to sing *Amazing Grace* in the church, and Donnie had no idea how she held it together because none of the parishioners did. There hadn't been a dry eye in the pews.

As the earth was thrown in on the coffin, old Alfie sang *The Galway Shawl* as an uplifting farewell to a long life well lived.

IT WASN'T UNTIL the next evening that Donnie noticed the tensions in the house between his mother and father. They were no longer sitting in the same room. His mother was quiet and seemed to tip-toe around Mickey-Joe, which was never her way.

His father entered the kitchen, kicking off his wellies and not lining them up as he knew Elizabeth would want. Kathy followed closely behind him as Donnie put the kettle on. He knew there were some heavy discussions ahead. First, he would have to come clean about *Dwarfland*. He would have to tell them the truth. He would have to share his concerns about Francis with Kathy, who strangely had asked nothing about him since Donnie had arrived home.

Mickey-Joe washed his hands under the kitchen tap as he looked into the lounge to Elizabeth asleep in her chair. Donnie wasn't sure if his mother was actually sleeping or if she just didn't want to talk to anyone.

'Are you okay, Dad?' Donnie asked.

'No, son, we're up shit creek.'

Sheena jumped down the stairs, repeating him, 'Up shit creek!' She laughed wickedly for full effect.

'What's happened?' asked Donnie.

'We might lose the farm,' Mickey-Joe disclosed, hanging his head.

'That's impossible,' Donnie said, thinking that surely it must be. 'What's happened? Everything was fine, and you had that money from Uncle Pete!'

'Everything was not fine,' Mickey-Joe answered gloomily. 'That's why I was keen to get Francis involved. I knew we were overstretched. The money from Uncle Pete got us out of a huge hole.'

Donnie looked at his father questioningly.

'And then,' his father continued, 'the money was gone.'

'What? How?'

'You'll have to ask your mother about that. She was on a winning streak. She thought she could solve all our problems.'

'Oh no,' Donnie sighed. He knew the only direction this was leading.

'Gambled. Gone,' Mickey-Joe seethed through gritted teeth.

'Gone,' Kathy nodded as if she had already dealt with this devastating blow.

Donnie thought he might vomit from waves of conflicting emotions—as if a lie had been revealed, and he wasn't sure if he felt angry, sad, pity or shame. Worse still, he had more lies to confess.

'It's a shit show. An ungodly mess,' Mickey-Joe said, his jaw clenching. 'Come through, come through.'

He motioned to Donnie to follow him into the lounge. It was dimly lit, and his mother was awake but sitting crumpled in the armchair.

'Hey, mum, are you okay?' Donnie asked, hoping she would refute his father's claims, but she nodded solemnly, a tear running down her cheek.

'We had a large tax bill to deal with and a few debts,' Mickey-Joe explained. 'Your uncle's money would have saved us, for a while at least.'

Elizabeth gave a small sob.

'The money is gone,' Mickey-Joe affirmed.

'Gone, Gone, Gone,' repeated Sheena like a backing singer.

Elizabeth hung her head even lower.

'Jesus Christ. Are you okay, Mum?' Donnie asked.

Elizabeth barely nodded.

'She's in the same mess as the rest of us,' Mickey-Joe stated, 'but she was trying to help. She knows now that gambling is a fool's game, don't you, Elizabeth?

Elizabeth nodded earnestly.

'Many a family fortune has been lost on a poker table, and a sure bet seldom is,' proclaimed Mickey-Joe. 'I don't have to tell you that we must keep this quiet. Francis knows nothing of this. We don't want to appear like we're going to need handouts to get our heads above water. We're a respected family in this community. This is our family matter, and we will resolve it.'

'Mum has our support,' said Kathy as if Elizabeth wasn't in the room, 'and we'll all help get the finances back on track.

I know Francis will help, but Dad is adamant he doesn't want him to get wind of it until we can figure things out. I'd already purchased some new equipment for the bakery, which might help make us more money, but at this rate, I might be better off returning it. The rest of the money I had is invested in the farm. We were all praying you had some good news on *Dwarfland* or maybe some cash left over to help?'

All eyes were on Donnie, and he thought he was going to collapse. He said nothing but stared at his mother, wondering if he, too, would be sitting in the opposite chair in half an hour with the same expression on his face.

'What did you bring me from America?' Sheena interrupted.

'Oh, you'll see,' Donnie replied as Sheena's eyes lit up.

'Go out and play, Sheena. You'll get your present later. This is important,' barked Mickey-Joe.

'It's pitch black outside, Dad!' Sheena pointed at the window in protest.

Sheena, realising she was not to be involved in the conversation, wandered around the room in her own little world. She picked things up on the mantelpiece and replaced them back to front. She looked to see if her mother would react, but she didn't. Taking it one step further, Sheena opened a drawer in the coffee table, pulled out some scissors and a piece of paper and started cutting the paper into tiny bits. Every so often, she would glance at her mother but received no scolding. Donnie found it upsetting that Sheena would prefer her mother's wrath to no reaction at all.

'Kathy said the investor is very positive,' Mickey-Joe said, poking Donnie on the arm to regain his attention. It was not a situation Mickey-Joe ever thought he would find himself in, being reliant on his son's abilities to pull him out of financial ruin.

Donnie's face revealed an internal battle that made Mickey-Joe uneasy. Maybe it had been foolish to expect anything of Donnie.

Donnie took a deep breath. He couldn't bear the deceit a

second longer.

'I've got something important to tell you all.'

Just as he was about to spill his guts, the phone rang. Mickey-Joe put his hand up to Donnie. 'Just a minute, son. I have to take these calls. It doesn't stop, but we have to face the music.' He lifted the receiver, clearing his throat before speaking, 'Mickey-Joe McNamara. Yes, who's calling? Yes, he's here, just a moment.'

Donnie wondered if it was Tommy the Thesp wanting to go for a pint. *Would it be hugely inappropriate to deliver his news and then run for a high stool? Probably.*

Mickey-Joe covered his hand over the mouthpiece and whispered to Donnie, 'It's an American. Abe Rockefeller, he says. Is that the partner?'

Donnie nodded and, with trembling hands, took the phone. He wasn't sure if he had been saved by the bell or if the bell was only serving to delay the inevitable.

'Hello, Abe.'

Abe was in his kitchen, pacing up and down the floor with excitement.

'Donnie! You got the fucking part! Get your ass back here!' he exclaimed.

Donnie's legs were buckling under him. He held onto the mantlepiece for support.

'Are you sure?'

'Of course, I'm sure. I just spoke to George. You need to get back here now!'

Donnie rocketed from the depths of desolation to euphoria.

'I'll get there as fast as I can,' he assured Abe.

'You need to be back by the weekend. The table read is Monday. See you then.'

Donnie heard the phone go dead, and it took him a moment to process what Abe had said. *How could this even be possible?* A joyous scream of elation bounced inside his head, but he had to keep calm.

Donnie replaced the receiver and took a deep breath, calculating his next step. What would his explanation be to his family? He couldn't confuse matters by saying he'd landed a part in a Hollywood film. His father would probably call the doctor. Within a millisecond, he decided to stick to the bumpy road he was on. He turned and faced them with a smile.

'Yes, I'll be able to help. Like I told you, this project is liquid gold. That was my beta partner on the phone. I need to get back. We've got a win.'

'A win?' Mickey-Joe didn't know what he was talking about, but it sounded good.

'A win, yes, I need to book a flight back and get over there as soon as I can.'

He turned to his mother.

'Don't worry, mum, it's going to be all right.' Donnie saw a glimmer of hope behind her eyes.

'But you only just got home,' Sheena looked devastated.

Mickey-Joe put a hand on Sheena's head. 'If he has to go. He has to go. This is important.'

'I'm important too,' Sheena pouted.

Donnie's heart melted. He picked her up into the air and whispered into her ear,

'You are very important. You're my best girl, and I promise I'll be back again soon. Anyway, I'm not going right now!'

Mickey-Joe had hoped there would be a day when Donnie would come good. He clapped Donnie on the back.

'Well, well,' he said, 'a tattered foal can grow into a splendid horse.'

Donnie wasn't sure if he'd been insulted or complimented, but his father's hand thumping his back felt good.

'Have you the money for the flight, son? Have you anything left?' Mickey-Joe asked.

'Yes, I've enough, and I'll send you money as soon as I can.'

Kathy rubbed Donnie's shoulder.

'I knew Francis would be a help to you.'

Donnie opened his mouth and quickly closed it again—one battle at a time. Then, he turned back to Sheena.

'Come on, let's open my suitcase and see what I got you. I think you're going to love them.'

CHAPTER THIRTY

THE VERY NEXT DAY

Sheena had woken Donnie far earlier than he would have liked. She sat on his bed, swinging her legs and admired the present he had given her—shiny silver roller skates with pink flashing lights. Compared to her old leather and metal ones, they were positively futuristic.

'I'm never taking them off,' she declared.

Donnie smiled, his eyes only half open.

'Please don't go,' Sheena pleaded, 'you only just got back. Mum and Dad are in terrible form, they're so grumpy all the time, and that only leaves me with Kathy, and she's always busy.'

Donnie put his arms around her.

'I promise I'll come back soon, Sheena, but I do have to go.'

'Are you going to fix everything? Make everyone happy again?' she asked with hopeful eyes.

Donnie had never felt pressure like it. The reality of his undertaking was setting in hard. He was the one carrying this family back to a happier place, and his little sister was depending on him.

'I will, Sheena,' he reassured her, 'I'll make everything right.'

After phoning the travel agent, he had breakfast with his family. His mother stared out the window, fixating her gaze on nothing in particular. His father emitted involuntary sighs as he cooked the eggs, and Kathy was engrossed in the special offer on the back of the cornflakes box. An air of tension lingered around the kitchen, affecting everyone. Donnie tried to lift the energy by hanging his spoon on his nose to entertain Sheena.

'I'm going to go visiting,' Donnie announced. 'I'll take Sheena.'

Sheena jumped up.

'Can I wear my new roller skates?'

'Well, I don't think the skates will—'

He saw her face crumple.

'Yes, I'm sure you can. We'll manage.'

Sheena held onto Donnie's jacket as she sat behind him on his Honda 50 with her roller skates on. Donnie drove through the gate at the bottom of the drive and headed for the care home. He didn't know why he felt such a pull to visit, but since the death of grandmother and Flo as well, he imagined Maureen sitting on her own, staring out of a window—her train to the next world delayed, all her friends gone without her.

Roísín met him at the door and welcomed them in.

'Hello, stranger,' she said and gave Donnie a hug he was definitely not expecting. 'I'm so sorry for your loss, and I'm so sorry I wasn't at the funeral. My aunt died the same day, and I only just got back from Dublin. A very sad week altogether. I'm really going to miss your Nana. She was such a colourful lady. It was a pleasure to have known her.'

'Thank you,' Donnie replied in a voice that squeaked. 'I'm sorry for your loss too. Were you close to your aunt?'

Roísín let out a breezy laugh.

'Not at all. She was wicked—a battle-axe! God forgive me, I don't want to speak ill of the dead, but she used to lock me in cupboards and hit us round the ears with a brush. She was lucky I didn't boycott her funeral and go to your Nana's instead! I had a lot more time for your Nana, that's for sure!'

Sheena looked horrified at what Roísín was saying and waited for her to say she was only joking, but she didn't.

'No, she doesn't sound great at all,' Donnie agreed. 'Makes the wooden spoon not seem quite so bad.' He quickly changed the subject because he wasn't sure what else to say. 'It's only a flying visit today, I'm afraid.'

'You're as good! Coming to see us when you're only home for a bit. You're such a dote.'

She squeezed his arm and smiled at Sheena. 'Oh, look at your fancy roller skates! I might have the perfect corridor you can wheel down if you promise not to knock anyone over!'

Donnie noticed the empty chair where his grandmother had sat—the doilies slightly worn where her arms had rested for the last five years, but the beaming face of Maureen soon warmed him. Maureen sat next to a tiny woman, Nora, who was so fragile, she could have been a hologram.

'Look who's here, Nora,' Maureen smiled.

'How are you, Maureen?' Donnie smiled back at her.

Maureen grabbed onto Donnie's arm tightly.

'I'm still here, Donnie. Maybe God still has some great plan for me,' she said, winking at him, 'but I'd rather be up there,' she continued, pointing up to the ceiling for emphasis, 'drinking brandy with your grandmother! I am sorry for your loss, Donnie. You were the apple of her eye.'

Donnie tried to fight back the tears welling up in his eyes. He poked himself in the eye when he saw Roísín appear beside them with a pot of tea and biscuits.

Roísín smiled at Donnie as she poured the tea.

'Thought we'd go for the chocolate ones today for our special visitor.'

'Thanks, Roísín, I've missed my tea. It's all coffee in America,' Donnie said, beaming at Roísín before she headed off to tend to an old man who looked like he was going to take half the day to zimmer himself across the room.

Sheena had been hovering at the arm of Nora's chair, and now Nora had a hold of her hand so she couldn't take off roller skating. Sheena made one attempt to pull her hand away but succumbed to Nora's tightening grip.

'Well,' said Maureen, 'Roísín told us you were off in America doing something with computers.'

Donnie felt the guilt stab his chest. How could he lie to Maureen? It felt like he was lying to his grandmother.

Nora released Sheena's hand to pick up a chocolate digestive, and Sheena seized her opportunity to wheel off down the corridor.

Donnie leaned towards Maureen.

'Can you keep a secret?'

'Oh, yes,' Maureen said. It wasn't something she had been asked often because, throughout Maureen's life, she had been notorious for her inability to keep secrets. No matter how hard she tried, they just leaked out. It had been several years since she had even heard a secret, let alone have to keep one, and there was no way she was missing out today.

'You really mustn't tell anyone,' Donnie urged.

Maureen put her finger to her lips and nodded.

'I'm not actually working on computers in America.'

Maureen clapped her hands.

'Are you bootlegging?'

'No, no,' Donnie replied, shaking his head. 'Do you remember the plays we used to do here?'

'Of course,' Maureen said, 'what fun they were.'

'Well,' Donnie continued, 'I couldn't tell anyone because they would think I was mad, but I went to Los Angeles to become an actor.'

'What kind of acting?' Maureen asked, unconvinced.

'Proper films. I got a role in a really good movie.'

'You mean Hollywood?' Maureen's eyes widened.

'Yes, Hollywood.'

'Oh my goodness, isn't that wonderful? Your grandmother would have been so proud!'

After half an hour, Donnie noticed Maureen's eyes were beginning to close. Roísín came over and put a blanket over her lap.

'It was so good of you to come, Donnie,' she said. 'Please come back next time you're home, and hopefully, one day, you'll be home for good.' She gave him a beautiful smile, squeezed his arm for the second time, and walked away.

As Donnie stood up to go, Maureen caught his hand and whispered,

'She likes you, you know.'

Donnie felt his face go red. 'No, she doesn't. She's lovely to everyone.'

'I might be ancient and half blind, but I see more than you think,' Maureen said sternly. 'That girl is smitten with you. You're a fool if you've not noticed it.'

Donnie looked blankly at Maureen.

'And you won't do better than Roísín. She's an angel. That's what she is.'

'She is, Maureen, but I think you're wrong. She isn't smitten with me. She's just nice to me.'

Maureen narrowed her eyes.

'Hmmm ... why don't you ask her out, and then you'll see I'm right?'

'No, I can't, Maureen. You see, I'm going back to America.'

'Not forever,' Maureen stated. She then called out, 'Roísín!' at the top of her voice.

'Jesus, Maureen, what are you doing?'

'I'm an old woman, Donnie, and if there's one thing I've learned in life, never let a good thing go by, and I want to prove to you that I'm right about this.'

Donnie hunkered down beside Maureen.

'Look, maybe you are right, although I doubt it, and she is, for sure, an angel. I would have given my right arm to go out with Roísín, but there's someone else.'

'Oh?' This was obviously Maureen's day for secrets.

'Yes, an American girl.'

Maureen was less pleased.

'You have a girlfriend in America?'

Donnie thought about how he was delivering this.

'No, not as such. I had a date with her. A sort of date. Look, I haven't had many dates with girls, and I really like her, so there's no point in asking out Roísín, is there?'

Maureen shook her head solemnly.

'I suppose not. Not if you're infatuated with some American girl who hasn't even agreed to be your girlfriend.'

Donnie wasn't sure what to say, but Maureen still had a point to make.

'Court abroad, Donnie, but marry at home,' she instructed as she patted his hand.

Donnie seized his opportunity to say goodbye.

Donnie and Sheena were at the door of the care home when Roísín called out,

'Here, I thought you might want to bring these back with you.' She handed him a box of tea bags.

'Christ, no, I can't take the teabags. I'll pick some up at the shop,' Donnie insisted.

'No, it's okay, I'll replace them. I wanted to give you something to take with you from home, and under short notice, this was the best I could do … unless you want incontinence pants or some haemorrhoid cream? You said you missed tea,' she said, pushing the box into his hands. 'Thanks for coming to see Maureen. It meant a lot to her.'

She hugged Donnie and walked back inside.

Sheena was grinning at Donnie as she skated backwards, wobbling towards the bike.

'She likes you.'

Donnie shook his head but felt a little glow of happiness rush through his veins.

HE ARRIVED BACK at the house and saw his Dad pulling some feed out of the shed. He walked over and stood beside him. His father was silent.

'Can I give you a hand?' Donnie asked.

His father smiled. 'Yes, son, you can.'

CHAPTER THIRTY-ONE

THE JOURNEY BACK WEST

onnie was up at the crack of dawn the following morning, and the whole family was at the door to see him off this time. Kathy packed some fruit scones into his hand luggage. His farewell felt fraudulent—they thought he was off to invent some incredible piece of technology that might help save the family farm when, in fact, he was off to Hollywood to star in a film directed by the legendary George Lawless. Of course, he couldn't possibly tell them this. Taking aside his father's disdain for acting, he could not expect them to believe him after the lies he had already told. The idea that he was going to star in this movie was like a parallel universe where dreams were fulfilled. This was not a reality he had ever experienced before, and so until he lived it, breathed it and could touch it, he wasn't telling his family.

The film on the plane was *Indiana Jones and The Last Crusade,* and he studied every expression Harrison Ford made. Maybe one day, he'd be working with him. However, he doubted very much that he would be cast alongside Connery— it had probably gotten back to him by now that he was trying to steal his part. The film finished, and Donnie realised he had another six hours ahead of him. He was restless and desperate to get off the plane. The icky smell of food from the galley filtered through the cabin, and he found it strange that all plane food smelt the same, whether it was fish, chicken or beef. Despite the lack of a tantalising aroma, Donnie couldn't help but get excited about plane food. It marked a milestone on the journey, and everything was so neatly packaged— little gifts for him to open up. They even included pudding. No sooner was dinner over, and he was agitated again. A mild feeling of anxiety swept over him that no matter how much he wanted to get off the plane, he couldn't. How would he get through the next five and a half hours when he was wide awake, uncomfortable and bored shitless? The biggest problem with travelling, Donnie concluded, was the travelling.

Donnie closed his eyes and tried to process the last couple of days: the funeral, the dark family revelations—but he kept drifting to his conversation with Maureen and Roísín handing him the teabags. He was playing out the moment in his head in such detail that he could see the strands of Roísín's black hair dancing in the wind, the goosebumps on her arms, her smiling blue eyes, and the box of Barry's teabags in her hands. Donnie opened his eyes and stared at the roof of the plane. His heart was in America, winning back Summer, explaining everything to her, so why was he thinking of Roísín? He shook his head and pulled out his walkman, turning up the volume to *Don't Go* by The Hothouse Flowers.

The plane touched down, and Donnie woke up, wondering when he had fallen asleep. He felt refreshed and happy. He wondered how long he would be able to walk through LAX without people recognising him. He indulged in the fantasy that in times to come, he would probably be travelling first class with a lovely PA and someone to carry his suitcase. Climbing inside a cab, he felt like the LAX expert now, not the lost Irishman reading signs and sweating in a foreign heat.

DONNIE ARRIVED AT his apartment and had to knock as he had left his key behind, believing he would not be returning. Francis answered the door with an expression Donnie could only read as mild relief.

'You're back!' Francis exclaimed.

Donnie pushed open the apartment door and tried to sidle past Francis, but Francis caught him by the arm.

'So, did you come clean to your parents? I'll be telling them you lied to me as well, of course.'

'Lying about lies. That's a good one,' Donnie retorted.

'What did you tell them, then? Kathy said nothing about it on the phone.' Francis was beginning to sound a little anxious.

Donnie smiled with a hint of smugness.

'No, I imagine she wouldn't have.'

Francis's face prickled with heat. *The socially inept little shit was getting far too big for his boots.*

'So you went to Ireland to your grandmother's funeral and still lied to them about *Dwarfland?*'

'I will tell them the truth, Francis, when I'm ready. I'm going to be incredibly busy, so why don't you go home and leave me alone? I have a lead role in a film directed by ...' Donnie held his silence for effect.

'Directed by who? Some unwashed student?'

'Directed by ... George Lawless!'

'That will be right,' Francis scoffed. He pushed his face closer to Donnie's. 'Is this another one of your little *Dwarfland* fantasies?'

Donnie scouted the room, looking for his belongings, picked them up and shoved them into his case.

'No, Francis, I have the part and go into rehearsals next week.'

Francis couldn't read the situation. Was he being made a mockery of, or had the little moron actually achieved the impossible? What possible God could there be that would pour this kind of good fortune on the likes of delusional Donnie? *No God*, Francis surmised.

'This is horseshit.' Francis hoped it was.

'No, it isn't. It's great news. It's the launch of my career. It's everything I've ever dreamed of. So it certainly isn't horseshit.' Donnie stuffed a few more t-shirts into his suitcase. 'Anyway,

I'm moving out of the apartment to stay with Abe and Melanie, and you need to go home to Kathy.' Donnie gave him a little wave goodbye even though he was still standing in front of him.

Donnie hadn't asked Abe and Melanie if he could move in. He'd only just thought of it, but it seemed like a great idea, and he hoped for a warm welcome. He would have slept on a floor—anything to get him away from Francis.

'Seriously, you need a doctor. You're still going on about Abe Nelson—and who the hell is Melanie? Melanie Griffith, I suppose?'

'Don't be ridiculous. Melanie is Abe Nelson's sister.'

Now Francis knew Donnie was full of it.

'Ha! And why wouldn't you tell your family if you've landed such an amazing part?'

Donnie was getting bored of Francis. Surprisingly, he didn't care that Francis didn't believe him—it would make it all the sweeter when he saw Donnie's name in lights. Donnie knew Francis might vomit if he witnessed that, and the thought made him feel smug.

'Because I want to wait until it's done,' Donnie said. 'I don't want anything to go wrong, and they've got enough on their plate.'

Francis laughed. It was a laugh that Donnie had heard so many times before, but it still held its sting. It descended on Donnie like a toxic haze, wrecking his head and making his blood boil.

'George Lawless. As if!' Francis sneered through his laughter.

Donnie's arm shot up and punched Francis in the chest, but his hand bounced, making no impact whatsoever.

'What the hell was that?' Francis was now amused.

Infuriated, Donnie picked up his suitcase and turned in the doorway and screamed, 'That's for ruining the nativity play, you fucking asshole!'

Donnie could still hear Francis's laughter as he walked away from the apartment.

CHAPTER THIRTY-TWO

LATER THAT DAY

onnie picked up several beers, chocolates and flowers in the hope that bearing gifts might make the question, '*Is it okay if I live with you for a bit?*' a touch easier. He stood on the front step of Abe and Melanie's cottage, two suitcases at his feet, his arms laden with offerings, and pressed the doorbell with his elbow.

Abe answered, upbeat and looking healthier than usual. His hair was brushed, he'd trimmed his stubble back, and he wore a t-shirt with *Frankie Says Relax* written on it. He was notably in a good mood which comforted Donnie.

Abe beamed when he saw Donnie and then looked down at the suitcases.

'Moving in?' he asked as if he had asked Donnie if he fancied a coffee.

'If it's okay? Could I stay? Just for a while. I'll pay you, of course, and I'll help with—'

'Shut up, for Chrissakes. Of course, you can stay.' Abe pulled Donnie in the door.

'Abe, I can't believe I got the part,' Donnie said, hugging him.

Abe relented for a second and then unhooked Donnie's arms.

'Well, it's a complete mystery to me, given your reaction after the audition. You had me convinced you'd fucked it.'

'I don't understand how I didn't.'

'The last thing you want to do is question it. He liked you. Thought you were right for the part. Keep proving he was right, and you'll be fine.'

Donnie followed Abe into the kitchen.

'Melanie! Donnie's here!' Abe hollered.

Melanie got up from the kitchen table, wearing an apron that looked like it had been in a food fight. Flour was dusted all over her face.

'Oh good, you can have some of the cake I baked. It's yummy!'

Abe whispered to Donnie, 'Push it up your sleeve or something. I think she has mistaken a few ingredients. I tasted vinegar in mine.'

Donnie handed Abe the beers.

'You two going to get jingled?' asked Melanie.

'We'll be having a beer or two if that's what you mean,' laughed Abe. 'Cake's a bit dry without it.'

'Dry?' Melanie scowled.

Donnie handed the flowers and chocolates to Melanie, and she hugged him.

'You know how to make an old woman smile! Take the weight off your feet,' she said as she pushed him into a seat at the table and landed a slice of cake in front of him. 'Here you go, Steven.'

It had all been going so well. Donnie wondered how long Melanie had thought he was Steven. Since he came in the door? Was it because he had been away, or had Melanie thought Donnie was Steven all along?

'Donnie,' Donnie corrected her and smiled apologetically at Abe.

Melanie rested a hand on Donnie's shoulder.

'I don't know why you want to change your name. Steven is a good, strong name—a screamer's name. Donnie sounds like a saddle bum.'

'A what?' Donnie and Abe asked in unison.

'A drifter,' she said matter-of-factly.

'Okay,' Donnie conceded. He had never debated whether

his name was a screamer's name or not; whatever it meant, he didn't think he wanted to be a screamer.

'But I'm not Steven, though.'

'Fair enough,' Melanie shrugged.

Donnie was feeling right at home. He had made the right choice coming here and was so glad to have received the welcome from Abe and Melanie. He felt like he had found a second family. Donnie ate a bite of the cake. *Oh God, what was in it?* He swigged his beer and swallowed most of it whole, causing a partial blockage in his throat. He gulped more beer to try and dislodge it.

'So you've got a read-through on Monday,' Abe said, smiling. He was full of smiles today. Donnie had never seen him so happy.

Donnie took another drink, hoping that the cake would collapse down his throat.

'Where?'

'At the studio.'

'It's happening. It's really happening!' Donnie said, choking.

'You've got some big nuts to crack!' agreed Melanie.

Abe looked at Melanie. He sometimes wondered if she knew exactly what was going on all the time and just entertained herself by confusing the shit out of everyone else.

'You'll want to be on top of your game,' Abe continued.

'For sure,' Donnie croaked out. The damn cake was going nowhere.

'Romi Miller has been cast.'

'FUCK!' Donnie shrieked.

The cake came up rather than down and presented itself on the kitchen table.

'What are you flipping your wig about?' demanded Melanie, staring at the regurgitated cake on the table.

Abe put his hand over Donnie's and tapped it. Donnie reached for a napkin and collected the mess he had made.

'Look, Donnie, we've all been star-struck at some point

in our lives. When I met Jimmy Stewart, the guy must have thought I was a bumbling freak.'

'Jesus! You met Jimmy Stewart?' Donnie was gobsmacked.

'Yes, it didn't go well. I stood and stared at him for a moment, and then, I did something awful ... really awful.'

'You pissed yourself?'

'No!' Abe snapped. 'Worse, I quoted him.' Abe stood up, re-enacting the moment. 'I didn't even say hello.' Abe put on his best Jimmy Stewart voice and pushed back his hair before quoting, '*Clarence! Clarence! Help me, Clarence! Get me back! Get me back! I don't care what happens to me! Get me back to my wife and kids! Help me, Clarence, please! Please! I wanna live again. I wanna live again. Please, God, let me live again.*'

'*It's a Wonderful Life,*' Melanie stated.

Abe and Donnie shared a look of surprise at Melanie's clarity.

'Yep, one of my favourite films and Jimmy ... he's one special actor. He's the everyman,' Abe said wistfully.

'So what happened? What did he say?' asked Donnie.

'He didn't say anything,' Abe laughed.

Donnie nodded slowly, 'Yes, I see your point, but with all due respect Jimmy Stewart doesn't look like Romi Miller.'

'True. Tell you what ... I'll work the script with you. I'll be Romi.'

'I'll be Romi!' interrupted Melanie.

Abe waved his hand. 'All right, Melanie. We can both be Romi.'

Melanie smiled, satisfied.

'Who is Romi, Melanie?'

Melanie screwed her face up.

'She's some big gun that's got Steven's knickers in a twist.'

Abe and Donnie laughed. Melanie did, too, but she wasn't sure why.

CHAPTER THIRTY-THREE

ON SATURDAY NIGHT

Donnie had managed to persuade Abe to come with him to Bar Boulevard. He desperately wanted to see Summer and explain everything. Bar Boulevard was intimidating enough without having the added problem of being dragged out by the cops the last time he was there. Donnie needed some solid support.

Abe looked incredible. He had a great sense of style when he wasn't wearing the clothes from his floor, and with Abe by his side, Donnie thought miracles could happen. They reached the door, and Donnie grinned at Brett. To Donnie's horror, Brett shook his head when he saw Donnie.

'Sorry, buddy,' Brett said as though he didn't even recognise Donnie, 'private function this evening.'

Donnie poked Brett as if Brett was having a laugh with him, but Brett wasn't joking and didn't appreciate being poked.

Donnie stood back, a little embarrassed.

'I see. Is this about the cops arresting me here?'

'No, but we can make it about that. You're not getting in.'

Abe put his arm on Donnie's shoulder and whispered, 'Come on, let's go.'

'Who's function is it?' Donnie wasn't giving up.

'Corey Haim's,' Brett said curtly and then looked above Donnie's head as if he was no longer standing in front of him.

'Well, this is Abe Nelson. You know Abe Nelson?'

Abe looked annoyed, but Donnie continued, 'You can't tell Corey Haim that you refused entry to Abe Nelson!'

'I won't,' said Brett. 'Abe is welcome to come in, but you can't.'

'Come on,' Abe insisted, grabbing Donnie by the arm and marching him back across the road. Donnie sensed that Abe was furious.

'Unbelievable! That guy knows me! What is his problem?' Donnie ranted.

'Don't ever use me like that again,' seethed Abe.

'What?' asked Donnie, genuinely shocked.

'I haven't been in this industry for years. I don't attend parties anymore. I have never met Corey Haim. He's half my age. I came here to support you so that you could speak to Summer, and you have abused that trust. That was fucking embarrassing.'

'Oh God, Abe, I'm sorry. It's not like that for me. I've never been famous, and I'm used to getting knockbacks from any local club. We'd say anything to get in, and I thought there would be no way he'd refuse me if I was with you. I'm sorry. It wasn't like that.'

'It was exactly like that!'

'Please don't be mad. I can't bear it. Please, Abe. Please, please, stop being cross. I'll do anything.'

Abe softened a little.

'The best thing you can do is focus on your part. Forget the girl for now. Knuckle down and get your career sorted. I'll help you but don't ever do that again.'

'Never, ever, ever,' said Donnie, suppressing his disappointment. He had a friend like Abe and couldn't even use his name to get into a club. He could see Abe's point but felt deflated—it seemed like such a wasted opportunity. Donnie had imagined himself basking in the glory of being next to Abe as Hollywood's hottest came over to chat, thinking he, too, must be *someone*. Even if they didn't think he was someone, he was a friend of Abe's, and that was plenty. He was a friend of Abe's, and he couldn't even fucking use it. Donnie decided it was worth one more prod.

They walked down the street, slower now.

'I wonder if I'll ever see her again,' Donnie said wistfully. 'She was one special girl. I mean really, really special.'

'You are still in danger of being punched by me.'

After finding a taxi and a silent ride home, Abe opened the door, and Donnie trudged down the hall to the bedroom Melanie had made up for him. The bed was covered in faded yellow silk cushions. He sat on the bed, clutching a cushion and stared at the ceiling. His boredom levels were high, and he surveyed the room. Then, in the corner, he noticed a stack of screenplays, seven or eight on top of each other. He wandered over and picked one up. The title page read: *The Last Drop, an original screenplay by Abe Nelson.* Donnie sucked in his breath and took it over to his bed. He lay down on the bed and started reading.

CHAPTER THIRTY-FOUR

THE DAY OF THE TABLE READ

A be had been out most of Sunday with Melanie. He took her to a Gospel church that she liked to attend and then to meet some of her friends. He hadn't asked Donnie to go with him, and Donnie was worried that he hadn't been invited because of the Bar Boulevard fiasco and decided to keep a low profile. So he had taken himself for walks on the beach, studied his script and quietly panicked about the table read. He had also read the whole of Abe's screenplay and loved it so much he thought he had to mention it, but was concerned that Abe might see it as an invasion of privacy and that Donnie had, once again, overstepped the mark.

Donnie found Melanie in the kitchen, burning toast.

'Here, I'll sort that. You sit down,' Donnie offered.

Melanie smiled. 'Thanks, sweetie.'

Donnie leaned against the sink as the bread was toasting and wondered if Melanie might have some insight.

'I didn't know Abe was a writer.'

'He is? Oh yes, he is. Well, he writes. Does that make him a writer?'

'I think it does,' replied Donnie.

'Where does it end, though, sweetie? Am I a baker because I make a great cake?'

'His screenplay is outstanding. I read it.'

'Are you saying my cake wasn't good?' demanded Melanie, narrowing her eyes.

233

'Of course not. It was delicious.'

'I'm only tickling you,' giggled Melanie. 'Yes, he can write all right. He used to write wonderful poetry for the girls he was mashed about, but he hung up his fiddle on that too. God only knows what he's doing now. I always wonder.'

Abe wandered into the room, looking more relaxed.

'What are you two talking about?'

Donnie decided it was best to come clean.

'I think you're a terrific writer.'

Abe looked confused. 'That's a unique opinion. What makes you say that? What have you read?'

'Well, I hope you don't mind, but there was a stack of screenplays in the bedroom I'm staying in …' Donnie noticed Abe's face flush. 'I didn't want to invade your privacy.'

'But you did anyway,' snapped Abe.

'Don't go off your chump,' Melanie interjected. 'He's given you the thumbs up. Don't get all hot under the collar when he's presenting medals.'

Abe half-smiled at Melanie.

'Yeh, well, anyway, which one did you read?'

'*The Last Drop*. It's excellent,' Donnie gushed.

'Not according to the twenty agents I sent it to. I think there's a high possibility it's shit. Do you want a lift to the studio?'

'You're driving?' asked Donnie.

'Yes,' Abe said as if that was perfectly normal.

Even Melanie looked shocked.

'Been a long time, honey, since you drove. You're normally suffering from barrel fever!'

'Not today. Do you want a lift or not?'

Donnie landed the toast down in front of Melanie.

'Sure thing, I'm good to go.'

'Good luck,' Melanie waved. 'Where's he going, Abe?'

'He's off to the studio for the read-through.'

Donnie grinned at Melanie and, under his breath, repeated, 'I'm off to the studio'. It all felt so surreal.

'Say hi to everyone from me. Give them my love,' Melanie said, waving.

THEY DROVE DOWN the freeway in Abe's convertible. The atmosphere had softened, but Donnie still felt the need to raise the other night.

'I'm sorry again about Bar Boulevard. I honestly didn't mean to upset you.'

'I know. I'd probably have done the same at your age. I shouldn't have overreacted and I wanted to say—'

Donnie cut him off, delighted all was fine, 'This car is pretty cool. You must've missed driving this little beauty.'

'Yes,' said Abe throwing him a look for interrupting, 'but I wanted to say I'm proud of you.'

'What?' Donnie had only ever heard people say they were proud of him when he was making something up, except for the time his mother said it when he won the bottle of brandy at the school's Christmas tombola.

'I'm proud of you,' Abe repeated. 'You got yourself here— believed in yourself, taken some rejection. Although you landed a part quickly, we all need a little luck and opportunity, and now you're on track to fulfil your ambitions.'

'I still don't know how I got here. I keep thinking it's going to be taken away from me.'

'Yeh, I think most people feel that way when they succeed at something. Why me? Am I a fraud, or am I as talented as they think I am? A dose of insecurity and self-doubt is healthy. Without it, narcissism takes over.' Abe fell silent for a moment. 'And that's never good, take it from me— you become a complete pain in the ass to everyone around you, and you also stagnate because you're not trying to improve, nor will you listen to anyone. Of course, too much self-doubt, and you can't get past the start line. It's a fine balance. The truth is, it has more to do with perseverance. I know for sure there were other actors out there way better than me, scraping to make a living, but I was there too, and the difference between them and me was that I didn't give up.'

Donnie thought about this for a moment.

'But you did give up.'

Abe shot him a look. The kid could get right under his skin when he wanted to.

'Yeh, all right, fuck off.' Abe put the pedal down, taking his irritation out on the accelerator.

'Don't you want to get back into acting?' Donnie continued, unaware he was making Abe even more tetchy.

'Nope,' Abe said, looking straight ahead and pressing down on the pedal hard enough for Donnie to be thrown back in his seat.

'Why do you keep all those screenplays piled up in the bedroom if you've thrown in the towel?' Donnie persisted. He couldn't understand why, when Abe had it all, he wouldn't want it back. The film premiere debacle should have been a distant memory.

'I might run out of toilet paper,' Abe snapped. 'Look, Donnie, I have my reasons, and I don't think that—'

The sound of sirens stopped Abe short.

'Fuck!'

Donnie looked in the wing mirror and saw the blue flashing lights. He twisted his neck round as far as he could see as Abe slowed the car and pulled over.

'Not good, not good,' Donnie muttered as Abe shot him another look.

Donnie opened the car door when Abe came to a stop.

'What the fuck are you doing?' Abe shouted. 'Stay in the car.'

'Why?'

'Do you want to get frisked? Handcuffed? ... Shot?'

'Not really, no,' muttered Donnie and hastily shut the door again.

An officer approached the car, looking very serious. Donnie wondered if these American police officers were auditioning for *Terminator* because that was all he could think of as he watched them stride robotically towards the car.

One of the terminators approached the car. He was the stockier and heavier of the two, more Arnold than the other guy. But, to Donnie's disappointment, he didn't speak in Arnie's staccato voice.

'Do you know why we've pulled you over?' he asked—more Californian than Austrian.

Donnie desperately wanted to blurt, '*Because you're looking for Sarah Connor,*' but managed to stop himself.

'No, Officer,' replied Abe.

'You were speeding. Can I see your driving licence?'

Abe hadn't driven in a long time and stopped carrying his licence in his wallet because he left so many wallets in bars that he would have been through ten licences by now.

Abe looked up at the officer and said apologetically,

'Unfortunately, I don't have it on me. I took it out of my wallet and forgot to put it back in.'

'I'm going to have to take you down to the station,' the officer asserted.

Donnie shook his head. This was different from how things were done in Ireland. A ticking-off, maybe, but down to the station for breaking the speed limit?

'Don't you recognise me?' Abe asked.

'No, sir, I do not.'

'How about now?' Abe said, lifting his sunglasses.

'No, sir, I do not recognise you.'

'I'm sure you've seen *Vicious Cycle,* the cop series?'

The officer shook his head.

Abe's frustration increased as he persevered.

'*Death Valley? A Trip to Insanity?*'

'You need to come to the station. It's an offence not to carry your licence, and you were ten miles an hour over the speed limit.'

'Abe Nelson? Have you heard the name, Abe Nelson!'

'Not recently. Perhaps you should step out of the vehicle.'

Oh shit, thought Donnie. This was rapidly going tits up.

Donnie put his hand on Abe's shoulder to calm him and pleaded with the officer.

'He's been under a lot of stress.'

Abe grabbed the steering wheel dramatically and started to cry … although it sounded more like a wounded bear to Donnie. Big, fat teardrops rolled down his cheeks as he shook his head at the futility of it all.

The officer looked at Abe, confused.

'Why are you crying? Please stop this at once.'

'I'm not a criminal!' Abe wailed. 'Why are you going to take me to the station? I'll get my licence when I get home and bring it in. I promise. I *promise!* Please don't charge me. *Please!*'

Donnie watched Abe open-mouthed.

'Pull yourself together!' the officer barked.

Abe looked at him again, woeful eyes filled with tears. The officer was at a complete loss.

'All right, all right!' he conceded, against his better judgement. 'You take your licence to the station tomorrow.'

'Thank you, oh thank you!' Abe beamed at him, eyes still wet.

The officer shook his head and walked away as Abe turned and grinned at Donnie.

'If all else fails, cry, but that lying bastard knew exactly who I was. What cop hasn't watched *Vicious Cycle*, for fuck's sake!'

Donnie agreed vigorously, 'Oh, he knew you all right, the bastard.'

Abe started the ignition, and the radio burst into life with George Michael's *Faith*.

Donnie could see that Abe still had a desperate need for recognition. Had he witnessed Abe's insecurity or his narcissism, or just a display of talented acting? He wasn't sure, but as he glanced sideways at Abe, he knew at that moment that he loved him so much—he couldn't imagine a world without him.

Donnie turned the radio down to Abe's mild annoyance.

'You know, we should work together.'

'Is that right? Doing what?' Abe asked, looking dubious.

'We should make an independent film together and star in it. One of your screenplays—it would be an amazing comeback!'

'No thanks,' Abe replied, turning the radio back up. 'I'm more likely to fly around town on a pig.'

Donnie closed his eyes with a big grin on his face.

'What are you doing?' asked Abe.

'Trying to make it happen by thinking about it.'

'Me flying on a pig?'

'No, us doing a film together—your film.'

'You know you haven't got superpowers, don't you? Someone has told you that by now?'

'We've all got superpowers. You just have to believe.'

Abe laughed. 'Who are you, Peter Pan?'

Abe pulled the car up outside the studio and shook Donnie's hand.

'Good luck, kid, and for God's sake, shut up about super-powers in there.'

Donnie looked up at the building in front of him. On the top of it was a huge golden sign, *20th Century Fox*. He stood there, unable to move for a moment, before uttering the words, 'Oh … My … God.'

He managed a wink at Abe. He was filled with excitement but, equally, felt the urge to vomit. Half of him wanted to run after Abe's car, climb back in and never leave his side, and the other half was itching to be inside the studio, seeing and feeling everything first-hand—not as a visitor, not as an imposter, as an *actor*.

GEORGE LAWLESS HAD been looking forward to today. He loved sifting out any crap in the script during the read-through and visualising the glorious picture in his mind. He was re-read-ing the script with his fourth cup of coffee of the morning, mulling over a scene he thought needed more punch. He'd spend some time on this today and see what the actors brought to it. He could smell Barbara's dense perfume before he saw her.

'Morning, Barbara, you know you don't need to be here today.' *Or, indeed, any day,* he thought.

Barbara wasn't expecting a welcome.

'I always go to the table reads, George, you know that, and I want to ensure you haven't made a mistake. He's a huge risk.'

George reluctantly put down the script.

'Look, if he sucks, we've got plenty of time to recast.'

'I think you've chosen him because he's Irish,' Barbara had said it. She wasn't planning to say it, but out it spilt.

'Now, you're being ridiculous, Barbara!'

'And,' Barbara continued, 'it might surprise you to know that I am also of Irish descent. My lineage is Irish, Scottish, German and Dutch.'

George stared at her. 'That's quite a mix, Barbara, but I can't see what your family tree has to do with casting Donnie.'

George stood up, and straight in his eye-line was Donnie, like a rabbit in the headlights, looking round the room for somewhere to bolt to. George strode towards him with more gusto after Barbara's irritating comment.

'Welcome, Donnie!' George said, offering a firm handshake. 'We'll be starting the table read in thirty minutes. Go and grab yourself a coffee and a doughnut before Barbara eats them all,' he laughed and then went so far as to point at Barbara, stuffing one into her mouth.

Donnie laughed with him and then wondered if laughing at Barbara was appropriate.

Standing on his own, drinking lukewarm coffee, Donnie decided to avoid the doughnuts in case anyone pointed at him shoving one into his mouth. His stomach was queasy anyway, and a doughnut might be too risky.

And then in she walked, more beautiful in life than on screen—if that was possible. Donnie felt his mouth open and his eyes fixate. He tried desperately not to stare, but he couldn't help it. Romi Miller was walking towards him casually, with no fanfare, no red carpet, no chasing paparazzi ... she simply walked. She wore jeans and a green jersey that looked so soft that Donnie wanted to stroke it. She picked up a cup and smiled at Donnie.

'Hi,' he managed to say.

'Hi,' she said, looking at him with her hazel eyes, 'I'm Romi. Pleased to meet you.' She put out her hand.

Donnie's hand trembled.

'I'm Donnie McNamara.' When he touched her cool hand, he realised his own was sticky and damp. 'I'm your co-star,' Donnie said, but it came out as a whisper, like a secret or a lie he dared to utter.

Romi flashed him another smile.

'Great.'

There was something in her tone that left Donnie wondering if she thought it was great at all.

George called everyone to their seats. More doughnuts were in the centre of the table. Donnie found it strange that there was temptation and offerings everywhere in an industry where everyone tried to eat nothing.

'We'll start with everyone introducing themselves,' George suggested. 'I know a lot of you know each other and certainly have seen each other's work, but we do have some first-timers at the table, and as with all my projects, we are a family until we wrap, so it's good to get the introductions out of the way before you escape into your characters.'

George was looking directly at Donnie, and then Donnie noticed, so was everyone else. Perhaps he was the only person at the table that no one knew. George gestured towards Donnie.

'First off, someone from my homeland, Donnie McNamara. Donnie, do you want to tell us a little about yourself?'

Donnie didn't want to do that. At all. He hadn't prepared for this question. His face now felt as damp as his hands.

'Well, as you said, George, I'm from Ireland, from a small

town on the West Coast called Bellvara. I came from a farming background.' Donnie could see he was losing his audience already, but Romi's eyes were on him, and he had to jazz this up a bit. 'I didn't like being up to my knees in cowshit and always wanted to act.'

There was a mild chuckle from George and a hint of a smile from Romi, which was enough to spur him on.

'The plays I was doing at the nursing home weren't really cutting it for me. Maureen preferred to play dominoes, and Flo couldn't remember her name, let alone anything we had just performed.'

A full smile from Romi and a roar of laughter from George.

'Then my sister married some flute called Francis, and he is taking over the family farm, so I bolted to California and thought, it's now or never, and here I am in a dream come true.'

He looked straight back at Romi, hoping perhaps for applause, but instead, she gave him one last smile and then looked away.

George clapped his hands together, which made Barbara jump. She had been miles away thinking about the clauses in Donnie's contract that would help release him immediately.

'This is the stuff,' gushed George. 'Okay, we'll go round the table with brief introductions now that everyone knows Donnie, and then we'll get on with the read.'

Donnie had loved every minute of the read-through. He'd done his homework and had benefitted from Abe's guidance. The subtleties he added were well received, his execution was the best he could have hoped for, and he even asked some relevant questions that generated discussion rather than ridicule. George was happy. Romi looked relaxed, and Barbara had stopped glaring at him for now. The rest of the cast was supportive, fun and thoroughly professional. Donnie did indeed feel like he was joining a family. Donnie was thinking this over another coffee at the end of the session when Barbara approached; her lips clamped together as though her teeth were sinking into them.

'Donnie,' she said, 'I want you to go to the production office and meet with Sable Vonderhyde.'

'Sure,' Donnie agreed, not knowing what was coming.

'Sable Vonderhyde is our main publicist,' Barbara explained.

'Sounds exciting!' Donnie said, but by the look on Barbara's face, he wasn't sure if that was the correct response.

'I will ask Felix to take you down to the office,' she said.

'Thanks,' Donnie replied and realised the conversation had come to an end.

Felix picked up Donnie in a buggy. He didn't say much, and what he did say wasn't positive. Unlike Chris, the Irish guy from the Warner Bros studio lot, who gushed with enthusiasm, Felix was a part-time actor with a chip on his shoulder, and Donnie felt that his chip was growing into a potato.

'How did it go?' Felix asked, not caring about the answer.

'Oh, it was one of the best days I've ever had,' Donnie replied, refusing to be taken down by Felix.

'Yeh, I bet. Some sucky script that's only going to sell because Romi's in it.'

'I have to stop you there, Felix. We all know Romi does not do 'sucky' films. It's going to be a hit.'

'At the Razzies, maybe,' snorted Felix.

'No such thing as bad advertising!' retorted Donnie, and then wished he hadn't because he didn't want to create any possible reality of a Razzie. Then again, *Cocktail* had won worst film this year, and Donnie had found it entirely watchable. Especially the bit with Elizabeth Shue in the waterfall, albeit it was Tom Cruise who was there with her, and not Donnie … and he'd learned how to make a few decent cocktails from that film. So what was there not to like about it?

Felix braked harder than necessary outside the production office and pointed half-heartedly towards it.

'In there.'

'Well, thanks very much, Felix. It's been a pleasure meeting you.'

Donnie stuck out his hand with a smile, and Felix reluctantly offered his hand back for the shortest handshake in history.

Donnie entered through the glass doors to a reception area with plush purple velvet chairs. A friendly-looking girl sat behind reception.

'Hello, how may I help you today?'

'I'm here to see Sable Vonderhyde. My name is Donnie McNamara.'

'Take a seat. She's on a conference call but should be wrapping up very soon. She's always on time,' the receptionist said, smiling.

Donnie took a seat in what he thought was the most comfortable seat he had ever sat in. He found himself shuffling back into it and resting his head on the wing of the chair. His eyes were just about to close when he heard the distinctive click-clack of stilettos coming towards him. From a distance, she looked stunning, with soft curls around her face, but as she loomed closer, there was a hardness to her face—it was like seeing a white sandy beach in the distance only to arrive there and find that the sand was, in fact, hard shells that hurt your feet.

Donnie stood up quickly, but she still towered over him in her heels, at well over six feet. She was lean and chiselled, and her green eyes felt like lasers on his face.

'I'm Sable Vonderhyde,' she clipped her sentences with a European accent that Donnie couldn't place.

'Donnie McNamara,' Donnie said, offering his hand as he felt a grip as firm as he expected in return.

She turned on her high heels and strode ahead of him down the corridor. They entered an office with a polished red tile floor and a shiny black desk with leather chairs. Sable motioned for Donnie to take a seat as she sat in the high-backed chair across the other side of the desk.

'Welcome to Hollywood,' she said, without a hint of welcome in her voice. 'Did you enjoy the table read?'

'I loved it!' Donnie exclaimed and then wondered if he should tone down his enthusiasm. 'But no one told me not to get out of my seat. You know, it's simply a read-through. No need for miming!' he chuckled, but Sable didn't, creating an awkward silence.

Eventually, after shuffling some papers, Sable looked up at Donnie.

'You see, Donnie, this is all new to you.'

'It is,' agreed Donnie.

'And no one knows who you are. No one at all,' Sable continued.

Donnie smiled and couldn't help himself.

'Some people know me quite well.'

He managed not to drop Abe's name, but she was obviously aware that he knew George Lawless and Romi Miller.

Sable grimaced, which made her look even scarier. Donnie wondered if she was of Viking descent. He could see her landing one of her boats on foreign shores with a horned helmet, leading the charge, and bashing native men out of the way like skittles.

'I'll get straight to the point,' Sable announced. 'We need to get you into the public eye somehow, and we need to do it now so that everyone knows who you are when the film comes out. Understand?' The word *understand* was barely audible, causing Donnie to cock his head to the side like a spaniel.

'Of course,' agreed Donnie. Perhaps this conversation wasn't going to be so bad after all—they just wanted to raise his profile a bit.

'So, George is good friends with Randolph Lettering—'

Before Sable could finish her sentence, Donnie sucked in the air between his teeth, creating a whistling sound.

'*Thee* Randolph Lettering?'

'Yes, and *Thee* Randolph Lettering has agreed to interview you,' she said, speaking as if she had an unpleasant taste in her mouth that she was trying to spit out.

'Oh my God, in New York?' Donnie's eyes were dancing. He wanted his feet to dance, too, but Sable's presence was enough to keep him rooted to the chair.

'No, he's doing a music special at The Troubadour tomorrow night, and we've managed to squeeze in a slot for you.'

Donnie's excitement turned to anxiety.

'Do they want me to sing or something?'

'No, absolutely not. As I said, Randolph is a friend, and he has agreed to include you on the show. There will likely be a couple of A-listers being interviewed on the night too.'

'You are shitting me?'

Donnie was back to excitement.

Sable handed Donnie the papers she had been shuffling.

'No, I am not *shitting* you. We have scripted what you are going to say. So you will stick to the script as best you can, and hopefully … all going well … we can get past the fact that no one knows you.'

Donnie could tell by her manner that she didn't have complete faith in him. Hoping to offer her a little comfort, he said,

'I love Randolph Lettering.'

Sable came out from behind the desk. Donnie could tell that his words had not reassured her and may have had the opposite effect and provoked her. She gripped his arm but squeezed it gently with a smile that didn't reach her eyes.

'But we must not mess this up,' she whispered.

Subtly, Donnie tried to pull his arm back.

'I won't.'

Sable gave him another quick smile before pointing towards the door.

'Nice to meet you. Good luck, Donnie.'

Donnie hastily got up and wobbled a bit before he reached the door, floated past reception and out into the glorious sunshine with a grin that would soon hurt his cheeks.

THE SUN WAS setting as Donnie took his taxi journey back from the studio. It had been a long and brilliant day—one he would always remember. He knew it was Abe that had made today happen.

Donnie arrived back at Abe's house. Abe was on the couch, playing his guitar as Melanie listened, her eyes closed, smiling.

Abe put his guitar down when he saw Donnie.

'Well, how did it go?'

'It was one of the best days of my life. Thank you, Abe!'

Donnie ran over and hugged him.

Melanie clapped her hands together in excitement.

'Good for you, Steven, good for you!'

CHAPTER THIRTY-FIVE

ON THE WAY TO THE TROUBADOUR

Donnie had never looked sharper. He had spent longer getting ready than he ever thought possible and barely recognised the result in the mirror. Tonight, he was going live on *The Late Entertainment Show* with Randolph Lettering. Donnie McNamara was going to be on television ... and it was being filmed at possibly one of the coolest venues in the world.

Donnie was on such a roll and feeling so good about himself, that he decided to stop at Bar Boulevard and make one last attempt to explain himself to Summer. He desperately wanted to tell her to tune in and watch him on Randolph Lettering's show. Perhaps all of his dreams might come true in one single night.

Donnie approached the velvet ropes, wondering if Brett was friend or foe tonight.

'Can't keep away?' chuckled Brett.

'Is Summer working?' Donnie asked. He was still licking his wounds over the whole Corey Haim birthday party incident.

Brett shook his head.

'Is she really not working, or are you just saying she isn't working?'

'Why would I lie to you? Hey, man, she hasn't got a barring order on you or anything, has she?' interrogated Brett.

'Brett? Seriously?'

Brett shrugged, offering Donnie the faintest of smiles.

'Sometimes it's the ones you don't suspect that are causing all the problems.'

'Sure, but no one would have any reason to take out a barring order on me.'

'I might! She isn't working, though. She hasn't been in for a while. Maybe ask Duke behind the bar?'

'Okay, thanks.'

Brett caught Donnie's arm as he passed. 'Duke's an asshole.'

'Thanks for the heads up.'

'Anytime. Anytime,' Brett affirmed and returned to his military stance.

Donnie walked into Bar Boulevard. It was fairly quiet, only a few after-work people finishing meetings before the night-time scene arrived. He spotted Duke washing some glasses behind the bar.

'Duke?'

'Yeh?'

Donnie was sure Duke knew who he was, so he was hoping for a more cordial welcome.

'I was looking for Summer.'

'Well, she isn't here.'

'I can see that, Duke. Do you know where she is?'

Duke stopped washing the glasses and looked up at Donnie.

'Even if I did, I wouldn't tell you. All your bullshit lies about being an actor. The last time I saw you, the police were escorting you out. So why would I tell you where she was?'

'That was all a big misunderstanding,' Donnie protested.

'I bet.'

'I came here to explain, and I did come out here to be an actor. I've got a part in a big movie. A George Lawless movie.'

Duke scoffed.

'I'm going on *The Late Entertainment Show* with Randolph Lettering tonight. They are interviewing me about it,' Donnie persisted.

Duke roared with laughter.

'Were the police taking you back to the mental institution?'

Donnie checked his watch. He didn't have forever to waste

convincing Duke; within hours, Duke would have to eat his words.

Donnie looked up as a shadow loomed over him … Francis. *Fuck*.

'I don't fucking believe it,' Donnie muttered.

'I thought I might find you here,' Francis said, smirking. 'What's happening?'

'Absolutely nothing,' replied Donnie, deciding it was time to leave before his whole night and life went tits up.

'Hardly nothing,' interjected Duke, his voice laced with sarcasm. 'He's going on *The Late Entertainment Show* with Randolph Lettering tonight. You might want to get a move on to get to New York on time.' Duke feigned a check of his watch before adding, 'Oh, no, look, I think you've missed it.'

'It's not in New York,' Donnie countered. 'He's doing a music special at The Troubadour.'

Francis narrowed his eyes.

'Is that so?'

'Of course it isn't!' Duke retorted.

Francis was unsure. Donnie looked better dressed than Francis had ever seen him, and something about his demeanour made him think that the little shit might have made some progress.

'If you want to prove it,' said Francis, 'you can take me with you.'

'As if,' objected Donnie, but Francis's comment made him nervous.

Francis shrugged and walked out of Bar Boulevard without another word. Donnie found this both comforting and strange. He turned to look at Duke, who had returned to washing glasses.

'Will you tell Summer I was here?'

'Sure, I'll tell her,' Duke said, shaking his head.

CHAPTER THIRTY-SIX

THE LATE ENTERTAINMENT SHOW
WITH RANDOLPH LETTERING

Donnie's cab pulled up on Santa Monica Boulevard outside The Troubadour. Donnie thought it was hugely understated for an iconic venue, with its dark brown facade and old English lettering on the sign.

Euphoria swept over Donnie as he stepped onto the kerb. He wasn't here to see Bob Dylan, Poison, or any other great band that had played here. He was a guest—a guest of Randolph Lettering, no less. He felt like he was having an out-of-body experience, watching himself in slow motion in this wonderland as he savoured every moment of his new reality. There was a long queue of people waiting to get in. Donnie knew he didn't have to stand in line but wondered how many people would complain if he walked straight to the front and knocked. Was there a back door? Why had no one given him this information? What had been a surreal moment was turning into a potentially embarrassing one.

He made polite excuses to the heavy metal contingent and gently elbowed his way to the door. He knocked—nothing. He turned and gave a small smile to what looked like hell-raising bikers, bearded and heavily pierced. They stared back, saying nothing. Donnie offered them a playful shrug of his shoulders and turned back to the door, his face burning hot. He knocked again, with a little more force this time.

A bouncer opened the door a fraction and peered out at Donnie.

'Oh, Hi!' Donnie said as casually as he could muster. 'I'm Donnie McNamara. I'm on the show tonight.'

The bouncer opened the door wide enough to pull Donnie through and shut it firmly behind him.

'You're at the wrong door.'

He muttered something into his radio, and a warm but somewhat harried woman appeared instantly.

Donnie heaved a sigh of relief.

'Hi, I'm Donnie McNamara. I'm on the show tonight,' he said, smiling now that the humiliation of getting in the door was over.

'Donnie McNamara. Yes, I'm Anita.'

Anita shook his hand firmly and quickly as if it was a task she needed to complete before doing the million other things on her exhaustive list.

'Follow me.'

She walked so fast that Donnie had to break into an awkward jog beside her.

Donnie had no time to gawp at the stage set up or the folk milling around, getting ready for tonight's show. Over his shoulder, he saw the bouncers open the doors, and a mass of people traipse in.

Anita reached into her pocket as they were hurrying backstage. She handed Donnie a piece of paper.

'There was a phone message for you.'

A phone message was delivered to me at The Troubadour, thought Donnie. *I really have arrived.*

He unfolded the note, which simply read: *For Donnie McNamara from Abe Nelson: Try not to shit yourself tonight.*

Donnie chuckled and put the note in his pocket. Perhaps he'd keep that note as memorabilia forever.

As Anita and Donnie reached the Green Room door backstage, she said,

'Oh, and your manager is here.'

'My manager?'

Donnie didn't have a manager, at least not one he was aware of. Maybe they had appointed him a manager. That would be good, someone that could manage him. Donnie could see how that could be very useful.

Anita opened the door and pointed towards a chair with its back turned towards the door. All Donnie could see was a hand resting on the arm of the chair, holding a can of beer. Two long outstretched legs protruded from the chair. The manager was tall. A head turned round, and Donnie let out a high-pitched gasp.

'What the fuck?' he squealed.

Donnie's triumphant moment was taking an unwelcome twist.

Anita, oblivious to Donnie's distress, pointed to the drinks cabinet.

'Help yourself to drinks. Let me know if I can get you anything.'

She was out the door before Donnie could say anything, and now Donnie was face to face with Francis in the very last place he wanted Francis to be.

Francis grinned, enjoying the look of panic on Donnie's face.

'This is fantastic. Free beer. Celebrity treatment.'

Panic turned to anger in Donnie. He was not going to let this dickhead ruin everything—not this time.

'Jesus Christ! This stops now.'

Donnie wagged his finger at Francis, an unfortunate reflection of his mother's mannerisms.

Francis shrugged and raised an eyebrow.

'I'm not Jesus Christ, but I am your manager, it seems. So, you weren't lying about being in a movie.'

Donnie felt his throat start to constrict.

'You need to get out of here. You can *not* be here.'

Francis dismissed Donnie with a wink, further infuriating him.

'You really need to fuck off, please.'

Donnie knew that Francis had no intention of fucking off. He was far too comfortable with his beer. He was far too comfortable being an asshole.

Anita appeared again, ushering in Alabama 3—Larry, Harpo and Rock. They appeared beside Donnie like guardian angels.

'Donnie!'

Larry stretched out his arms and gave Donnie a hearty slap on the back.

'You remember me?' Donnie asked, momentarily forgetting about his big problem with Francis as he felt the swirl of rock 'n' roll around him.

'Course I do, Brother!' Larry replied, giving him a bony hug.

'Which is amazing,' quipped Rock, the guitarist, 'considering how many drugs he does.'

Francis was beginning to feel left out and was seething that Donnie knew anyone as cool as Alabama 3. Finally, he stood up and put out his hand.

'Hi, I'm Francis Brawley.'

Donnie rolled his eyes at Larry, Harpo and Rock. It was the kind of eye-roll that said *seriously, avoid this one; he's a complete prick.*

The meaning of the eye-roll wasn't lost on them. Harpo left Francis's hand dangling and helped himself to a beer. Harpo had met enough assholes throughout his life and had an uncanny ability to smell them out. He had a good whiff of Francis's arseholery the minute he walked in the door. Harpo gulped his beer and pulled out his harmonica.

Rock had no plans to say hello to Francis. Rock was the intelligent socialist, not the comfortable sandal-wearing type, but the kind who viewed *Thatcher* as a swear word. Francis smacked of some toff school or just some nobhead. So rock decided to turn his back. Francis looked thick, and if Rock couldn't have the stimulation of challenging opinions or debating quantum physics, then he couldn't be arsed wasting his time conversing with him.

Larry was luckily two steps to the right of Francis, so nowhere near his outstretched hand. To walk forward and take it would look awkward and unintentionally enthusiastic, so he, too, left Francis's arm dangling in the air. Besides, Francis looked boring, and that was worse than being a psychopath. According to Larry, being boring was a cardinal sin, and tonight was not the night to be bored.

Donnie turned his attention back to Francis.

'You need to take a fucking hike, please.'

'No, no, I'm here for the long haul. I'm your manager,' Francis said, laughing.

'No, you're not. I'm going to get security.'

'Are you? A quick long-distance call to your parents might make you want to rethink that one,' Francis scoffed.

'Go right ahead. They've got more things on their mind now that they're broke.'

Francis did a double-take.

'What do you mean, they're broke?'

'They're probably going to lose the farm, so you calling them up telling them I'm about to be in a Hollywood movie isn't going to rock the boat too much. The only reason I haven't told them yet is because I wanted to wait until we were filming. But you go ahead, tell them the good news.'

'What about the inheritance? Your family has that money! She's meant to be rich!'

'What the fuck do you care? You're rolling in it.'

Francis's face was ashen. He screamed in Donnie's face,

'But I haven't got any fucking money!'

Harpo found the conversation more interesting and decided to contribute.

'Neither do we. Someone got a swimming pool out of our last album, but it sure wasn't any of us.'

Francis's eyes grew dark, and his facial muscles tightened, making him look troll-like.

'All I've got is a mountain of fucking debt, inheritance tax and leaking house and your fucking sister was meant to sort all that!'

Donnie felt like someone had awakened him with a stinging slap on the face.

'Hang on. You married my sister for *money*?'

'Well, it fucking helped.'

Donnie had no idea where his arm came from, but it arrived at light speed, fuelled with anger and knocked Francis straight to the floor, blood pouring from his nose.

Anita entered the room, momentarily observed Francis on the floor, and as if nothing was unusual, she smiled at Donnie.

'You're on, Donnie.'

CHAPTER THIRTY-SEVEN

MOMENTS LATER

Abe and Melanie had been positioned in their armchairs long before Randolph Lettering started. With a beer in one hand and a prayer in his mind, Abe willed the interview to go well. Melanie clapped her hands.

'Oh, I love Randolph Lettering!'

Abe turned up the volume as Randolph strode onto the stage.

'Welcome to our music special at The Troubadour! We also have a couple of film stars here tonight. Here to save the world … Bill Murray! And our *Big* guest, Tom Hanks!'

SUMMER WAS SITTING in her small apartment on her bed, already wearing her pyjamas. She unwrapped a Baby Ruth chocolate bar and took a swig from a bottle of Bud Light—the loneliness of her evening was going to be filled by Randolph Lettering. An hour would pass, at least. The problem with living in LA was that she had many acquaintances but few friends whom she could share anything meaningful with, and this evening seemed to sum that up. She watched Randolph introduce the evening line-up.

'But first up, we have someone you have never heard of because this is his first film. He's landed on his feet in a new George Lawless movie, *Cracked*. Maybe he'll join the walk of fame one day, but it all starts here. Ladies and Gentlemen, please welcome Donnie McNamara!'

Hearing Donnie's name made Summer's stomach lurch. 'What the hell?' she spoke out loud.

Summer stared at the television screen. *Oh my God, it's him*, she thought. Then, a million more thoughts ran through her brain like an electric current: the conversations about acting, the police taking him away, his awful brother-in-law that night, and suddenly, the realisation that perhaps she had been wrong. She couldn't believe she was watching Donnie about to be interviewed by the most prominent television host on the planet. She noticed how nervous he looked. Waves of remorse flooded her mind, knowing she could have been there to encourage him.

'It's okay, I won't bite,' Randolph said. 'So, Donnie, you're a farmer from a remote village in Ireland, and now you're making a George Lawless movie! Tell us how this all came about?'

ABE COULD FEEL Donnie's nervousness through the television. He began to sweat himself. *Please make this go well*, he prayed.

'Ooh,' Melanie squirmed, 'he looks as nervous as a drug mule at a border crossing.'

BARBARA, THE CASTING Director, had a lot riding on this interview. If she had been frank with herself, she wanted Donnie to fuck up. Better now, on national television, than two weeks into filming. She wasn't having her name associated with casting this idiot, and she was pretty sure an early interview with Randolph Lettering would unleash the obvious—the obvious to everyone except George. She smirked as Donnie looked like a bullock entering the abattoir, and Randolph had to repeat the question.

'Donnie? How did it come about?'

Barbara was stunned to hear a heckler in the background. This never happened on Randolph's show.

'Everyone knows you can't fucking act!' boomed the voice.

MELANIE WAS STARTLED when she heard the loud heckle. She looked to Abe for an explanation.

'Who's shouting at him?' asked Melanie, upset.

Abe was on the edge of his seat.

'I don't know, but it's not good.'

Abe was relieved to see that Donnie ignored the shout and was finally answering Randolph's question.

'Well, Randolph, for as long as I can remember, I wanted to be an actor, and I don't think anyone took me seriously—'

'Took you seriously? Why would they? You fucking suck, you useless little, lying bollox.'

Melanie and Abe gasped at the same time. This was a catastrophe.

SUMMER RECOGNISED THE voice. *Oh God, the asshole brother-in-law from the bar. What is going on?* She watched as Randolph Lettering tried to control the situation.

'Seems you have a bit of a fan already.'

Summer heard the audience laugh and gasp as a figure made straight for the stage. Then, as if, things couldn't get any worse, she stared in horror as Donnie swore on live television.

'WOULD YOU EVER FUCK OFF, FRANCIS!'

She jumped off the bed as the camera panned to follow Donnie hiding behind Randolph's chair. She pulled on her jeans, t-shirt and Converse boots, with her eyes glued to the show and witnessed Donnie walking, trance-like, towards the camera.

'Hi, Mum, Dad, Kathy, Sheena. I've got a lot to tell you.'

Summer ran out of her apartment and slammed the door behind her.

ABE SAT WITH his head in his hands as Donnie's voice continued, but Melanie listened intently.

'It's not so bad, Abe,' she soothed. 'He's just popping his corn, but I might get the tissues. This could be a bit of a tear squeezer.'

BARBARA SAT BACK IN her chair and smiled. A weight had been lifted from her shoulders as she proved, once again, that she was right. Normality had been restored.

GEORGE LAWLESS WAS watching Donnie on Randolph Lettering, and the whole fiasco had resulted in him losing his grip on the ten-year-old Irish malt he was enjoying. Just as he had poured himself another, Barbara called to gloat. George made a mental note to unequivocally never work with Barbara again. There was nothing worse than someone waiting in the wings to be proved right. *That po-faced crone willed this to happen*; George was sure of it. George hung up the phone, his face stinging with a combination of frustration and anger. He sat back, took a long swig of his whiskey, and continued to watch Donnie disembowel himself on live television.

'I never wanted to be a farmer, but I love my family,' Donnie declared to the camera.

George listened to Donnie's rambling and had no idea what it had to do with his film.

'So you can imagine, for me,' Donnie continued, 'Kathy marrying Francis was like a burst sewer pipe in our home. One that filtered into everything with its rancidness. Even rooms that were seemingly untouched started to smell.'

George was glued to every word.

'No one took me seriously. I am a terrible farmer. As thick as pig shit but only half as useful. I had notions of being an actor. My acting debut was when I was six years old, and this is where my problems with Francis started.'

THE PRODUCER DIDN'T want Donnie's interview to finish, but by the time he got to the end of the story of the nativity play, he was under pressure. Just a few more words because he could not leave Bill Murray and Tom Hanks waiting any longer, but this was too good not to air.

Donnie hadn't finished.

'I promised my little sister, Sheena, I would fix things for our family, and I haven't managed that tonight, but I want to tell you all the truth. I lied about being in computers. To be fair, I'm not much use with technology either. I lied about what I was doing out here. I was auditioning, and Francis knew. He blackmailed me, and maybe I deserved that, but my sister, Kathy, deserves to know the truth. He has married her for money. I'm sorry, Kathy, he told me that himself. Ironically, money we don't have, and if all I achieve in my life is to reveal to my sister that a low-life snake is deceiving her, then … at least there is that.'

Donnie opened his mouth to speak again, but he was rushed off stage. The audience was silent, but within moments, there was the sound of a solitary clap, which did not break into thunderous applause or a standing ovation—it merely fizzled out with looks of confusion and a few sniggers.

CHAPTER THIRTY-EIGHT

TEN MINUTES LATER

Donnie staggered off stage in a daze and was shepherded towards the exit. Anita rushed towards him and handed him a note.

'Another phone message for you,' she said, her voice oozing sympathy.

For the briefest of moments, Donnie felt a glimmer of hope. Then, he opened the note to see Anita's scribbled words: *From Barbara Beatty: You're fired.*

Donnie reached the exit door in a trance. He hoped he would wake from this nightmare, but it all felt too real. He could feel the sharp intakes of breath in his chest, the thudding in his head and the clattering of the end of his career, and yet the image in his mind that he kept playing over and over was of his little sister, Sheena, and her hopeful eyes.

Tears streamed down his face as he hailed a taxi. The idea of returning to Abe's, with a fist full of failure, didn't appeal, but he had nowhere else to go. It was either Abe's house or a leap from an exceedingly high bridge. The taxi pulled up outside Abe's cottage, and Donnie felt glued to the backseat. The cottage door opened, and he saw Melanie, her arms outstretched towards the taxi. He heaved himself out and walked towards her, his head low. She wrapped her arms around him as he sobbed on her shoulder.

'You know,' she said, trying to calm him, 'don't worry about biting off more than you can chew. Your mouth is probably a whole lot bigger than you think.'

SUMMER COULDN'T HAVE gotten to The Troubadour any faster, but as she stood face to face with a militant security guard, who informed her that Donnie had left after the debacle, she knew she was too late. She rushed to the phone booth and tried calling his apartment, not knowing he was no longer there and left a message. She hung up the phone and watched cars whizz past, wondering what might have been.

ABE HAD NO idea what he was going to say to Donnie. Having melted down at the film premiere and embarrassed himself in front of the whole world, he was hardly in a position to lecture. Donnie's situation wasn't entirely his fault, but Abe only had himself to blame for the intoxicated mess he had fallen into that fateful night that ended his career. He felt bitterly disappointed and realised how much he cared about Donnie's success as if his own happiness depended on it.

Melanie towed Donnie into the lounge, and Abe offered an empathetic smile.

'I'm so sorry,' Donnie apologised and crumpled into the nearest chair.

'I don't need an apology,' Abe replied.

'It was all going so well. I hate him. I hate him,' Donnie blurted and then started to laugh. 'The irony is, I spilt my guts to my family on national television, and they don't even live in this country. They'll never get to see it. As far as my sister knows, she's still married to a man that loves her. My father will still lose the farm, and I can't fix any of this for my little sister.'

It suddenly struck Abe that in Donnie's deepest despair, when his dream was reduced to a pulp, his biggest concern was his family. A family that had ridiculed him.

'You know what I think? I think you'll be all right,' Abe

said. 'You can see past yourself … and, if I'm honest, that was always my biggest flaw … I couldn't see past myself—my ambition, my dreams … and then I met you, and it was like a light switched on, to be filled with hope for someone else.'

This hadn't been the conversation Donnie was expecting. He would have grovelled at Abe's feet for forgiveness and wouldn't have been a bit surprised if Abe never spoke to him again.

'Maybe we should do something together after all,' Abe declared, his mood swinging from disappointment to excitement. 'Like a phoenix from the ashes, we'll rise together.' Abe wasn't sure if it was the beer talking or if he had just had an epiphany, but the idea swelled inside him, and he felt the first adrenalin rush he'd felt in years.

'How?' asked Donnie.

The word *how* flummoxed Abe. He looked into space, contemplating that he and Donnie were now swimming in the same endless cesspit, albeit Abe had been paddling around in it for a long time before Donnie splashed in. He was trying to find the right words for Donnie to offer him hope. A hope he had always denied himself, but no words of wisdom poured from his mouth. He just looked away, willing a metaphorical ladder to appear that would let them climb out.

Melanie, who had been listening intently, leaned in and whispered,

'This is just a hair in the butter. I bet they'll love you out there. You told the truth. You weren't some plastic actor following a script. You were you. Of course, you were a bit sappy again, but some people like that.'

'You're so kind,' Donnie said, wiping a tear that reached his chin, 'but I've been fired from the movie. I don't know who I was kidding, thinking I could do it. My parents need me to help—they don't need me to disgrace the family. I'm going to go back to Ireland. I'm going to help on the farm and try to forget any of this happened.'

CHAPTER THIRTY-NINE

THE FOLLOWING EVENING, IRELAND

Kathy had not heard from Francis for six days. She marched down to The Pier Head bar, a wrathful look on her face. Locals, who would usually stop and chat with her, nodded and kept walking, head down. Kathy's mind was chattering, overloaded with questions and self-doubt.

She loosened her jaw, aware that she looked enraged, as she opened the door to the pub, where she was meeting her friend, Marie. Marie and Kathy were creatures of habit. Every Friday after Marie finished work at Dunnes stores and Kathy closed the bakery, they met for a few drinks, dissected the week, slipped gossip to one another and got nicely merry. Like Kathy, Marie had grown up in the village, and like Kathy, Marie was a grafter, sometimes holding down three jobs at a time. Fridays were her night off, and there was always some hope that something exciting might happen, and maybe she would be swept off her feet by an unknown stranger that entered the bar.

Marie knew all the local men—some were friends, two were ex-boyfriends, and none were what she was looking for. She was beginning to wonder if there was anyone out there at all. Kathy was now with Francis, and although Marie was happy for her, she always thought Francis was a weasel. She worked hard to conceal these thoughts, often praising him to mask her dislike. Marie had known Kathy all her life, and when Kathy walked in the door, Marie had never seen her more livid.

'Looks like you need a drink,' Marie noted.

'The fucking bastard!' Kathy said, throwing herself onto a barstool next to Marie.

Teresa appeared from behind the bar—right on cue.

'Harp or is straight to Bacardi?'

Kathy managed a smile.

'Bacardi, please. A double and another for Marie.'

'I haven't heard from Francis in six days,' Kathy whispered to Marie, although most of the bar could hear her.

'What? Why?' Marie wasn't sure what to say.

'I have no idea. At first, I was a little concerned when he hadn't returned my calls. Then I got even more worried—has he had an accident?'

Marie nodded, chewing her lip and endlessly fidgeting while repeating a little mantra in her head not to say anything too defamatory about Francis.

Kathy's speech accelerated, 'Has he been mugged in downtown LA where they shoot first and ask questions later? Has he been eaten by a Great White?' Kathy paused and leaned close to Marie. 'I tell you what, Marie, if he's not dead, in a coma, or seriously fucking injured and lacking the ability to use both hands and his mouth, I'll be eating the head off him. There will be murder.'

Marie was unsure whether to wholeheartedly agree or smooth the waters. Teresa's interruption was welcome.

'C'mere to me,' Teresa said, leaning over the bar, out of earshot from the other punters, 'is Donnie out there doing a movie?'

'Eh? No,' Kathy answered. 'Where did you hear that? He's working on some computer yoke. *Dwarfland*.'

'Yeh,' Teresa was unsure whether she should continue, but her nose was bothering her so much, she had to know, 'see, I heard that he made that up. I heard that he's starring in some big movie.' Teresa raised her eyebrows, looking for clarification.

Old Alfie was at the end of the bar, and his ageing ears pricked up.

'Good on him!' Alfie shouted from the other side of the room, raising his pint high into the air.

Kathy shifted uncomfortably on her bar stool.

'Where … Teresa, did you hear it?'

'My cousin heard it from Lisa at the Bingo, and she heard it from her sister, who lives with one of the nurses who works in the care home, who said that Maureen Walsh said it.'

'Maureen Walsh in the care home?' Kathy repeated.

'Yes, but the girl said that Donnie told Maureen Walsh.'

'Did she hear Donnie telling Maureen Walsh that, or did Maureen Walsh say that Donnie had told her that?'

Teresa leaned back, one hand on her hip.

'Look it, I don't know about that. That's just what I heard.'

'I see,' replied Kathy, wondering if this story had some legs or was just Chinese whispers in the village. Either way, she had bigger fish to fry and looked directly into Marie's eyes.

'What do you think, Marie?'

'Well, I heard some rumblings about Donnie but not from any reliable source … so I paid no heed.'

'No, Marie, not Donnie. What do you think about Francis?'

Marie was on her fourth drink. She was on the bridge—the bridge between her mantra working or her mouth about to reveal an endless list of concerns.

'Well, I mean, I'm not sure.'

'Come on, Marie!' Kathy pushed.

'I think he's a bit of a prick,' Marie said, her bridge creaking.

'He is a prick for not calling me,' Kathy agreed.

'No, I think he's a prick, generally. Him not calling you is just symptomatic of the fact that he's a prick.' Marie swigged her drink, now utterly impervious to the fact that her bridge had entirely collapsed.

'Right,' said Kathy, confused, 'how long have you been harbouring this thought?'

Teresa had heard every word and, being a pro, she landed at their side of the counter.

'Another drink, girls? The truth is they are all pricks. Look at mine …' She pointed over to Bernie, sulking in the corner of the bar. 'He doesn't even like soccer, and he's over there looking like a wet weekend just because Man United lost tonight. No doubt I'll get it in the neck later. Not before some unsuspecting customer, mind.'

When Teresa was allegedly out of earshot, Kathy said to Marie, 'Poor Teresa. He's some fucker.'

'He is,' replied Marie and clinked her glass with Kathy, relieved her earlier comment about Francis had been lost in some frenzied husband-bashing fog.

Kathy and Marie had now been in The Pier Head for a couple of hours, and Kathy felt no improvement in her mood. She was acutely aware she was sucking the life out of Marie and everyone else around her.

'Right,' said Kathy, looking at her watch, 'I'm going to get going. Sorry, I'm not able for it tonight.'

Marie squeezed her hand. 'No, you go. Get some rest. He'll call.'

'He will, yeh.'

Kathy was no longer sure.

'Well, if he doesn't …' Marie was going to say more, but she was trying to rebuild her bridge. 'If he doesn't,' she continued carefully, 'something has definitely gone wrong.'

Kathy got on her bike and cycled back to the farm, with a few wobbles and near misses with the ditch. She wasn't sure if the imbalance was caused by Bacardi or her inability to focus on anything except that Francis hadn't called.

When she arrived at the house, she saw a dinner had been left aside for her. She put the plate in the fridge, too annoyed to eat, and followed the noise of the television to the living room.

Sheena was lying on the back of the sofa, and her mum and dad were in their armchairs—the television was the only communication between them.

Kathy tickled Sheena's foot on the way past.

'I would never have been allowed to lie like that across the furniture,' she said.

Mickey-Joe looked over from the television.

'Get down, would you, Sheena? How many times do I have to say it?'

'Did anyone call?' Kathy asked as casually as she could.

'No, he didn't,' Elizabeth answered with a shake of her head. Elizabeth was growing more and more unimpressed with Francis. Her antenna was up the minute he stayed out to help Donnie. Everyone knew those two had a hatchet that refused to be buried. Now Elizabeth quietly observed her daughter's pain when he wasn't calling from California. *The bollox.*

RTE news had started. The nine o'clock news was a family ritual, casually observed by the older children and painstaking agony for Sheena. The presenter, Derek Davis, was talking about the growing backlash against mining for gold on Croagh Patrick, a sacred mountain in County Mayo.

'They can't go reducing a holy mountain to slurry and contaminating the waters with cyanide,' Elizabeth uttered.

'Let me tell you this,' Mickey-Joe said bitterly, 'if there was a mountain of gold on a hill outside our door, I'd be the first out there with the cyanide.'

'You don't mean that,' Kathy said, knowing he probably did. 'Anyway, our farm doesn't have thousands of pilgrims climbing it each year.'

'Just get the gold from the end of the rainbow,' Sheena suggested.

'Why are you not in bed?' Mickey-Joe barked.

The news was wrapping up, but there was always time for a light-hearted story at the end, and it would have been light-hearted entertainment if the story hadn't been about Donnie.

'A Galway man who had secured a lucrative role in George Lawless's new movie, *Cracked,* has been cut from the film due to a disastrous live interview with Randolph Lettering. Donnie McNamara from Bellvara—'

Mickey-Joe's eyes just about popped out of his head, and Elizabeth stared, open-mouthed. A small clip was being played of Donnie on Randolph Lettering.

There he was on the television—their Donnie.

'Hi, Mum, Dad, Kathy, Sheena—'

'It's Donnie!' screamed Sheena.

'Shhhhh, for God's sake!' Mickey-Joe's blood pressure was rising.

'What in the name of Jesus is he going on about the nativity play for?' Elizabeth asked.

'Why the hell is he on the TV?' shouted Mickey-Joe.

Donnie continued, his voice booming around the living room.

'My sister, Kathy, deserves to know the truth. He has married her for money. I'm sorry, Kathy, he told me that himself. Ironically, money we don't have, and if all I achieve in my life is to reveal to my sister that a low-life snake is deceiving her, then … at least there is that.'

Kathy stormed out of the room.

SHEENA FOUND KATHY lying on her old bed, staring at the ceiling, with tears trickling onto her pillow. She made no sound and didn't so much as glance at Sheena when she entered her room. Sheena eyed Kathy cautiously as she knelt in front of Kathy's record player in the corner of the room. Flicking through a few singles propped up against the wall, Sheena selected Alison Moyet's, *All Cried Out*. She pulled it from the sleeve, placed it on the turntable and blew the fluff from the needle before carefully placing it on the record.

Kathy turned her head slowly towards the sound of the music as Sheena turned up the volume bit by bit. The faintest of smiles appeared on Kathy's face as Sheena twisted the knob to full volume and started singing along with Alison. Kathy sat up, wiped the tears from her face and sang loudly with Sheena. After a few moments of their cathartic duet, Sheena shouted over the music,

'I never liked him anyway.'

CHAPTER FORTY

DONNIE'S LAST DAY IN LA

Donnie woke up to the sun flickering through the curtains. His instinct was to pull the covers back over his head and remain in the foetal position until the end of time, but the smell of bacon cooking and the sound of Abe's whistling filtered into the room, and he knew Abe and bacon would offer more comfort than the cold sweat he was suffering in bed.

He pulled on his jeans and picked up a t-shirt from the floor, smelling it first, before discarding it and fishing for a fresh one in his case. As he shuffled towards the bathroom, armed with a toothbrush, he met Melanie at the door.

'Did the sleep not ease the despair?'

After a moment of processing what Melanie had asked, Donnie replied,

'I feel better, Melanie, but I'm sad to be going home. I feel I've let everyone down.'

'Life is not about how fast you run or high you can climb, but how well you bounce.'

Donnie smiled. Talking to Melanie was like hearing an old favourite song—she instantly lifted his mood.

Abe piled extra bacon on Donnie's plate when they sat down to breakfast.

'Still going back to Ireland?' Abe asked, hoping Donnie might have had a change of heart.

'There's a flight this evening. I have to go, Abe.'

Abe nodded, feeling a weight of sadness on his shoulders.

Donnie walked along the beach early that morning, partly
to clear his head but mostly clinging to the hope that he might
see Summer out surfing. He sat cross-legged on the sand,
not far from where he had beached himself after the terrifying shark incident, and scanned the surfers on the waves.
Pelicans plunged into the water beside the surfers; their sheer
size would have frightened Donnie so much that he would
have fallen off his board, but these surfers were oblivious
to the enormous birds diving down beside them.

And then he saw her. Riding a wave elegantly and effortlessly, like a feather floating in the breeze. He stood up
and watched her for a minute, but his excited smile faded
quickly. *What was he doing here?* Like his ambition of
being an actor and smashing Hollywood, Summer was a
pipe dream—even when his desire was within reach, Donnie
had managed to clumsily drop it and watch it fade out of
sight into another world for another person. He felt like a
fraud: LA, Summer, Hollywood, none of it was his life—he
was merely a gatecrasher that the bouncers were now ejecting.
He watched as she got back on her board and paddled back
into the waves. Then, with a swell of pride for her in his heart,
he turned and walked away.

ABE ENTERED DONNIE'S room and saw his things packed
into his suitcase. He felt a genuine sorrow, a loss of a dear
friend, and that the house would never quite be the same again
without him. With a heavy sigh, Abe wandered back to the
kitchen and cracked open a beer. He walked out onto the front
step of the cottage, where Melanie was sitting in the sun and
put his head on her shoulder.

'I know, Abe. The jig is up. I'm going to miss him too.'

A few hours later, Donnie's taxi was waiting. He hugged

Melanie and Abe and found it gut-wrenching to look back. With tears rolling down his cheeks, he waved farewell with a heart that felt like winter.

CHAPTER FORTY-ONE

BACK IN IRELAND

Donnie got the bus from Dublin to Bellvara, and as it approached the town square, Tic was waiting for him. Donnie hadn't told anyone when he would be arriving, so although he wasn't expecting Tic to be at the bus stop, he wasn't entirely surprised. News in the village seemed to travel by telepathy, or perhaps Teresa at The Pier Head was indeed some village spy with a global network who could transmit any scrap of news across the town.

The reality was close. Tic had a CB radio in his chest pocket and was radioing back to Teresa in the bar, and when he saw Donnie's forlorn face through the misted window on the bus, Tic covertly pressed the button on the CB radio.

'The blue tit has landed, Teresa.'

Donnie almost fell into Tic's hug. He was so relieved to see a friendly face.

'Good to have you home, fucking idiot,' Tic said, pounding his back.

'I've got a lot to tell you. I totally fucked up.'

'Yeh, everyone knows. It was on RTE news.'

'What?' Donnie felt instantly weak.

'Although … you might be surprised at people's reaction.'

Tic pulled Donnie's arm to see a banner roped across the street that read, *Welcome Home our star, Donnie!*

Donnie's eyes welled up, and he stared back at Tic.

'Come on, let's get a pint. Fucking leaky-eyed loser.'

'I can't face it, Tic. I've let everyone down.'

'No, it was Francis that did that. He's such a prick that he's made you look good. Turns out he wasn't liked in the village at all!'

Donnie walked into the pub, and it was filled with people raising a glass to him. Through the haze of smiling faces, he saw his father, and to his amazement, his face wasn't smacked red with anger. Perhaps someone had plied him with enough booze that he had forgotten everything.

Although still unsure why everyone was so happy to see him, Donnie made straight for his Dad.

'I'm sorry, Dad, I'm sorry I lied to you—to you all.'

Mickey-Joe patted Donnie on the shoulder.

'I've had time to think, son. I stopped you from doing what you wanted, so what choice did you have but to lie and here's the thing … you were going fine, ticking away … succeeding even, until that gold-digging, see-you-next-Tuesday stuck his oar in. If I see that weasel, I will stick my foot so far up his arse, he'll be licking my boots.'

Donnie was more than a little taken aback. Never in his life could he imagine his Dad taking his side over Francis's—and he even detected a hint of an apology. This was unprecedented, and Donnie wasn't sure if he could handle any more without bursting into tears or running out the door. His father knew Donnie's emotional buttons, but now Donnie realised there was a certain relief knowing a berating was coming. When it didn't, and something foreign and fuzzy appeared instead, his psyche malfunctioned entirely, causing salty water to leak from his eyes.

'And the other thing is, son, you stood up for your family. For your big sister … and while it might have helped us a whole lot more to have your name up in lights, you did a good thing doing that. Of course, it would have been great if you could have done that *and* saved your acting job, but look, everyone makes mistakes, and I never expected perfection from you.'

Mickey-Joe laughed a little as if it was a joke that Donnie might get.

Donnie's soul was now running ragged inside his body, focused on the fact that his father had commended him for something and mentioned the word 'acting' and 'job' in the same sentence. This transformation was alien, unsettling, and the opposite of the homecoming he had dreaded.

'Just as well I didn't jump off a cliff then. That would have been a mistake!' laughed Donnie, feeling adrift, like he was on lilo caught in a tidal stream at sea.

'Eh?'

'I mean, if I'd jumped off a cliff thinking you were mad with me, that seems a bit like a silly idea now.'

'What are you raving about?'

'It was just a joke,' Donnie replied, aware the conversation was headed in the wrong direction.

'There's nothing fucking funny about jumping off a cliff,' Mickey-Joe proclaimed and shook his head, giving Donnie comfort that his father was still his father and his lilo was floating back to shore.

The door to the pub opened, and Kathy and Sheena came in. Sheena ran over and hugged Donnie.

'Donnie!'

'Sheena! I missed you. I'm sorry I didn't fix things like I said I would.'

'You got rid of Francis. I NEVER liked him.'

Sheena ran to the bar to order her red lemonade as Kathy stepped forward and smiled at her brother.

'I was white with rage when I saw you on RTE. You hung me out to dry.'

'I'm sorry, Kathy, it wasn't my intention to—'

'Yeh, well, after a while, I saw that you did me a favour. I can see that parasite for what he is, but I can't see how I didn't see through his lies.'

Sheena stuck her head between them.

'Kathy wants to become a lez bean.'

Kathy laughed.

'It's one solution. I can't even get a flipping divorce. It's such a mess.'

Mickey-Joe leaned over.

'Nothing my shotgun and Gerard's digger can't fix. There's plenty of land in Connemara where no one will notice a six-foot ditch.'

Teresa nodded to Donnie.

'Welcome home. Pint?'

'Harp, yes, thanks, Teresa.'

Old Alfie had been sitting at the end of the bar, watching Donnie closely. He called Teresa over.

'Let me get that for him,' Alfie said, tapping the side of his pint glass. 'I'm going after this one and want to get him a drink.'

'It's from Alfie,' Teresa said, landing the pint in front of Donnie, 'and you've one on tap from me. It's good to have you back.'

Tic was beside him now. He grinned at Teresa.

'Teresa, he's been off gallivanting, and I've been here, supporting your pub. So where's my free pint?'

'I'll give you ten free pints if you'd fuck off for a few months, Tic,' Teresa laughed.

Donnie walked over to Alfie.

'Cheers, Alfie. I'm sorry I'm not home victorious after our last chat.'

Alfie smiled, his eyes twinkling.

'If a baby falls, it gets up again and only starts walking when it learns how not to fall.'

'Right,' said Donnie.

'Whether you tripped or took a nose-dive into the slurry pit doesn't mean you can't keep trying.'

'No, Alfie, I appreciate all your support, but my acting days are over.'

'Pity,' Alfie said and winked at Donnie as he took a sip of his pint.

CHAPTER FORTY-TWO

A COUPLE OF WEEKS LATER

Donnie's life had been returning to the familiar normality of life before he left. He was unaware that the locals were chasing reporters from the village but acutely aware of his father's increasing stress about the farm's future and his mother's slide into a more profound sadness. Kathy had been surprisingly upbeat, but Mickey-Joe had noted it was because she was becoming more imaginative about the various ways she would murder Francis when she saw him.

Mickey-Joe was confident that Francis wouldn't have the nerve to show his face at the farm, but he made sure there was always a bullet in his shotgun, all the same. He didn't intend on killing him, although lately, he'd been fantasising a little about it—he just wouldn't feel the same satisfaction pointing a gun at him if it wasn't loaded.

The day they had not been expecting arrived. It was a filthy day. Grey skies and rain had been over their heads for days, but today it lashed down, flooding the fields and turning everything to muck. Kathy and Donnie had been out feeding the cows when they saw him dashing towards them. He didn't so much as look at Donnie. Instead, he pulled his hood down and looked at Kathy imploringly.

'Kathy, I know what you've heard, but it's all lies,' Francis shouted over the howling wind.

Kathy, who had a head full of clever rebukes, stood speechless, with the colour draining from her face.

'I think you'd better go!' Donnie shouted back, sensing an escalation that may involve the emergency services.

'YOU!' Francis pointed his long finger towards Donnie. 'This is all your fault, you little lying fucker.'

Kathy stood in front of Donnie.

'Get out of here, Francis. I have nothing to say to you, and I'm going to take it to the fucking Bishop to get you out of my life.'

The roar of Mickey-Joe's tractor could be heard over the rain, and as Donnie whirled around, he saw the mud spurting from the wheels as Mickey-Joe sped towards Francis. Francis looked up and saw the fury on Mickey-Joe's face. He had about two seconds to get out of the way as it was pretty clear Mickey-Joe was using him as a target. In a flash, Francis would be squashed, but he showed no signs of moving. Donnie leapt forward and shoved Francis to safety, the two of them sliding in the mud together.

Francis jumped up and ran, slipping all the way to his car. He started the engine with the door of the car still open and skidded out of the drive.

Donnie had a reassuring feeling that he might never see Francis again.

After the excitement, Donnie walked towards the house to get cleaned up and noticed his mother looking out the kitchen window, smiling at him. He smiled back and felt a surge of hope for his family. He entered the kitchen just as the kettle was boiling.

'Good riddance to that *baaaaasssstard*. He brings nothing but misfortune and lies,' Elizabeth said as she poured Donnie's tea.

Donnie noticed that when his mother cursed, she took so long to say the word as if she would incite the devil if he were listening.

'You know, Mum, it would be good if you could get out. Why don't you and Dad go to a dance? Go and see Big Tom or someone.'

Elizabeth sighed. 'Can't be doing that just now, Donnie. We're skint.'

She looked away, her face still carrying the guilt of what she had done.

As Donnie sipped his tea, an idea came to him. He was so excited that he almost dropped his mug. He pulled his waterproof trousers back up and ran out to the yard.

'Dad!' he hollered after his Dad, who was walking with Kathy towards the field. 'Dad!'

Mickey-Joe turned around.

'You all right, Donnie? He's lucky I didn't shoot the hole off him.'

'I've had a brain wave.'

'Oh, fuck no.'

'No, it's good. Just listen for a minute. You and mum can't afford to go and see Big Tom, right?'

'Right.'

'How about if we bring Big Tom here?'

'What are you raving about?'

'How about we use the barn? Charge for tickets. Bring the bands. Bring the dancing. Turn this farm around.' Donnie stood back and pointed towards the barn. 'Make it a venue! They will come from miles around!'

Mickey-Joe wanted to protest, but he was silent for a moment.

'It would work, Dad. We could make it work. Build it, and they will come!' Donnie insisted.

'Son, build it, and they will come does *not* apply to everything.'

'It's an idea, Dad,' Kathy said, joining the excitement.

'It's an idea,' agreed Mickey-Joe, 'but I'm not sure it's a good one.'

'The barn would be perfect,' Kathy agreed. 'I can do it up with fairy lights and hay bales. Let's give it a try. If nothing else, we'll all have fun, and I need some fucking fun.'

'Mind your tongue,' Mickey-Joe barked at Kathy, 'but I agree we all need some fucking fun.'

CHAPTER FORTY-THREE

ONE MONTH LATER

onnie took his Honda 50 to the care home to visit Maureen. It was the first time he had been there since he got home. Donnie was the type of person who liked to visit others—neighbours, old relatives, and friends. He enjoyed 'popping in for a chat' and seeing the joy it brought to those who had less contact with the outside world. Today, however, he had convinced himself he was going to see Maureen, but a little voice laughed inside his head, taunting him, *who are you kidding?* The voice kept repeating itself until Donnie consciously acknowledged that he desperately hoped Roísín would be there.

He bumped down the narrow road in his Honda 50, easily avoiding known pot-holes and narrowly missing new ones. As he passed the weathered gates to Francis's manor house, he couldn't help feeling smug when he saw the 'For Sale' sign. Francis was out of his life for good, and the oppression he had felt in the past when seeing Francis's house finally dissipated. If anything, he felt a little sorry for him—Donnie knew what it was like to live a lie, and Francis perhaps had been doing everything he could to survive in his realm. But, Donnie concluded, Francis had unfortunately set his sights on the wrong family to exploit.

Donnie's heart bounced when Roísín opened the door of the care home. Her warm, bright smile was infectious. Donnie beamed back at her.

'Welcome home,' she said.

'Thanks. Good to see you. How're things?' Donnie asked, trying not to look into her hypnotic eyes. He suddenly felt that he shouldn't be here—that it was all too obvious, but Roísín kept talking, her hands expressing herself all the time as she spoke.

'Much quieter round here without you, but I hear you've been busy.'

Donnie laughed. 'Don't believe everything you hear.'

'I hope it's true,' replied Roísín. 'Sounds like the most fun around here in a long time. Big Tom coming to your farm, and you all over the news. From Hollywood back to Bellvara! How does it feel?'

Donnie was taken aback by Roísín's enthusiasm. She seemed to emanate sunbeams. They radiated out of her and spread warmth everywhere.

'It feels like I'm home,' Donnie said, and he meant it.

When Donnie entered the lounge, Maureen was dosing in her chair, but Roísín gave her knee a little tap, and she opened her eyes and was delighted to see Donnie standing in front of her.

'Well, well, how's Hollywood?' Maureen slapped her thigh.

'It came to an abrupt end,' Donnie said, secretly wishing everyone would stop going on about it. He realised it was something that was never going to go away. Like a surname, it was now a permanent attachment.

Roísín was still beside him. She squeezed his arm and said, 'I don't think it's the end of the journey at all. You'll be back on the horse in no time.'

'That's right,' agreed Maureen, 'just you wait and see.'

Donnie didn't have the heart to tell them it didn't work like that. If you take an opportunity and blow it up into smithereens, people are less likely to offer another. He had come to terms with the fact that he was probably his own worst enemy—that his dreams had been within his grasp, but instead, he'd pipped himself at the post by goring himself on a spear of failure. He was home now, and it all seemed like some distant hallucination, but one that he was sure he wouldn't be experiencing again.

Roísín walked away smiling as Donnie sat beside Maureen, following Roísín with his eyes.

'You're surely not here to see me?' Maureen laughed, with devilment in her eye.

'Of course I am. I'm sorry it's been so long.'

'A long time, all right. A long time is taken you to come here and ask that lovely girl out.' Maureen's voice was stern now. 'What happened with your American girl?'

'Ah, nothing,' Donnie replied, his face reddening, 'she was never my girl. I see that now.' Donnie felt he could see a lot of things now. Summer wasn't his girl; he didn't belong in LA, and he wasn't an actor. Yet, he felt strangely at ease with it all. Not having to try all the time felt so liberating.

Maureen gave a satisfied nod.

'Well, what are you waiting for? A sign from God?'

'What do you mean?' Donnie asked.

'Ask her out. You know that's why you are really here.' Maureen smiled knowingly.

Donnie stared at his interlocked hands and twisted them around like a child might when caught lying.

'She does like you. It's obvious. She's always talking about you,' Maureen said, pressing him. She couldn't understand why he wouldn't just get off his ass and ask her out. Men seemed more cock-sure and determined in her day. There was a feeling of urgency back then that certain decisions had to be made to survive. These days it seemed young people walked around as if time and choices were infinite.

'Everybody's talking about me just now. That doesn't mean anything,' Donnie replied in a whisper.

'Fair enough,' Maureen folded her arms, 'but you'll never know, will you? Unless, of course, you ask.'

Donnie was desperate to ask her out but terrified of rejection. Rejection itself wasn't what he feared; it was rejection from Roísín that he would have found too humiliating and too much to bear. If she said no, there was no flying home or moving away. And right now, Donnie was happy not trying. If you didn't try, you couldn't fail.

'Trying doesn't kill you,' Maureen said as if reading his thoughts.

'I know,' agreed Donnie, but he was seriously worried that it might.

Maureen gave Donnie a nudge. 'Go on. Make an old lady happy.'

She noticed a hopeful spark on Donnie's face and gave him another push.

'Go on. Will you!'

Donnie saw Roísín across the lounge putting some biscuits on a tray and casually walked over to her. Maureen made it all the harder by watching him like some form of entertainment.

Roísín dazzled him with her radiant smile when she saw him approach.

'Did you want some biscuits?' she asked. 'No chocolate ones this time, I'm afraid.'

'No thanks, but I was wondering if … maybe you might like to come to the gig at our farm. You know, Big Tom.'

'I've already bought my ticket,' she said happily.

'Oh, you did?' Donnie hadn't expected that. 'Maybe you could come as my partner because I would have liked to have given you a ticket.' The words fell out and hung in the air. Donnie desperately wanted to catch them and swallow them again as she stood looking back at him curiously.

'As your partner?' she asked with a tone that made Donnie repeatedly blink, wishing he could fast-forward the next five minutes.

'Unless you're going with someone else. No problem.' Donnie wanted to run out of the room as fast as he could.

'No, I'd love to go as your partner,' she said, smiling.

'Really?' Donnie couldn't believe his ears.

'For sure!'

A wave of elation washed over Donnie, and as he turned around, he saw Maureen beaming back at him. The thought crossed his mind that sometimes life was easier than he had made it all these years.

CHAPTER FORTY-FOUR

BACK IN LA

Geeorge Lawless's schedule had been crazy during the shoot of the movie. His heart wasn't in it, which made his days even more exhausting. After the meeting with studio bosses when Donnie got fired, the dynamics changed, and he felt a constant tightening of the reins around his decision-making. George had felt stifled and frustrated. Not that he was always right, but their attempt at eliminating failure also annihilated creativity. So he was glad to be taking a break from it all and meeting his old buddy, Abe, for dinner. George knew it wasn't just dinner—there was a project on the table and one that could mean the world for Abe to re-ignite his career. George was the kind of guy who liked to do favours for people and give them a leg-up—but he was also shrewd, and if he was totally honest about his motivations, there needed to be something in it for him too.

George pulled up outside Dan Tana's restaurant on Santa Monica Boulevard in his black Merc. Dan Tana's was an understated place, painted bright yellow with a green awning. The kind of place you could eat dinner with an old friend and get quietly smashed with no one to bother you except the waiter offering another bottle of wine.

When George arrived, Abe was already sitting at one of the red leather half-moon booths, sipping on a beer. Abe had deliberately arrived early as a token effort to reassure George that he had his life back on track. He wore a navy short-sleeved linen shirt—the one that made him feel smart, even when everything else about him was a mess. Before George arrived, Abe had lifted the napkin and refolded it three times, studied the bland still-life paintings on the wall, averted the eyes of other customers, examined the cleanliness of his fingernails and picked at the label on his bottle of beer. Abe wasn't used to being early, and it felt like purgatory. Added to this, Abe had a feeling of trepidation. Discussing projects again was like trying to climb back into a plane he had already jumped from.

'Good to see you, Abe. You're looking well!' George grinned, winking to the waiter for a beer. George looked effortlessly suave. His silver hair, still peppered with black, had retained its thickness—not a bald patch or receding hairline in sight. Abe had noticed that George had an edge over most people he met, not simply because of his good looks, but because his colourful presence was loud and fun, if not sometimes out of place, like a rock star leaping around the altar at a funeral.

'I'm still alive,' agreed Abe, 'turned a corner. Not off the booze, though, just less. I'd rather be dead than not drink at all!'

'Me too! Hell is a place with no bar!' George rubbed his hands together. 'So, I read your script. Thanks for sending it to me,' he said, raising his eyebrows at Abe as the waiter handed him a beer.

'Ah,' Abe replied, a little taken aback that George had mentioned it so quickly, 'I'm amazed you had time with all you've got going on. Donnie enjoyed it, and I thought, well, see what you thought.'

George took a long drink from his beer and placed it down with a bump on the checkered tablecloth.

'I loved it!' he cried with an enthusiasm that surprised Abe. 'You did?'

Abe had battled over sending it, and he had hoped for a spark of encouragement from George, but 'love' was strong … although arguably over-used in Hollywood. However, Abe knew George was a straight-talker, and his endorsement of the script made Abe's stomach flutter—a feeling he had thought he would never experience again.

'I loved it, Abe, and I want to do it.' George grinned again. 'You want to do it?'

'Yes, except for one major difference, which I don't think will take away from the story.'

'Sure, sure.' Abe was all ears. He'd fucking re-write the whole thing from start to finish if George was 'in'.

'It's set in Canada, right? Well, what if we set it in Ireland?'

George sat back, his eyes wide, hoping Abe would bite.

'Okay, but I've never been to Ireland—it could be hard for me to write it authentically.'

George was silent for a moment. He had to get Abe to buy into this. George was a big respected fish in Hollywood and could thrash out commercial hits one after another, but none of them meant anything special to him. None of them caused his heart to sing; none gave him the feeling of self-fulfilment he was looking for. No matter how big his house was or how expensive his car was, there was an aching void that George had never managed to fill. Then he met Donnie. To George's surprise, the encounter with Donnie made him feel homesick—a desperate feeling to return to Ireland and create something that his own people were proud of. He wanted to bring something home.

George finally answered, 'I'll finish this shoot in a few weeks. Let's go to Ireland, and I'll help you fill in the gaps on anything you're unsure about.'

Abe stared at him anxiously.

George raised his hands dramatically and tried to ease Abe's mind.

'Don't worry, don't worry. We'll make sure it's authentic. It has to be,' George said, with a hint of apprehension himself.

Abe didn't answer.

'Look,' George said, 'I've never shot anything in Ireland, and I've reached a point where that seems wrong. I want to go back. Let's go and create some magic together!' George clapped his hands as Abe's eyes lit up. He felt his head perspire with the thrill of it all.

'Donnie's back in Ireland, you know. I'd love to look him up when we get there,' said Abe.

'I fought like a bastard to keep him in the movie after his interview with Lettering!' George explained.

'I know. He knows he fucked up, but he's a good kid. Melanie and I miss him.'

'Fucked up?' George's voice was getting louder, 'It was the most hilarious thing I've seen in a long time, and those fuck-tards at the studio wouldn't know a breath of fresh air if it was blown up their asses! He was honest, Abe, and for Christ's sake, we need some candour in this town. Yes, let's get Donnie. He's a good tonic for you, too—I see that. Obviously, I want him in it, and you—a great father and son story. You'd be great on screen together.'

George was talking so fast that Abe was barely able to keep up.

'You want me to be in it?' The idea alarmed Abe. He could cope with a return to the industry as a writer with relative anonymity, but to be back in front of the camera again was like smearing himself in blood and swimming with the sharks. Abe scrunched the napkin into a ball on the table. 'No, no, no, George. I've written it—that's enough.'

'Yes,' George said, ordering another beer from the waiter. 'I'm not doing this without you starring in it. Like old times. You'll be playing the father.' George stated this as a fact, not an idea.

'What? No, George. If we set in Ireland, then the father is Irish. I'm a fucking yank.'

'So what?' George laughed and waved his hand. 'We can get over that. You're an actor, and you're good at accents.'

Abe leaned forward. 'George, I gave you the script to see what you thought, but I can't get back in front of the camera.'

'Why the fuck not?' asked George, his face a little stern now.

'Well, because—'

'—Because nothing. Let's fucking do this!' George thumped his fist on the table with infectious excitement.

Abe closed his fingertips in front of his face, thinking deeply before responding,

'George, if we do this, can I bring Melanie? I can't leave her behind.'

'Of course!' beamed George.

Abe's smile arrived slowly as the fog of fear lifted and was replaced by a tantalising surge of excitement.

CHAPTER FORTY-FIVE

THE NIGHT OF BIG TOM

Despite growing up in Bellvara, Donnie had never felt as much part of the community as he did today. They had rallied around the family, helping with every tiny detail to make the Big Tom gig a success. Teresa and Bernie from the pub had brought kegs of beer and taps and worked the bar in unusual harmony, proving that there was nothing like a common cause to sort out individual problems. Donnie had noticed Bernie smile twice at Teresa. Perhaps Bernie didn't want her to die after all.

But the problems between Teresa and Bernie were only ever speculation. Donnie had first-hand knowledge of the plight facing his parents' marriage. A crisis that seemed insurmountable until this evening. Micky-Joe had been up a ladder in his suit, trying to find which fairy-light bulb wasn't working, resulting in the whole string of them going out. He was muttering and swearing as he worked his way along the bulbs when Elizabeth walked into the barn smiling. She wore a beautiful green dress—the same dark green colour as the dress she had worn when she first met Mickey-Joe at the dance in Salthill decades before. Mickey-Joe sucked in his breath and stared at her. He felt an old familiarity that filled him with contentment and joy, as if his wife had returned from somewhere far away, and he was seeing her again without the shadow of endured bad times and heartache.

Elizabeth smiled up at him on the ladder.

'Try the next bulb, love. I'm sure it'll be that one.'

Mickey-Joe tried the next bulb, and the lights twinkled across the barn. He hurriedly came down the ladders, a beat to his step and walked over to Elizabeth.

'You look mighty!' he said, his arms clutching her waist.

Elizabeth smiled. Years seemed to have vanished from her face. 'It's a new start, isn't it?'

'Yes, it is,' Mickey-Joe grinned back at her. 'It's a new start for us all, and I've got my dancing shoes tightly laced.'

Standing beside Donnie, Kathy was also watching her parents. She turned to Donnie and squeezed his arm.

'You're a genius, Donnie,' Kathy whispered.

'Hardly,' Donnie laughed, and out of the corner of his eye, he spotted a white Fiat Uno pulling up and felt a thrill of anticipation.

'Who is it?' asked Kathy, following his gaze.

'It's Roísín,' Donnie said, unable to dial down the smile on his face.

'Aha! You dark horse!'

Roísín got out of the car, wearing a layered skirt, a cropped shirt tied in a bow at her waist, Doc Martins boot and a flowing overcoat. She looked softly bohemian. Donnie had only ever seen Roísín in her nurse's uniform, and he was captivated by her unique sense of style. He could imagine her in an iconic music video, like Eddi Reader from Fairground Attraction, or running through a meadow of flowers advertising shampoo to the masses. Her dark hair fluttered in the wind as she helped Maureen out of the passenger seat. Donnie was enthralled by her. His stomach was tied in so many knots that he was sure he would never be able to eat again. Roísín struggled to get Maureen out of the car as Donnie stood rooted in a trance, watching her.

Kathy gave Donnie a shove.

'Stop standing there like an amadan and go and help her, for feck's sake.'

Donnie gathered himself together and ran over to help Roísín, but Maureen was already bundled out of the car, and with a grateful smile, she tapped Donnie with her walking stick.

'Here we are! Ready to party!' Maureen hollered, breaking the ice for Donnie.

An hour later, Big Tom was on stage with his band, wearing a cowboy hat and belting out the tunes. The barn was a mad whirl of known and unknown faces, laughter, and legs flying in all directions. In the centre, Roísín was thrown around like a rag-doll in Donnie's arms and laughing so hard that she thought she might get sick. Big Tom's voice echoed around the mountains like an open-air amphitheatre. The strong smells of the country combined with burgers and perfume were a vibrant melody for the senses.

Donnie felt the music pumping through his body, beating a rhythm to the happiness he felt jiving with Roísín. His hands were sweaty, and he lost his grip on her hands, but she laughed, wiped her hands on her beautiful skirt, and shouted to him over the music,

'Sweaty hands! What can we do?'

Tic was in his element—he'd danced with every girl in the barn and been on the stage twice with Big Tom. Big Tom didn't seem to mind Tic's colourful additions to his lyrics, but when Big Tom started singing a slow number, Tic leapt from the stage and straight to the bar.

Donnie looked over at his parents. They slow danced, and Elizabeth's head rested on Mickey-Joe's shoulder. He had never seen them look so peaceful. Donnie pulled Roísín in a little closer and wrapped his arms around her waist.

'Thank you, Roísín,' he said.

'For what?'

'For being here tonight.'

He leaned in an inch closer, and when she didn't pull back, he kissed her and thought his heart might burst. Donnie felt that whatever search he had been on, he had surely found what he was looking for.

Sheena had been on just about everyone's shoulders. She had also asked most people for a sip of their drink, and the majority had obliged her. However, it took over two hours before Elizabeth spotted what she was up to.

'Ah sure,' they all said, 'it's only a sip.'

Elizabeth tried to explain, 'It might only be a sip from you, but she's getting the same from everyone, and there are two hundred people here. She'll be polluted—she's bold, don't indulge her.'

Before Elizabeth could chastise Sheena, she seized her moment and was off—straight over to Maureen.

'Hi, Mrs Walsh!'

'Ah, you're Donnie's sister, Sheena!' Maureen stroked her hair. 'Great little girleen, you are. I saw you dancing. Do you want to be a dancer when you grow up?'

'No way,' laughed Sheena, 'Dad would kill me. He wants me to be a vet but guess what?' She leaned in close and whispered to Maureen, 'I'm going to be a pop star!'

'I'll bet you will,' Maureen clapped her hands.

Elizabeth whispered into Mickey-Joe's ear, 'Now she's over there about to talk Maureen into giving her a sip of her sherry.'

'The apple doesn't fall far from the tree,' Mickey-Joe said, laughing. 'I'll distract her.' He called out to Sheena, 'Sheena, would you ever go into the house and get my fags out the kitchen drawer?'

Mickey-Joe had smoked his whole pack before Big Tom arrived, wracked with nerves, but now, as he saw a smile on his wife's face, he was finally relaxed.

Just as there was a lull in the music, Sheena came running from the house clutching the cigarettes and shouting for Donnie,

'Donnie! Donnie! It's the phone for you. It's that guy, Abe Rockefeller, from America!'

THE END

ACKNOWLEDGEMENTS

A huge thanks to you, the reader, for choosing my debut novel. I hope you enjoyed it and I would be very appreciative if you could leave a review or share your thoughts. You can get in touch via my website www.fionagrahamwriter.com

I would like to thank Vanessa Mendozzi for the wonderful work she has done on the cover and interior and for her incredible patience with me.

So many people have taken the time to encourage me and show their support. I am deeply grateful to Emma Heatherington, internationally best-selling author, for all the helpful advice, great chats, advance review and for promoting me to her fan base. A massive thanks and appreciation to Sean Maguire for his review and continual support and encouragement. A huge thank you to Olaf Tyaransen for taking the time out of writing his own book to read and review mine. Thank you so much to Anita Stratton, for all the help and encouragement, for reviewing the book and for all the laughs along the way. Huge thanks to Chris Harvey for taking the time to read and review the book and for his constant show of support.

I have been incredibly blessed to have the support of fantastic friends and family, and every word of encouragement has helped me on this journey—the first of many novels, I hope!

To my husband, Sean, and daughter, Sheena, your support has been immense. Sean's wit is infamous, and he thought of the title. It takes one to know one, they say! Sheena is a ray of sunshine and inspired the character by the same name.

To my amazing friends and family, thank you for all the support, inspiration, and encouragement and for helping to spread the word: The Stratton Family, Aisling Byrne, Mairi McLellan, Lara, Eriskay and Ella, Tracy Parkinson, Konrad Begg, Fionnuala Tarpey, Maree McNamara, Micheline McNamara, Roisin McNamara, The Togher Family, Meredith Adam, Gordon Dundas, Neil Fullerton, Julie Waites, Ruth Sexton, Valerie & Mike Forkan, Mary Donnellan, Andrew Nelson, Ruth Wilson, Calum & Katie Graham, David Graham, The Connolly family, Michelle MacDonald, Mick Walsh and Emma Pyne.

A massive thank you for the support from my wonderful parents, Iain & Sheena, and sister, Mairi—growing up in the mad house gave us all a sense of humour.

I'd like to thank Sean O'Shea (back in the day, our work was made so much more entertaining by Sean's funny stories), my cousin Andrew Nelson (partner in crime since birth), my farmer neighbours John, Joe, Micheál and Pat for the night we calved the cow and every pint since, and finally to the dearly departed Iain Murray, my father's cousin and possibly one of the funniest people I've had the pleasure to know. Iain was the publican at the fantastic The Ship Inn in Irvine, Scotland, now run by his son Christopher, and his humour is still legendary.

Heartfelt thanks to The Alabama 3 and their manager Jonathan for supporting this book, and I'm looking forward to being led astray by them again soon.

I am unbelievably fortunate to be part of an amazing community in Kinvara—an incredibly special place with the best pubs and restaurants. To the people and businesses of the town, a massive thank you for all your support.